S0-COH-241

Pressure Points

Judy Tucker

Also by Judy Tucker

THE SHAPE OF DARKNESS

BOILING POINT

RUN

All characters appearing in this work are fictitious. Any resemblance to real persons, living or dead, is purely coincidental.

Copyright © 2018 Judy Tucker

All rights reserved.

ISBN-13: 9781791555139

1

The plane hurtles into the sky, corkscrewing upward in a gut-wrenching spiral. The goal is to stay over the airspace of Baghdad International Airport until they're above the reach of surface-to-air missiles, which means the pilot has to force the aircraft into this stomach-churning maneuver until they hit an altitude of least 15,000 feet.

The angle seems impossibly vertical. And the rear hydraulic ramp is open: an escape hatch, just in case. All Grady can see is the ground—and it's spinning. He clutches the M4 carbine that was handed to him after he boarded and lets out an involuntary, "Shit!"

A loud "Fuck, yeah!" explodes out of the guy next to him. He's holding his own carbine. On this flight, each of the twenty-or-so passengers has been armed for takeoff. In the event of a crash and confrontation—assuming they survive—they can fight their way out. At least that's the idea.

Finally, the plane levels off, and Grady realizes he's been holding his breath. A couple of sergeants come by to collect and stow the weapons. As the man next to him hands in his M4, he turns to Grady. "How many times you done this?"

"Three."

"Five for me."

Grady gives an approving grunt, acknowledging that his seat mate has some good-sized cojones.

"Never gets old does it?" the guy says.

Grady has to admit that it never does.

\#

"Play it again." Rachel tries not to let her frustration show in her voice. She thought they were past this kind of crap. Gil clicks a mouse six thousand miles away, and the screen of a laptop in Baghdad's Green Zone fills her screen. She sees a young man's face in awkward close up: sunburned nose, pale blue eyes, blond hair cut almost Marine boot camp short, grown out enough that a curl's just beginning to reappear. Tears roll down an unlined face that hasn't yet lost all its baby fat.

"I'm sorry," the young man says. His voice is choked. "I love you. But I have to do this. Tell Mom and Dad that I love them, too. It isn't anything you've done, not any of you. And there's nothing you could have done about it. I just can't go on."

He's sweating profusely. Stress. His face is liquid.

"Mom and Dad, you raised me right. And I let you down. I disgraced you. I can't live with it. The other guys, they can, but I can't. And I'm such a fucking coward I can't do anything about it either. I can't go through all that. So I'm leaving it to Geezer to take care of it. I'm counting on him. He'll do the right thing." His voice trails off. "I'm sorry. I'm so sorry…" The last words are barely above a whisper.

The video ends. Rachel knows what came next: the gunshot to the right temple. And the stupid kid got the timing wrong. He meant to send the video to his girlfriend back in Ohio, had it all set up. But he didn't click the right button, somehow closed the thing down instead. Shaking? Too scared that if he slowed down he wouldn't go through with it? Who knows?

She takes a sip of warm diet soda, catches herself drumming her fingernails on the desk, tells herself to stop.

Gil's face comes into the frame. "Again?"

An icon flashes on her screen. Her copy has just arrived. She shakes her head. "No."

"So. Send it to the family?"

"Yes, but…"

"Clip it. So Mom and Dad and the girlfriend just get the first part."

"Yup. And about this Geezer. Find out who the hell he is."

2

She slips into the water. And realizes that the room is too dark.

When she was running the bath, she had the choice between the glare of the overhead and the soft glow of the seashell nightlight. She chose the nightlight. But now she's in the tub, below the level of the countertop where the nightlight casts its beam and it's damn black in here. Shit.

She could light a candle. In the movies, when a man and a woman are taking a bath together or even when a woman is relaxing all by herself—as she is tonight—there are always candles everywhere. Hundreds of them.

She's always wondered where they get all those candles. Do the screenwriters think everyone has a closet full of the things?

She'd have to get out of the tub (sopping wet, getting chilly), dig around in the cabinet next to the washing machine to find even one, then plunk its grubby stub down in an old saucer and hope she could get the wick to catch.

Too much trouble for what would be one lonely little flame.

C'mon, get over it. Why does she need to see?

The water is just right: hot, and slippery from the bath foam. And there's no problem reaching her glass of wine. Her hand finds it and wraps around the stem. There. Much better.

The music isn't perfect. Her playlist is too heavy on aggressive beats to be as soothing as she wants right now. But then she hears the opening notes of the latest from Hot Mud, one of her favorite bands. What a song. Cooingly romantic, then angry, even violent, then romantic again. Really puts the "alt" in alt-rock.

And she doesn't know much about wine, but she sure got lucky with this bottle. Whether it's officially classy or not, the taste is wonderful: soft and round. She drank most of it before getting into the bath. But there's enough left for some slow sipping. Plenty to top off the tank.

Life may not be perfect. But tonight it's all good.

She leans back in the tub. She pinned up her hair, but she didn't get it all. She can feel the small curls at the nape of her neck soaking up the water. Frizz city here we come.

Who cares? She doesn't have to be anywhere tonight, doesn't have to look good, doesn't have to smile or make nice to anyone. That never happens on a Friday! And even if this latest stuff—just some pills she had on hand—isn't instant bliss, it's working now for sure. She's reached her happy place.

She sets the wine glass on the floor next to the tub, slides down so that the water laps at her armpits, covers her breasts, then says to hell with the hair and slips down even further. Only her knees poke up above the surface. She exhales slowly through her nose. Blowing bubbles like a small, sleek mermaid, just like she learned to do as a kid in swimming class.

She lets herself go limp. Her body feels like liquid, merging with the water. She almost couldn't move even if she wanted to... But...

She surfaces. And hears... Is there someone in the room??

The overhead light goes on, nearly blinding her. She's never seen the man before. He's young, good looking. She knows she should be alarmed, but she can't quite manage it.

Then he tells her who he is. And she can handle it. Just stay loose. A little smiling, some flirting, share the wine…

But…he's pressing on her? Holding her down?

She's breathing suds, breathing water, hot in her nose, her throat, her lungs. She needs to struggle, needs to surface, but she's so tired…so…floaty…

The music changes. Shimsham's "Deep Six." She hears the opening words, "Down by the water, baby. Watching it roll. Foolish in love, foo-oo-ool…foo-oo-ool…"

Then she doesn't hear any more.

The water covers her. But she's not blowing bubbles this time.

The shaved-slick legs go slack. The knees are still in air, but they can't breathe. They drop to one side, leaning against the vertical white porcelain of the tub.

The form in the tub doesn't move. The nightlight casts its tiny beam. Bath-foam islands drift on the surface of the water.

3

Grady sits on the brand-new couch in his furnished apartment and waits for his ex-wife.

The security system on the downstairs outer door rings through to his cell phone, and he buzzes Jill in. He hasn't seen her in well over a year. But then he's hardly been in Tucson since he hit the road with his dog and his truck in spring 2008, more than eighteen months ago. He stopped in his hometown on his second break from the sandbox back in May, but he wasn't around very long. He picked up a rental car at the airport and drove by the house he grew up in, the house his mother lived in until she died. He killed some time, then went to the address he'd been given for the title company and signed the papers to close the sale. He deposited the check, drove to the south side, ate some good Mexican food. After that, there didn't seem to be much reason for him to hang around. So he left.

Why Jill's coming by now, he doesn't know. They're friends, at least in the sense that they've come through for each other when it's counted over the years. But, still, they're exes. They don't hang out.

When he hit town on Friday, he did leave a message at her office that he was back. (He doesn't have that many people in this town any more, and she's one of them.) But he didn't expect to hear from her for days. Maybe not at all. So he's puzzled at what feels like her rush to see him less than forty-eight hours later. Except for those few crises where they've helped each other out, he's been on the periphery of her life for a long time.

He steps out of his apartment into the hall, the elevator doors open, and there she is. Most of her face is hidden by a large potted plant that fills her arms. "Here," she says, handing him the greenery. "Welcome home."

She looks good. Sometimes she dresses like the precise, well organized professional she is—which he gets. Who wants a dentist to be sloppy? Other times, she's all done up in what he thinks of as her foothills costume: glossy hair, visibly expensive clothing. A member of Tucson's upper middle class. Today, she's wearing slim black jeans, a white t-shirt, and Keds, her blonde hair up in a messy knot.

He likes her this way.

Is he imagining it, or is Jill also assessing him—and maybe surprised at what she sees? The bathroom in this new place has one of those oversized mirrors covering most of the wall above the sink. The leasing agent said something about it "lighting up the room." Whatever. But it does mean he can't help checking himself out every so often. His hair is more gray than brown now, but it's still thick, and he sprang for a pricey haircut to welcome himself back to town. He'll always be a big guy because of his frame, but he's a hell of a lot trimmer and more fit than he was a couple of years ago. In fact, he's in better shape than he's been for a long time. That tired sop to the aging, "You're not getting older, you're getting better," is crap. He'll never be twenty-five, or even forty, again, but he feels pretty good about how he's holding up.

He sets the plant on what the realtor referred to as the "island" or "breakfast bar"—two fancy terms for what just seems like a hunk of detached counter with a sink in it to him, and Jill gives him a quick hug. "It's an aspidistra," she says, "also called the cast iron plant. You've been pretty mobile lately, and I didn't want to weigh you down. But I thought a plant… And the Internet says it thrives on neglect."

"That I can handle."

"So this is it!" she says, scanning the space. Then she's moving from one part of the area to another, poking her head into the half-bath, opening a door to look at a still-empty closet. He's always thought of her as a calm person, but right now she reminds him of a cat that can't settle.

The apartment is "open plan," something the leasing agent pointed out proudly, saying it was "great for entertaining." What it amounts to for Grady is that the living area is all one big room, with the kitchen at one side. There's a bedroom and a "master" bath and an assigned parking spot down in the garage. All he needs. "Yup," he says. "This is the new place."

Finally, Jill perches on one of the counter stools that came with the apartment. Grady pulls bottled iced tea out of the frig. "It's this or tap water," he says. "And I don't have any sugar."

"I don't take it," she says as he pours. She sounds annoyed, like he's supposed to remember every personal preference she ever expressed and maybe have kept up on the ones that have changed.

"To your new life," Jill says, and they bump paper cups. They sip in silence for a moment before she speaks again. "So," she says, "how are you?"

Before he can answer, she's up again. She walks over to the door wall at the side of the big room, slides it open, and steps out onto the small balcony. He follows.

"How nice!" she says brightly. "You can put a little table here and have your morning coffee." She illustrates where the table would go with her hands and ignores the pack of cigarettes and ash tray he's already parked on the wide railing. "The plant I brought won't survive outside, but you can get something else to dress up the space. You'll enjoy this."

She's stopped talking and, at least for the moment, stopped moving. They stand there on the empty balcony with its straight-across view of an office building, its rows of windows dark on a Sunday. The street below is empty except for two homeless people sitting on the sidewalk and a couple of teenagers rolling by on skateboards.

"It's still not much of a downtown," he says, looking at a scene that a few years ago would have been only a few steps up from post-apocalyptic.

Jill contradicts him. "So much better than it was."

From Grady's point of view, they're both right. Although it's still not exactly a bustling metropolis, downtown Tucson is (finally) showing signs of life. Bars and restaurants have been opening. Rents are rising after decades of stagnation, and new condos are going up. It seems like the right place for the "new" Jack Grady.

Because there are some differences between the old Jack Grady and the new one. He's gained some things, one of which is a certain amount of money. There are the proceeds from the sale of his mother's house, the income from his current gig in the Middle East. This is a level of financial security he's never known.

But he's also suffered some losses, of the kind that can't be undone. Even without cracking a self-help book, he knows there are times when you need to force yourself to look ahead. To make a clean break.

And when he's not out of the country, he needs a home base. The last eighteen months have taught him that. He wants that base to be in Tucson, even if he's not sure why. But the new Jack Grady does not want to be out in the desert, or in the kind of lower middle-class family neighborhood he grew up in, or in an area of low-rise apartments, or even in the flashy foothills. He wants a place that's different from anywhere he's ever lived or even thought of living. And where he can lock the door and go away for months at a time.

So here he is in a furnished apartment in a building in downtown Tucson that's just tall enough to need an elevator. It's the right choice.

He thinks.

The sun felt good when they stepped out from the chill of the apartment, but the balcony faces south and it's an early afternoon in mid-September. Within moments, it's uncomfortably hot. They retreat into the air conditioning.

Back inside, Grady watches Jill tour the space again, just as she did when she first walked in. He sees her examine the stove, run her hand over the granite counter, take in the tile floor, the two matching lamps, the sofa and occasional chair, faux walnut coffee table, end table, and entertainment center. Everything's brown or some shade of beige, something he hasn't really noticed before.

"It's so new," Jill says. "Like one of those model homes that's so shiny it's almost spooky." And maybe she sees the look on his face, because she adds, "It's nice."

But her tone makes it sound like faint praise, as if that polite word is the best she can say for it.

He's puzzled by her reaction. "You don't like it?" Can't she get that for once in his adult life, he wants a place that *is* new, and clean, and even—as Jill put it—"nice"? Where he can be absolutely, one-hundred-percent respectable?

"No, no, no," she says. "I didn't mean that. It's fine. There's nothing wrong with it. I just don't see *you* anywhere."

He doesn't know what she expects. He's only been in town a couple of days, signed the lease on the place less than twenty-four hours ago. "I haven't had a chance to get my turntable or my records out of storage yet. And I need to buy a lot of things. Right now, all I have are a set of sheets, a couple of towels, and some leftover pizza. Oh, and that iced tea we're drinking." You try it, he thinks. Leave a war zone on Wednesday and be back in the states getting criticized by your ex-wife on Sunday. He tries to keep the annoyance out of his voice. "Besides, I'm still jet-lagged."

"Of course," she says. She sounds upbeat but a little too loud, as if she's caught herself not being supportive and is overcompensating. "And you needed a furnished place."

He did. His last landlord sold, or dumped, most of Grady's stuff when he fled Tucson just over two years before, running from a frame-up for the murder of an ex-lover and a Federal investigation he wasn't even supposed to know about. When he was eventually exonerated, his furniture and other household goods, such as they were, were gone. After his mom died, he kept the few things that meant something to him or were precious to her (photo albums, her good dishes, a knick-knack or two) and let an estate sale company deal with the rest.

They sit on the couch facing the bare coffee table, the empty entertainment center, the blank walls, and he changes the subject. "So," he says. "Catch me up. How's Sophie? How's Charlie? How's the practice?"

Jill takes a sip of her tea and looks around again. "Where's the spot for the piano?"

She knows what the piano means to him. When he lost everything else, Jill rescued his sound system, his records, some keepsakes—and the piano.

"I'm not sure it'll fit. And then there's the noise, and the neighbors…"

"Oh, Jack." There's a note of despair in her voice. "Jack, what are you doing here?"

Where's he supposed to be? Frozen in time? Still living hand-to-mouth in some dump the way he did for all those years? Jill has a successful practice, a husband, a kid, a big house in the foothills. She moved on years ago.

Maybe she gets how damn insulting she's being because she shakes her head. "Scratch that," she says. "It'll be fine. You'll get your things. You'll hang something on the walls. You'll figure out the piano. You'll make it yours." There's that false cheer again.

She stands and picks up both their paper cups. "How about a refill?" she says, moving to the refrigerator.

He waits until she returns to the couch. "So," he says, "you were going to catch me up."

Everything is good, she says. Her dental practice is growing. She's thinking of taking on an associate, someone fresh out of dental school. Charlie's traveling a lot. His business is like that. Home for a while, then mostly gone for weeks or months. "You know how it goes, Jack." Sophie's a senior, busy with AP courses and friends, getting ready to do her college applications. She goes through it quickly, just a few sentences, almost as if she's reeling off a list: career, check; marriage, check; child, check. Then she turns the subject back to him.

She wants to hear about his time in Iraq, so he paints her a picture that's both less alarming and more interesting than reality. He emphasizes that he's basically a glorified security guard, shares (and embellishes) a few funny stories, and plays down the IEDs, the terror, and the loneliness. She doesn't look like she's buying.

"So," she says. "You're done with it?"

He shrugs. "Just got started," he says.

"Three tours. That seems like a lot."

He reminds her that each tour is only ninety days, with a mandatory, thirty-day out-of-country break before the next one. He doesn't mention what all contractors know: escort duty is high-risk. And escort duty is what he does day in and day out.

Acting as security for important personnel and for all kinds of equipment, from medical supplies to food to cook stoves to weapons, that need to get from the Baghdad airport to the Green Zone or from designated point A to point B doesn't sound all that hairy, but it's one of the most dangerous jobs in the country. A while back, somewhere between three and nine contractors were being killed each week. (There are no good statistics because no one official is counting.) These casualties aren't included in the numbers reported on the nightly news. And no high muckety-mucks are meeting the coffins when they arrive back in the States.

The death rate for contractors peaked, he's heard, in early 2007. That was going on three years ago, and things in the sandbox aren't as hot and heavy as they were, but still...

He expects Jill to probe, maybe express disapproval, or even concern that he's planning on going back—for the fourth time—to a war zone. But, to his relief (and surprise), she lets it go.

He's given her a sanitized version of the truth, and he senses that she's done the same thing. There's been something slightly off about Jill from the moment she stepped off the elevator. And she's always been slim, but now he's thinking she's lost weight, that maybe she's a little too thin.

They've known each other since she was in dental school and he'd just made detective in the TPD. They were married. He rescued her daughter, Sophie, from kidnappers a few years back. Then she kept the faith when the media and law enforcement were calling him a murderer and trying to hunt him down. Even if it's been years since they've spent any real time together, the two of them should have more to share than pleasantries.

He tries to break through. "You seem a little distracted," he says.

She gives a little chuckle. "Just busy. You know how I get when I'm overbooked."

He does. She becomes a whirlwind with only one goal: to get things done. Intense, tightly focused, the opposite of scattered. He's never seen her like she is today.

They've been moving toward the door. Jill has already looked at her watch, mentioned a commitment back in the foothills, expressed her regret that she can't stay longer, said she has to get going. She's slung her handbag over her shoulder.

Now they're out in the hall. "I shouldn't do it," she says. "Let myself get this busy. But I guess I'll never learn."

It's a dismissal. Butt out, Jack.

She reaches out to push the button for the elevator just as he decides to try again. "C'mon, Jill. You can't snow me. What the hell is going on?"

For a moment, his words hang there. Then she gives him a smile, a big one, too bright. "I'm good," she says. "I'm really good." She pats his arm. "No worries."

The elevator doors open. She gives him a little wave, steps in, turns to face him, and adds, "I'm leaving Charlie."

And before he can react or ask a question or even give her his sympathy, the doors slide in front of her, cutting across her too-bright smile.

4

Now she's done it. She's said it out loud. All the turmoil that's been churning around inside her for weeks came out in three flat words: "I'm leaving Charlie." And she was lying. Because Charlie's leaving her. At least it looks that way.

Her timing—announcing the catastrophe just before the elevator doors closed—left Jack without an explanation. She's known for years that, whatever his feelings for her, Jack has always admired (and maybe envied) her marriage. He must be shocked by what she said, with no idea what the hell is going on. If she had to open her mouth to someone, why in God's name pick her ex-husband? How dumb— and weird—is that?

She walks rapidly toward her car, parked just down the street. She doesn't look back. If Jack stands on that little balcony of his and leans out, he'll be able to see her emerge from his building and follow her progress all the way to her car. There's no reason on Earth he should go out there and stretch to see her scurrying along the sidewalk. Just the same, she needs to believe there's no possibility he's watching. She needs to pretend she hasn't exposed herself.

She reaches her Audi, slips inside, folds the sunshade. She was already on the elevator when she said those three words. Maybe Jack didn't hear her. *Yes, he did,* her interior voice insists.

Maybe he didn't get her meaning. *It wasn't subtle,* the voice reminds her. *You put it right out there.*

She starts the engine, pulls away from the curb. *Why do you care that you've "told"?* the voice asks. She chooses not to answer, but the voice won't stop. *Because you don't want to talk about it, do you? You don't want to admit that your marriage is going down the tubes. Not even to yourself.*

The radio is tuned to NPR. Radio Lab, a story about lucid dreaming, how one man learned to do it and took control of his nightmares. *The problem,* her internal voice says, *is that you're awake.* She hits the control to switch the source to her iPod, which picks up in the middle of a piece about K-Pop, teenage singing groups in Korea. *So you'd rather think about this,* the voice scolds her. *Something frivolous that has nothing to do with you and your problems.* Yes, I would, she answers. *Talk about avoidance!* the voice rebukes her. She turns up the volume.

#

Grady's dumbfounded. Maybe he misheard her. Or misunderstood. No. He heard her correctly. And what she said was clear. She said, "I'm leaving Charlie."

He always thought she and Charlie had one of those ideal marriages, that after she'd failed with Grady—or they'd failed together—she'd found her soulmate in Charles Whitehurst.

Back in the apartment, he finds himself oddly saddened by her news. He guesses everyone likes to think there are some constants in the world. And he thought Jill's marriage was one of those things that could be counted on.

A few years back, he might not have felt this way. For a long time, he carried a painfully blazing torch for his ex-wife. He tried to get out of the habit of aching for her but didn't really succeed until he became involved with another woman: Ally. And even though the romantic part of that relationship has ended, he's managed to keep the embers of his feelings for Jill tamped down.

He steps out onto the balcony where he left his cigarettes. He's promised himself he'll only smoke outside, hoping that this will be the first step on the road to quitting entirely. As he lights up, he spots Jill about a half block away, walking to her car. He watches as she hits the button to unlock the door, gets in, and drives off.

He nukes himself an early dinner, eats it in the silence of no TV, no sound system, then takes a walk around the echoingly empty streets, choosing his route to avoid the street with the few bars that are open on a Sunday evening, moving past the turn that would take him there and then walking some more. And he thinks about whether he should call Jill. Maybe he can help. Maybe she needs an ear. But she must have woman friends she can turn to if she wants to talk about it. Better that than pouring her guts out to her ex-husband. And other than that, what help could he give?

She told him because she's telling everyone, getting the news out. That's all. And she told him when she did, at the end of her visit, because that's all she wanted to say to him. She doesn't owe him details, or even an explanation. He decides that, for now, all he can do is respect her privacy.

5

"I've got the I.D."

Rachel's still half-asleep, up working till two and now…. It may be almost lunchtime where Gil is, but here in D.C. it's four a.m. His voice in her ear is a noise keeping her from her pillow.

Unprofessionally, she yawns. And stumbles toward the kitchen. "What I.D.?"

"On Geezer."

Now she's awake. She hits the button on the coffeemaker and flips open her laptop.

"Guy bunked in the same quarters. Rotated out only a few hours before Malone offed himself."

She retrieves the file. The name, beginning oh-so-formally "John Matthew …," doesn't mean much—at first. But the photo!

She laughs.

A surprised voice in her ear: "Rachel? Are you okay?"

"Fuck, Gil! I know this guy."

6

The numbers on the microwave flash 3:00 a.m. Jill pours hot water into a mug, drops in a tea bag. She leaves the tea to steep, walks into the powder room, can't avoid seeing herself in the mirror over the vanity. Her always narrow face is gaunt, its features too sharp, her thin nose a beak, her eyes more red than blue. She sees lines she's never noticed before, and they're all pointing down. She looks exactly how she feels: like shit.

The weekend has been hell. Except for that brief, stupid visit to Jack, she was on her own. Sophie was up in Phoenix with a friend and the friend's parents. And there's a teachers' in-service this Monday so she won't be back until tonight. Charlie is in Denver in the middle of an extended business trip and chose to stay there over the weekend instead of making the two-hour flight home. "Just not worth it, babe," he said. Her spirits rose when he called her "babe" because he hadn't used that casual, sexy endearment in… She has no idea how long it's been. But then he went on about how awful flying is these days, all the security crap he'd have to go through, the drives to and from both airports. She listened to the excuses pile up, their logic irrefutable, like he was making an argument in court. And she realized that the "babe" didn't signal anything at all. At least not in regard to her.

The old Charlie would have thought that even one night at home was "worth it." She remembers a weekend when he had been in Boston working late into the evening on Friday and had to be in meetings there first thing on Monday, and she had a heavy Monday schedule she couldn't change. He begged her to meet him halfway, screw the expense. And they had a wonderful most of a weekend in an airport hotel outside Chicago. But this Charlie...

It doesn't matter because when he is home, he isn't really with her anyway.

So she has rattled. She tried cleaning kitchen cupboards, reorganizing her closet, the kind of tasks that usually center her when she's being eaten up by worry about events she can't control. But it hasn't worked. The spices are still out of their cabinet, scattered across the counter, waiting to be culled. Her sweaters are off their shelves, out of their bags, in a jumble on the closet floor.

Theoretically, it's Monday now. TGIM. Work will be good. She'll be forced to focus on her patients. She's always been able to do that: flip a switch and become her confident, caregiving self—no matter what's going on in her life. If nothing else, she's a professional.

She's at the office by 6:15. She looks over the day's schedule, catches up on email and charts. Better, she thinks. This is better. These necessary tasks, the demanding routine of her days. It's exactly what she needs.

By the time she walks down the hall to the little kitchen to pour herself another cup of coffee, it's still nearly a half hour until her first appointment and she's almost cheerful, or at least can imagine being cheerful. Paige, one of her front-desk people, is stowing her lunch in the frig. "Oh, hi, Dr. Whitehurst," she says, "I didn't know you were in yet. There's someone waiting to see you."

"That would be..." She just looked at the schedule and can't pull the name of her first patient out of her memory bank. Oh fuck. So much for being rescued by routine. First in her class at USC. Phi Beta Kappa. And losing it right here in the breakroom.

"Mr. Harper. Prep for crown. He's your first." Paige is on it. And to Jill's relief, a visual of Mr. Harper's second bicuspid pops into her mind.

Paige is still talking. "But it's not him. There was a woman waiting outside when I unlocked the door. She says she knows you. I asked her name and she just said, 'Tell her it's Gina.'"

Gina?? Maybe someone she met at a charity event? Or the mother of one of Sophie's friends? But why would anyone like that be in her waiting room without an appointment at seven on a Monday morning?

When she opens the door beside the receptionist's desk, she can see the entire outer office. It's empty except for one person, presumably Gina. Not old enough to be the mom of one of Sophie's friends. Late twenties, tops. And not likely anyone she met at a fundraiser, either.

The girl (somehow Jill can't think of her as a woman; she doesn't look mature enough to be called that) is sitting in the chair nearest the door to the outside. She's bone-thin, wearing faded jeans, flip-flops, and a purple tank top, which doesn't hide dingy white bra straps or protruding clavicles. A tattered blue backpack rests on the floor in front of the chair. The girl's hands are clenching the armrests. Her legs are crossed, right foot bobbing furiously. If she were a patient, Jill would diagnose extreme dental anxiety. But as it is...

She's wearing sunglasses, classic Ray-Bans with white tape around one temple, but Jill can almost feel the eyes behind those lenses fixed on her as she crosses the room.

Jill stands in front of the girl, looking down at tangled light brown hair. "Gina?"

"Yes." Jill's still drawing a blank, and it must show on her face because after a moment, the girl says, "Jack Grady's niece."

Oh. That Gina.

The last Jill heard of Jack's niece she had disappeared from Tucson and—Jack feared and Jill assumed—back into a druggy haze. When Jack left Tucson in a hurry a couple of years back, on the run from a frame-up for a murder, Jill rescued his dog from his place out in the desert and took Bear to his mom's. In the one frantic phone call he'd been able to make, Jack had asked her to do that and to tell his mother and Gina that he loved them. When she dropped off the dog, Jill passed that message on to Jack's mom. But his niece wasn't around. Jill hasn't actually seen Gina since before her marriage to Jack broke up. Gina was still a little girl then… Jill's never been her dentist… She couldn't be here seeking meds, could she…?

Unless she's prepared to hold up the place, that isn't going to work.

Maybe she has a real dental emergency.

Whatever it is, Jill needs to handle this, get Gina out of the way before her patients start arriving. It may not be kind, it may not be politically correct, but she doesn't need an addict in her waiting room. Take the girl back to her private office? Or try to deal with her here?

Before she can decide, Gina says, "I need to reach my uncle. He sold the house. I went there, and the people said they're the new owners. I don't know where he is."

Gina vanished, what, eighteen months ago? No. More. And Jack left not too long after that.

Jill's not sure how to respond.

"He's in Tucson, isn't he?" Gina's tone makes it clear that she can't imagine him anywhere else.

Jill nods. Yes, he's here.

"I need his phone number."

Jill stands, frozen, still looking down at Gina. The girl is Jack's niece. But there's a privacy issue, especially given her condition. Gina doesn't look sky-high, but she doesn't look completely sober either.

Out of the corner of her eye, Jill sees the outer door open, and John Harper enter, white head a little bowed, leaning gently on his cane. Grateful for the excuse to break eye contact with Gina's Ray-Bans, she gives him her best professional smile.

"His phone number," Gina insists, her voice rising. She grabs Jill's arm.

Jill knows that Jack loves his niece. He's never been an enabler, but he's done everything he can for her. And she can't see him stopping now.

"He moved," she says. Gina's face says "duh."

"I think he just has the cell. No home phone yet."

"Uncle Jack actually using his cell phone. That's a new one." Gina's face says she finds that hard to believe, and Jill can see why. She's never known anyone as reluctant to adopt new technology as her ex-husband. "And I need his address."

Should she? Gina has always been so elusive, so often slipping through Jack's fingers, and her grandma's when she was alive. Jill remembers how desperately they tried to hold onto her as she careened in and out of rehab, on and off the streets. And Jack didn't send Gina away: she ran. Jack was still in town at that point, living in his mother's house, hadn't been to Iraq even once. But even though it was Gina who broke off contact, Jill can't imagine how Jack would feel if he knew his niece was in Tucson and tried to reach out to him through her and was turned away. "Of course," she says.

The girl picks up the backpack, unzips it, and begins scrabbling through the contents. Looking for a pen? Jill sees clothing, underpants, a t-shirt or two. She goes to the reception desk, grabs one of her business cards and jots Jack's number and address on the back. At the last moment, she adds her own cell phone number. First, she wasn't going to give Gina any information at all, and now she's giving her something she should never need and that Jill wouldn't normally want her to have. Why she's not sure. Maybe some misplaced sense of obligation, or sympathy—or just her own jangled emotional state.

She hands the card to Gina. "Okay," Gina says. "Thanks." She tucks the business card in her pocket, zips the backpack. Jill opens

the outer door for her, hoping that the hint that she should leave—
and leave now—comes across as more gracious than rude.

Gina takes the hint. Once she's outside and before the door
closes, she says, "I, uh, owe you one."

It seems to be a thank you. Jill hears herself mutter, "No
problem," a phrase she hates.

As she turns back to her waiting room and her day, Jill can see
that John Harper has been watching with interest. The odd little
interaction has probably been the most exciting thing that's happened
in his life in weeks. "Okay, Mr. Harper," Jill says brightly. "I'm going
to go get ready for you, and we'll see you in just a few minutes."

Making a quick stop in her private office, she sends Jack a text.
"Gina in town. Gave her your address & cell #."

As she hits "Send," the thought hits her. Is this about the baby?

7

Grady knew he'd have to wait around for the cable guy anyway, so he got a late, lazy start. Now he's got Internet access and cable, but he doesn't own a TV, and it looks like the TV shopping isn't going to happen today.

He's running behind the schedule he set for himself.

It shouldn't matter that it's already Monday mid-afternoon. He's on break, with twenty-five days left before he's scheduled to fly back to Baghdad. But he's promised himself that he'll get all the logistics of setting up his new home taken care of stat so he can… Do what? He's not sure. But he wants the option, whatever it is.

He's glad to be back in Tucson. He thinks. His new place doesn't feel like home yet. But he expects that if he keeps on doing what he's doing, getting the apartment the way he wants it, it will. He just hopes that will happen soon.

He'd rattled during his first two breaks.

In mid-January, he went to Memphis for the blues; then he "vacationed" in New Orleans. Great jazz, but not a town for a man who was trying not to drink, so he left and wandered up to Seattle, and finally to the East Coast, where he caught his flight back to Iraq.

His second break was much the same. Thirty days of trying to recreate, killing time. The wrapping up of the house sale in Tucson. Then California, Oregon. And back to...

"Home" can't—or shouldn't be—the house he shares with eleven other guys in Baghdad's Green Zone. Thanks to the Iraqi women who work there, the food is good and the place is clean. Or as clean as the women can keep it when they're dealing with a dozen men who don't much care about keeping anything except their bodies and their weapons in good shape.

It's a glorified, all-male dormitory—or a seedy frat house, except that the occupants are older and they have guns. There's no privacy. All of life is lived in common spaces. They bunk two or three to a room. Share snores, night terrors, and bathroom smells. The primary entertainments consist of nights drinking contraband booze on the roof (Grady stays downstairs) and watching Internet porn (blatantly crude stuff, so he tends to abstain).

And the days there are all the same. The men in the house kill time maintaining their gear, cleaning their weapons, lifting weights, playing video games, watching even more porn, and patting themselves on the back for managing to leverage their otherwise under-valued skills into sizable bank accounts.

The only possibility of a real break in routine lies in becoming the victim of an IED or a car bomb. Some people say this does things to your head. But it is what it is. He tries not to think about it.

Most days, he's assigned to a security detail for dignitaries or equipment going back and forth from Baghdad International to the Green Zone and, occasionally, to other destinations both inside and outside the city.

Twice, he was part of an escort that went as far as Mosul. Lots of desert. Everyone on high alert every klick of the way, guts in knots. But both excursions were uneventful.

Almost all their trips are.

You don't ever get used to it, though. And nobody acknowledges the fear. But he knows guys, men as tough as he's ever seen, who routinely come back from a detail and throw up. Everybody pretends they don't notice.

During his first tour, one of the guys in his house was blown apart by an IED. Just riding along when the transport he was in rolled over the damn thing.

Whenever you leave the house, you know you could be maimed—or dead—at any moment. No matter how alert you are. No matter how careful you are.

And there's nothing you can do about it.

Contractors don't patrol. Not allowed to. Their weapons are for defensive purposes only, and they've been warned to take these rules of engagement seriously. Not everybody does. Or so he's heard. There have been cases over the years where who started what never became totally clear, and there are always rumors…

He keeps his head down, does his job, pays no attention.

Grady's only seen something resembling action a few times. The first time, the detail he was on drove into a firefight. He and the other men all pulled their weapons, but it was over almost before it started. The other two incidents involved returning and then exchanging fire. But they were almost as brief. None of the encounters were what you would call a battle.

He turns the key in the padlock and pushes up the storage unit's rolling door.

There they are, his worldly goods, except for the piano, which is in a special climate-controlled facility up near Phoenix. They don't amount to much.

He carries the boxes with the stuff he's ready to deal with right now to the pickup, first the cartons containing the turntable and amp, then the ones with the speakers, then the other boxes holding his LPs, the photo albums that were his mom's, a few of her household items that have good memories for him. As he lifts the last two cartons—one marked "Keepsakes" and the other "Misc"—the tape sealing the top of the Misc box gives way, and it pops open. He doesn't have any tape with him, so he carries the Keepsakes carton to the truck and comes back for the other one.

As he bends to pick up the carton, he can see some of the contents. On the top: a dog dish, a compartment on the left for water, one on the right for food.

It hits him, almost knocks him over.

They, he and his dog, were in a remote part of Saskatchewan headed for Saskatoon on what Grady had come to think of as an endless, aimless journey when Bear got sick.

After it was over, Grady was convinced the German Shepherd had been as stoic as a dog can be, doing his best to be the cheerful, tail-wagging companion he'd always been. He thought he'd been taking care of Bear all those years. Now he saw that it was the other way around.

At first Bear was just lethargic. Grady thought, hell, sometimes I don't feel like doing much either. But when the dog stopped eating. Grady realized he was fooling himself, got them to the nearest town of reasonable size, and found a vet. By then, nothing could entice Bear to get up or even lift his head.

Bear lay there on the table, unmoving, letting out an occasional yip. The vet examined the dog and turned to Grady. "His name's Bear, right?"

Grady nodded. He stroked his dog's head. Bear licked his hand.

"How old is Bear, Mr. Grady?"

Grady told him.

"Hmm. Your dog has far exceeded the life expectancy for the breed. You must know that."

Grady supposed that he did, but he'd locked that knowledge away in the part of his brain marked "Things to Never Think About."

"In human terms, Bear is a centenarian. And he's very sick. I assume it's been obvious that he has arthritis."

It had been. Bear had been slower and visibly stiffer for years, long enough that his deliberate movements had come to seem normal. The vet in Tucson had prescribed some meds, and Grady had given them to Bear faithfully, but he was never sure they did much good.

When Grady looked back at it later, he realized that for any decent vet these were never easy conversations. And Grady wasn't helping. He continued stroking Bear's head. The vet cleared his throat. "I believe your dog has end-stage cancer. I could run tests, but given his age and condition…"

The doctor made a gesture that spoke for itself. It was a motion of letting go, forcing (or guiding) Grady to say the words: "So it's time to…"

The vet nodded. "Bear only has a few days left. A week at most. And he'd be in agony. I'm surprised he's doing as well as he is right now."

Grady didn't want that suffering for his dog. Of course, he didn't. But fuck!

They did it not more than thirty minutes later. Grady held Bear. And he cried. He didn't give a shit what the vet or his assistant thought of the big guy blubbering, he just cried.

He takes the dog dish out of the box. He wants to throw it against the wall. But he doesn't. He thinks about dropping it in the dumpster that sits outside near his truck. But he knows he won't. He considers just leaving it on the floor. He won't need this storage much longer. It would be a gift (or an annoying chunk of litter) for the next renter or whoever checks the units after someone's moved out. But he can't.

He puts it back in the box and carries the carton to the truck.

8

He sees her as soon as he steps off the elevator. She's sitting cross-legged on the hallway carpet, leaning up against his door, puffing away on a cigarette, using a McDonald's to-go cup as an ashtray. The hand that isn't holding the cigarette is tapping her knee. By the looks of the cup and the ashes scattered on the rug around it, she's been there a while.

Grady's heart takes a happy little leap. His only real family, back in his life! But his only real family is an addict. He's seen her (or tried to see her) through homelessness, casual prostitution for money, drugs, or a place to sleep, petty theft, and what for her was a revolving door of rehab and recovery. She was clean the last time you saw her, his heart says. But how long did that last? replies his brain. He can see that she's thin, which tells him nothing. She doesn't look grimy like someone who's been sleeping on the streets, which is good. But there's that rapid puffing, that nervous, rhythmic tapping...

And all the time he's thinking this, he's walking toward her. She hasn't seen you yet, says his brain. You can turn around, get back on the elevator, find some other place to be for the rest of the day. She won't sit here forever. But that will only postpone whatever is going to happen with Gina this time, says his more rational self. Might as well get it over with. And, says the spark of optimism and what there is of love that won't die (or won't let itself be killed), maybe everything will be fine. Maybe everything will be different. This time.

Now it's too late anyway. She looks up and sees him. As he nears her, she climbs to her feet, reaches out for a hug. "Uncle Jack!"

"Wow!" he says. He puts down the box he's carrying and wraps his arms around her, hoping that his tone hides his mixed emotions. "Gina!" And she bursts into tears, gasping for breath between loud sobs.

He picks up the cup-ashtray and her backpack, juggles them and his keys, manages to unlock the door, and get them both—and the box—inside.

He plops the cup and backpack on the kitchen island, leads Gina to the couch. She crumples onto it. He stands over her, thinking maybe he should get her a glass of water. She still has the burning cigarette in her hand, and he takes it from her, looks around for some place to stub it out, finally uses her improvised ashtray. There are already three other butts floating in a couple of inches of soda mixed with ashes. Nasty.

"How are you?" he says, thinking what a stupid thing that is to say to a woman who's crying so hard she can barely breathe.

"Good," she says between sobs. "I'm really good."

He decides to get her that glass of water whether she wants it or not. And he doesn't have any tissues, so he grabs a couple of paper towels.

He sets the water on the coffee table and sits down beside her. She seems calmer. He hands her the paper towels. "I couldn't find you," she says, blowing her nose.

"Oh." It's a non-response, but it's the only one he can think of.

She bursts into sobs again. "You sold Grandma's house!"

He can't imagine sharing his reasons with her, at least not in the state she's in right now. Can't imagine explaining that he needed to get away for a while, so he did, taking off to the Northwest and

Canada. Then he had a chance to make a living doing something that had some relation to his skills, and (he hoped) had some intrinsic value. To do that he needed to leave the country and didn't know how long he'd be gone. Unless he was going to rent the place out indefinitely… He couldn't imagine being a landlord for the long term, so he decided to sell.

And his mother, Gina's grandma, is gone. Gina was still around when that happened. Virginia Grady is no longer in that house, and neither is her spirit. Grady stayed there long enough after she died to be very sure that no ghost of his mother was hanging on there. But because he can't imagine explaining all this, at least right now, all he says is, "Yes, I did."

Gina's still crying, but she's up now, pacing the open area between the kitchen island and the living room furniture. "How could you? How could you sell my grandma's house?"

He gets how she feels. Her grandma raised Gina from the age of twelve when Grady's sister, Frannie, and her husband were killed in a car crash. And sometimes Gina treated her well, and sometimes Gina cursed at her, and stole from her—just used her in any way she could. He tried to do what he was able to, but he can't kid himself. He wasn't always much help, or even a positive role model, during Gina's crucial growing-up years. And before Gina turned eighteen, it was— or seemed to be—too late.

No, it was Virginia who bore the burden, and it was Virginia, above all other beings, whom Gina loved. Whom Gina depended on. Who made sure that Gina always, no matter what her behavior, knew she was loved.

Still, he can't help but resent Gina's claim to exclusive grief. She was *my* mother, Grady thinks. Do you imagine selling her home didn't cause me pain? Do you imagine that I let go of that house easily? You were the one who left. You were the one who ran away without a word to anyone. You are the one who vanished.

"How?" he fires back. "How could I sell it? I hired a realtor and went through the whole process. How do you think I sold it?" He's immediately sorry for the sarcasm, but he'll be damned if he'll let her know it. And now she's sobbing even harder.

Suddenly, she stops, as if something else has grabbed her attention. She looks around the great room, tries a door that leads to a closet, the door that leads to the half bath, then opens the door to the bedroom and disappears into that room. Within seconds, she's back.

"Where is he?" she yells through renewed sobs. "Where is he, Uncle Jack?"

Grady knows who she means. And he should have seen this coming.

Grady last saw Gina's little boy at Ally's place outside Seattle in late January. He was there for a visit during the break between his first two ninety-day tours in the sandbox. Mattie had just turned one. He was babbling like crazy and crawling all over the place, pulling himself up on furniture, getting ready to walk. Ally said he had Gina's eyes, but he just looked like himself to Grady.

The January that Mattie was born, twenty months ago now, was one shock after another. After months on the run, Grady had just been cleared on an espionage beef complicated by an accusation of murder. He liked to think of himself as vindicated, but releasing him without bringing charges was as far as the Feds were willing to go.

He left his jail cell to discover that his mother's memory was becoming frighteningly wobbly and that his drug-addict niece was both clean at the moment and heavily pregnant. Then his mother died of a massive stroke, and Gina gave birth and (she said) recognizing her own limitations signed her half-black son over to Grady and disappeared.

Grady was broke, grief-stricken, and, he realized, not equipped to parent the child. He arranged for Mattie's adoption by Ally. His romantic relationship with Ally was at an end, but they cared for each other, and she was longing for a child she couldn't have. It was unconventional, but that didn't matter. It seemed like a good fit. Mattie would be raised by a wonderful, competent woman who would love him. And Ally was black. Ally could guide him through the mine-field that growing up black still is in this country, especially for a boy.

Mattie was an "easy" baby, Ally said. When Grady didn't know what that meant, Ally explained. "He has a lovely disposition. For a baby, he's an awfully good sport."

He hasn't seen Mattie since that January visit. It was only a few days and Ally had welcomed him, but she was clearly relieved when it was time for him to go. Still friends. A good visit. But long enough. For them both.

Ally was happy, she said. It seemed to be the truth. And he could tell Mattie was happy.

He'd talked to Jill about that when she came to his new apartment the day before.

"You did a good thing," Jill said. "I thought maybe you were a little hasty at the time, that you might have been letting your grief control you. But it seems you were right."

The whole thing with Mattie and Ally was one of those rare times when the universe lets you fit a few of its puzzle pieces into just the right places.

And now here's Gina.

"Where is he?" she screams. "Where's my baby?"

Stay calm, Grady tells himself.

He keeps his voice steady, lets the words out slowly. "He's not here," he says. "But he's fine. He's safe. He has a good home."

If he thought he could easily talk her down, he was wrong. She's still screaming.

"What did you do? What did you do, Uncle Jack? I left my baby with you! Where is he?"

"He has a good home," Grady says again.

"You gave him away???"

"You didn't want him, Gina."

"Yes, I did."

"No. You didn't want him then. If you want him now, too bad. It's too late."

"I always wanted him. I just knew I couldn't do it."

"He's got a good life. He's safe. He's loved."

"Tell me where he is."

"No. You have a shitty track record, Gina. And you may want him now. And maybe you're clean now. I don't know. But what about tomorrow? Or three months from now? I'm not going to let you mess up his life."

"You should have kept him!"

"I couldn't. I'm not even going to list the reasons. But I wasn't any better able to take care of that little boy than you were. And he's black."

"Half-black."

"It's the same thing! If he looks even a little black, he's black."

"So? What kind of fucking racist are you, Uncle Jack?"

"God, Gina. I'm not a racist. I'm a realist. A black man in this country… you're looking at bias in hiring, harassment by cops. A shitload of infuriating—and dangerous—stuff. It can be a tough and painful life. I have no damn idea how to keep him safe."

"And whoever has him does?"

"One hell of a lot better than I do."

"I'll get him back."

"You can't."

"I'll go to court. Just watch me."

"You do that, Gina, and I swear to God I will hunt you down and no one will find even your bones."

Grady's astonished at what he's just said. Gina looks like she's been hit.

"You'd kill me????"

Grady doesn't answer.

"You wouldn't!"

He stands his ground. "To protect Mattie? Yes, I believe I would."

"Oh! So his name's Mattie."

"Matthew. After your grandpa. My father."

"Matthew what?"

Nice try on her part. Smart. No way in hell he's telling her that.

"This was finished a long time ago, Gina. Your son is almost two years old. You are way too late."

"You can't threaten people like this! I could report you."

"Who to? With your history, how much credibility do you think you'd have with anyone who has any brains? And if you do find some sleazy lawyer to take your case, it's all over. I guarantee it. I will never let it get that far."

Gina isn't in great shape. He realized that from almost the first moment he spotted her. She's not fully sober. No sane judge should ever even think about giving Mattie back to his birth mother. But the law can be tricky. Stupid decisions do happen in family courts. He can't take that chance.

He feels cold. He's perfectly willing to destroy this girl he's always loved if that's what it takes to protect Mattie.

"They'll catch you. They'll kill you. This is a death penalty state!"

"Doesn't matter. I'll do it anyway." And at that moment he means it.

Gina's sobs are gulps. She grabs at her backpack, swatting the to-go cup of cigarette butts, soda, and ashes off the counter and onto the floor. She runs to the front door, yanks it open, and disappears into the hallway. Grady follows and sees the door to the stairway swing shut behind her, hears her footsteps clattering down toward the street.

#

He keeps thinking she'll come back. He cleans up the mess she made, starts a pot of coffee, opens the boxes he was bringing in when Gina appeared, unpacks his turntable. Waits for her another hour. Makes several trips down to the garage for his amp, speakers, and records. Sets up his sound system.

By the time he's done, it's dark outside. He walks to the barbeque joint a couple of blocks away and treats himself to a pulled pork platter with fries and beans. He considers adding coleslaw, but he's not in the mood for rabbit food. He tells himself that he'll get around to a shopping trip tomorrow, promises the gut he can almost feel growing that he'll start eating right, working out, keep the weight off, stay in shape.

Back in the apartment, he pulls out John Coltrane's *Abstract Blue*, dusts the vinyl disc, puts it on the turntable. He sits on the couch, kicks his shoes off, props his feet on the coffee table, and tries to get lost in the music. But the sounds of laid-back mid-century jazz, which have always transported him to a peaceful, if slightly melancholy, place aren't having their usual soothing effect. He's still wound up, still angry, still feeling self-righteous about the things he said. God, she was unreasonable!

He brews more coffee, pours himself a mug, takes it and his cigarettes out to the little balcony and leans against the railing, sipping and smoking, looking down at the street below. The sidewalks have definitely rolled up. There is some action after dark in this city center, he knows, but clearly not in his corner of it. You're too old for nightlife anyway, Grady, he tells himself. And the thought of his middle age carries its own injection of angst. Any moment now he'll be slipping into self-pity. He can feel it coming.

Fuck! A paying gig, money in the bank. He's got it made now, right?

He doesn't have a TV yet. That's what he needs. He'll buy one tomorrow. One of those big flat-screens. And he'll increase his cable package, spring for all the movie channels.

He should be happy. He will be happy.

9

Grady lies there in the dark. There's just enough light creeping in around the edges of the curtains to catch the edge of the fan blade whirring overhead. The glint pulses in the blackness.

He meant what he said about protecting Mattie. Maybe Gina can't be saved. Who knows?

But Mattie can.

He was way too tough on her, though. God! Telling Gina he'd kill her... What the fuck is wrong with you, Grady? Why can't you handle the crap life throws at you without making death threats? How the hell could you have said something like that?

If he'd ever thought he was fit to parent anybody, the way he dealt with Gina this afternoon proved to him that he isn't. Shit. Fucking up with his already fucked up niece.

Some fresh start. No Ally. No Mom. No booze... He could... There'd be someplace still open. He could get himself a bottle. Just one bottle. Or a beer. Just one beer.

But he doesn't. Maybe he will later, or tomorrow. But not now.

So. No Ally. No Mom. No booze. No dog.

No dog.

After Bear died, he drove his empty truck back to his empty motel room and got very drunk, so drunk he vomited on the carpet by the side of the bed and passed out with his clothes on.

The next morning, he ran himself through a long, hot shower and got back on the road, hangover and all. He drove to the city of Prince Albert, saw the sights, and treated himself to dinner at his favorite kind of red leather and dark wood steakhouse. But it wasn't the same. He left the scraps on the table and dragged himself back to his motel.

As he drove through Prince Albert Park the next day, trying to pretend that he was having something resembling a life, he found himself thinking about the FBI agent who had seemed to hint that he might have a future in some sort of higher-level private security. He had taken her only semi-seriously, partly because he couldn't believe that any of those Feds held any kind of good opinion of him, of anything he did, or of anything he stood for, and partly because he had the impression that those gigs were usually overseas. Even though it was pathetic that his only family was a dog, Bear was his family, and he'd already been away too much. He wasn't about to put either of them through a long separation again.

But now... He'd been wandering aimlessly for months. And it had been getting old well before Bear died.

What did he have to lose?

She'd been the only one of the Feds to treat him in any way like he was a human being. The others acted as if he was not just a low-life, but a snake. If he managed to slither away this time, they'd still get around to cutting his head off someday.

In a way, this meant she was the only one to acknowledge that he was innocent of the major crimes they'd been chasing him for. And when she'd introduced herself— Rachel Greene, Special Agent— she'd given him her card, simple letters and a seal on white stock.

He still had it.

They met in Detroit. He drove across the Ambassador Bridge from the prosperous city of Windsor, Canada into the heart of the hollowed-out former greatness that was today's Motor City. The office building was non-descript. No major Federal bucks were being spent here. He showed I.D., passed through a metal detector and took the elevator to the tenth floor.

She was waiting for him when the elevator doors opened. He was surprised that she wasn't taller. The only other time he'd seen her, he was already seated across from a couple of standard-issue male agents when she walked into the room. She was thin with dark-rimmed glasses cutting across a long, angular face and dark hair pulled back severely. A black pant suit teamed with high-heeled black pumps increased the appearance of height. He'd pegged her at 5' 7" or more.

Now the outfit and the hair were the same, giving the same impression of tall and narrow from a distance. But as she approached, he realized that without heels she'd stand 5' 4" at the most, and depending on how much lift she was getting out of the shoes, she might not top 5' 2". A v of white blouse at the neckline contrasted with skin that was on the paler side of healthy. Either she wasn't an outdoors girl, or she regularly dipped herself in sunblock. Her eyes were her only spot of color. They were a stunning shade of green. He wondered if they were the only attribute she couldn't force into cookie-cutter FBI conformity, and if she disliked them.

She led him down the hall to an anonymous door with only a suite number, 1017, unlocked it with a key, and waved him inside. The room was small, no more than ten by twelve. It held a vintage government-issue metal desk and three metal chairs. There was a small bookcase that contained a phone book from 2002, six years in the past. The desk held a phone and a closed laptop.

"Sorry for the spartan surroundings," she said. "They're overcrowded here, and I'm a visitor and not a very distinguished one at that. I get the annex."

They settled themselves in the standard places, she behind the desk and Grady in one of the two chairs facing it. "I don't have coffee or even water," she said, "but if you like, I could go down the hall and get you some."

He let her know he was fine. Truth was, he could have really used a cup of coffee, but sending her on an errand didn't seem like a good way to start the conversation.

"So you're interested," she said.

He nodded. He wasn't sure what he was interested in, but he figured she would tell him.

She pushed her chair back from the desk, crossed her legs right over left, jiggled her top foot rhythmically. He was certain that if she'd been born a little sooner, or into a less privileged background (he figured her at about thirty-five, with an Ivy League education that followed an upper middle-class childhood), she'd be a smoker. Her nervous system was crying out for nicotine, and she didn't even know it.

"What do you know about the use of private security companies in Iraq and Afghanistan, Mr. Grady?"

"Mercenaries?"

She gave him an indulgent smile. "No, no, no. That's a misconception. Private security companies—contractors—supplement our military personnel in a number of areas, everything from food preparation to construction. They free our troops to focus on the job at hand. They're cooks, dishwashers, carpenters. They clean the latrines and mop the floors. Yes, they do provide security for personnel and equipment. But they do not fight. Even the most heavily armed, most highly trained of these personnel act in a protective capacity only. It's an important distinction."

She seemed to be waiting for Grady to acknowledge his faux pas, so he did. "My mistake."

She nodded, which he assumed meant "no problem." "I thought of it for you initially because, well, you have the right background, and you've shown you're resourceful."

"And I got a bum deal."

She shrugged. "And then when you called… Well, I was going to be in your general area, so why not have a chat."

"Help a citizen out?"

"We're not villains, Mr. Grady."

"I know. I've been reminded. My tax dollars at work."

The foot stopped jiggling. Any warmth that had been in her voice vanished. "Look. I have other things I can be doing. If you're interested, we can continue this conversation. If not, you can leave and I'll go on with my day."

He'd been reprimanded, and there was no point in getting his back up about it. Time for a little remorse. "I'm sorry. That was uncalled for."

"Yes. It was."

"So you have me in mind for one of these positions?"

"Not me personally. But it occurred to me that I could point you in the right direction. People with your qualifications, they're, well, unusual."

His qualifications?

"There aren't that many men with a background that includes both experience as a Ranger and significant time in law enforcement."

"They're not breaking my door down. Never have."

"Well, these companies are looking for either. The combination is a big bonus from their point of view."

"You know how I left the force. I was fired. That's got to be a deal-breaker."

To his amazement, she smiles. "Hmm. You signed a lot of papers, correct?"

He did.

"There were a lot of harsh consequences. No question about that. But my understanding is that, technically, according to those documents, they let you resign. Right?"

Huh. He didn't think so, but it occurs to him that when he was being investigated by the Feds a couple of years back, this agent or her colleagues would have been through all that, every dotted i and crossed t. She must know better than he does.

"I guess so."

Another nod. "So you'll get through the background check. It's not like a dishonorable discharge. You get a couple of your former colleagues to write letters of recommendation. How loyally you served, how professionally, how they believe that if it hadn't been for media over-reaction, you'd still be on the job. That you were a real loss to the department. If one of them happens to be a former superior, so much the better. Some of these contracting companies, well, they understand these things."

A good old boy soldier-of-fortune network? Was that what she meant? "Okay," he said hesitantly. "Okay."

Apparently, she heard the doubt in his voice and took it for continuing concern about his credentials because she went on. "Also, you're big. You're solid."

Did she mean fat?

"You know your way around policing and hand-to-hand combat. And you look like you could be one of those large, aggressively macho guys, but you're not."

Grady didn't get it. "And that's a good thing?"

"Yes. You have more sense than that. Oh, your type isn't for everybody. There are some real assholes in high places in this business. But there are also people who appreciate men who have the skills but who don't want to play Rambo. They make the best protective personnel."

So she was talking about him going to a war zone and playing fancy security guard. It was hard for him to imagine it was something he'd want to do no matter how lost he felt at the moment. But...

"I don't want to kid you. Some of the assignments are high pressure. There's risk involved. But you'd be making a contribution. And the pay is good."

She couldn't give him an exact figure, she said. It would depend on who hired him and who the particular contract was with: the Army, the State Department. But an approximation? For a man with his skills, he'd be looking at $600 per day, seven days a week. He did the math quickly in his head. $18,000 per month.

He hated to bring it up, but he had to. "What about my age?"

"Not a disqualifier. Not at all. Most of the men are younger, many significantly so. But there's not any formal age cut-off for this kind of thing, and most companies like a few older guys to even out the energy."

"Young guns can be dangerous."

An expression that was almost a smile. "You got it." Then all business again. "All this said, you'll need to pass a physical. You don't look too bad, but you'll need to start working out. Today. And you have to stop drinking."

She knew everything about him, or thought she did, he could tell. Including the drinking. He'd always liked a few beers, or a Scotch. But there had been times when he drank and times when he *drank*.

After he was ousted from his job as a detective, his boozing was worse than it had been in a long time. But once he got the job as security director for the group of gated communities, he knew he was lucky, knew he'd been more or less rescued, even if the lifeboat was leaky, small and unlikely ever to come within sight of any kind of promised land, and he managed to mostly sit on his drinking. To do it at night and at home, where the only witness to slurring or stumbling or the occasional sloppy sentimentality was his dog. And Bear didn't care. That German shepherd's love was unconditional.

His time on the run from false charges had led him down the rabbit hole again, but when he found out what really happened just before he left the Army back in 1981, he knew that his drinking could have been, and almost was, the end of him. And he got semi-sober.

But lately. Since Bear died...

"You won't be able to drink during your tours, no matter what you see the other guys doing—and, yes, people do manage to get alcohol into these Muslim countries no matter how officially it's banned. And you won't be able to drink during your breaks. No r'n'r binges. Can you do that?"

Could he? For a job that paid more money than he'd ever dreamed of earning? A job that might make him feel worthwhile?

He wanted to tell her he'd already stopped. But that would have been a lie, and lying to her seemed like a really bad idea. He had tried. But each day, especially each evening starting about sundown, was a teeth-clenching exercise in what felt like extreme self-denial. He told himself it would get easier, that he could do this. And every night, his need called him a liar. He'd only managed to string together two sober days at a time. But where there were two, there could be three, and four, and more. With this kind of carrot added to the motivation he already had, it would work. He could do it.

She was waiting. "Well, Mr. Grady? Can you do that?"

He nodded. "Yes, ma'am. I can."

And he did. He drank soda and sparkling water that night, and the next, and the next.

She gave him a card: Hammer, LLC, with a name, "J. D. Hammer," a title, CEO, and a phone number.

He made a quick trip back to Tucson to beg recommendations from former buddies in the TPD. With little confidence in his prospects, he approached Kevin George, old Two First Names KG, now retired, who'd been a lieutenant when his particular shit hit the fan.

KG hadn't spoken up for Grady back in the day, had even called him a fuck-up to his face. But apparently that was then and this was now. KG popped the tops on two bottles of beer, handed him one, and said, "Hell, Grady, I don't care if the fucking media smeared you six ways 'til Sunday. You tell me you got your shit together, you got your shit together. Good enough for me. Ask me, I think Captain Mackenzie had it in for you. Ever since that send-off for Fat Joe where you took a piss in Mac's hat and it was dark in the place and he'd a few himself and he put the damn thing on and the piss splashed all over him." KG chuckled at the memory. "After that, he was just waiting for an excuse. And you gave him one. Mac never did have a sense of humor."

They clinked bottles. Grady managed to unobtrusively empty the contents of his bottle into a handy potted palm and walked away with a recommendation just short of glowing. "Why are you doing this for me?" he'd asked Rachel Greene.

"Look, the first time I met you, back in Tucson, I implied that your situation—all that you'd been through because of a, well, less than optimally handled investigation—was just business as usual. That you should suck it up, smile, and get on with it. But you were right. You got a raw deal. You seemed like a nice enough guy, and, in the vernacular, you were royally screwed. So since I can do it, why not?"

Just what was she doing, he wondered. So he asked. "And that is?"

"As I said earlier, just pointing you in the right direction. That's all."

She vouched for him, he realized later. When he called the number on the card, J. D. Hammer (through his secretary) passed Grady off to another guy, the one who handled recruiting. As they went through the duties and the requirements, that man seemed almost solicitous. At one point, he mentioned that not many applicants came recommended in this particular way. It seemed to have bounced Grady to the front of the queue at the very least. Would he have gotten the job anyway? Maybe. His background was close to a private security company's ideal—if you overlooked certain things. And, he learned later, there were companies who did, whose vetting of prospects was a little too casual at best, slipshod at worst. But it was also very possible that he never would have even gotten his foot in the door without Rachel Greene. He owed her big-time. If he were one of those people who lit candles, he would have lit one for her.

It's after one when he finally gives up on sleep. He wanders into the kitchen and is looking in his nearly empty frig for a midnight snack, wishing he had something sweet, even one of those lousy fast food sugar bombs they call pies, when he hears a distant ringing.

It's the damn cell phone. Supposed to be convenient, but here he is trying to follow the sound to figure out where he it. Then he's trying to grab the pants he hung on a hook in the closet and dig out the phone before the call goes to voicemail.

No luck. But just as he gets the thing in his hand, it rings again. And he sees it on the screen: Tucson Police Department. What the hell?

"Mr. Grady?" It's a male voice, youngish, with the polite cadence of a rookie not too long out of the academy. "It's your niece, sir. When you didn't answer the first time, she said I should try again right away."

Gina. In trouble again. Drug possession? Prostitution? Shoplifting? An overdose? Fuck. He should have stayed in Iraq. He's used to dealing with the day-to-day crap there—and whatever emotional shit is stirred up by the ever-present threat of danger.

This is a whole different kind of pain.

10

Technology has exploded in law enforcement since Grady's day. Keyboards and flat-screen monitors are everywhere. Smoking in the building was banned long before he left the force, but the squad room still doesn't seem quite right without the gray haze and the smell of stale tobacco. The coffee hasn't changed, though. It's the standard cop brew, burned and thickened from hours sitting on the hot plate. He takes a slug anyway.

They've already been through the whole thing, and he still can't quite believe what he's hearing. "She found a body?"

Detective Moreno ("Pete Moreno," as he introduced himself) nods. "She did."

"In a bathtub."

"Yes."

Grady's sitting on a government-issue metal chair in front of Moreno's desk. Gina is slumped on a bench against the far wall. She looks like hell.

He puts his attention back on Moreno. "And she knows this person."

"Seems so. She's a little out of it now, but she was talking our ears off for a while."

"Is she being held?"

"No. Look, your niece is on something. But she's functional. Doesn't seem in any danger from whatever it is. No signs of an overdose. And she wasn't holding. She's free to go."

"Thank you."

Moreno shrugs. "We're not in the business of making more trouble for people than they already have. And it looks like you and the rest of her family have had plenty."

Grady acknowledges the truth of that statement with a nod.

"If it makes you feel any better, she did the right thing. She didn't run. She used the wall phone in the kitchen to call 911. She was hysterical when we got there, but she didn't leave. She fell asleep in the squad car, but once we got her back here and got some Coca-Cola into her, she perked right up. Told us what we needed to know."

"So you have her statement."

"Yup. We may want to talk to her again. But we're done with her for now."

When Grady answered the call from the TPD, the young male voice said, "Mr. Grady? This is Officer Gonzalez with the Tucson Police. We have your niece here at the main station." Then, without warning, he put Gina on the line. Grady could hear her crying, almost hysterical. Was this still about the baby? And how in God's name had she gotten the police involved? But all Gina kept saying through her sobs was, "She's dead, Uncle Jack. She's dead."

Then the male voice was back. "This is Officer Gonzalez again. Your niece is pretty upset. And she says she has nowhere to go. Could you come down here, sir?"

The knot of dread in his stomach tightened when the front desk directed him to the squad room. Those words: "She's dead." Who was dead? And how? Had a fellow junkie somehow OD'd in Gina's presence—or at Gina's hands? Could 'she's dead' mean something even worse?

But then he saw her sitting on a chair kind of out of the way. She wasn't in holding, she wasn't cuffed. It didn't even look like anyone was paying much attention to her.

She spotted him and stumbled across the room, fell into his arms, and began sobbing. "She's dead." She kept saying it. The same words. "She's dead." Over his shoulder, he saw a chunky dark-skinned detective seated at a desk make eye contact, then beckon him over. He got Gina calmed down, stuck her on a nearby bench, and made his way over to the guy.

He had to own up, no point in trying to hide it. So he introduced himself as a former detective with the unit, and got no reaction at all beyond a handshake, the words "Pete Moreno. Good to meet you," and a nod of acknowledgement that he had once been among the brethren. He was relieved—and then realized he shouldn't be surprised. Almost a decade down the road, his disgrace would be old news to those who were around back then, and the younger cops would never have heard of him at all. This guy looked to be early to mid-thirties, somewhere between the veterans and the newbies. Either way, it didn't seem to matter.

Now, having heard as much as the detective is willing to tell him, he thanks Moreno and gathers Gina up.

In the car, she looks like she might drift off again, so he decides she needs food, stat. He drives through the next Burger King he sees and gets double whoppers, fries, and large Cokes for them both.

They sit in the truck in the parking lot and eat. As the glucose hits her bloodstream, Gina begins to revive. And to talk.

11

She'd left Grady's really upset. "You tore me apart, Uncle Jack. You were awful."

Grady doesn't say anything. She's right. He was awful. But she was pretty horrible herself. And if Gina is who she is…well, he is who he is, too. Confronted by the same kind of unreasoning, off-the-wall behavior again, he'd probably do the same thing.

"I have friends. I know you think I don't. But I do. And they're good people."

She was going to look up one of those friends, she tells him. She'd only been back in Tucson since Sunday night when she took the last bus in from Phoenix, and she hadn't seen this friend since before her baby was born. Grady gets the impression that the friend is one of the few people Gina knows who manages to keep a roof over her head.

"I knew she'd be glad to see me. I knew she'd put me up for a while."

Grady figures that "a while" probably would have turned out to be a night or two. At best. Gina may not look like she's been deep into hard drugs again or sleeping rough, but she doesn't look like she's morphed into an upstanding citizen either. And the welcome mat tends to be yanked away pretty quickly from someone like that.

Gina didn't have a cell phone, so she had to find a pay phone. "That was hard, Uncle Jack. There aren't many around anymore." Grady hears those words and expects that she'll use this opportunity to hit him up for a cell. In your dreams, Gina, he thinks, if you have some wild idea that I'm paying for that. You'd only sell it the first time you wanted to get high and were short of cash.

Maybe she knows his answer, or maybe she just doesn't have the energy it would take to manipulate him right now. Either way, she doesn't ask.

It took a while, but she managed to find a pay phone outside a Circle K and called her friend. No answer. So she decided to go to her friend's place and surprise her. And if she wasn't there, Gina would wait.

"What was I supposed to do, Uncle Jack? I'd been up all night, and I didn't have a lot of money. I didn't have anywhere else to go. You didn't want me."

"I didn't say that, Gina."

"Huh. Sure sounded that way to me. The things you said!" And she's crying again.

He's supposed to reach out, comfort her, tell her he loves her, that everything will be all right. But he doesn't want to. He's tired of Gina's drama. He's tired of Gina's problems. He's tired of being dragged down and pulled apart by his love for her.

So he does the only thing he can manage to do at this moment. He says, "Eat your food."

It's a command, but with love somewhere behind it. And apparently Gina hears it that way because she snuffles, wipes her nose with a napkin, and takes another bite of her Whopper.

He prompts her. "So you went to your friend's place."

"Melissa. She goes by Missy. She has an apartment near Broadway and Country Club."

"And when you got there…?"

"I went up to her door. All those apartments open onto the outside. She's on the second floor, and there's, like, a balcony that runs all the way around."

Grady knows the configuration. Two-story buildings with an open-air stairway to the second floor and a walkway providing access to the apartments. Fronting a parking lot, or if the residents are lucky, backing on a parking lot and arranged in a "U" around a small swimming pool. Typical Tucson rentals.

"I rang her bell, but she didn't answer. There was a woman coming out of the next apartment over, and I asked her if she knew where Missy was. She just shook her head and said her car was there, but she hadn't seen her all weekend, since Friday afternoon."

"She could have gone away for a few days."

Gina shakes her head. "No. Missy worked weekends. Friday and Saturday nights were her busiest times."

"What did Missy do?"

Gina shrugs. She takes another bite of burger, fills her mouth with food. Grady has the distinct impression that she doesn't want to answer, that chewing is a delaying tactic.

"What was Missy's job, Gina?"

"She was an escort."

Of course. A friend of Gina's. A prostitute. Probably a junkie. What was it Moreno had said? "There may have been illegal activity involved. But it doesn't look like foul play." Illegal activity. Hooking. Drugs. In Gina's world, that's same old, same old.

"So you're at her apartment, and she's not there."

Gina shrugs. "Well, she wasn't answering the door. So I was going to wait. And then I realized I knew where Missy keeps...kept...her extra key. There's a metal railing that goes all the way around that balcony or landing or whatever you call it that the apartments open onto. The bottom railing's shaped like an upside-down U. Missy always had one of those magnetic hide-a-key things stuck up in there."

"And you decided to use it."

He hasn't tried to hide the criticism in his voice, the implication of criminal wrongdoing leftover from his years in law enforcement (or hasn't tried hard enough), and he can tell she hears it. "You don't understand, Uncle Jack. Missy wouldn't have wanted me to just wait there outside, especially when I was tired and getting hungry. And really upset about those things you said. Missy and I are really good friends."

Really good friends. An addict and a call girl. Who hadn't seen each other or—from what Grady has gathered—even been in touch for going on two years. Not that the heavily damaged, the people living in the cracks of society, can't form bonds. But in spite of all the movies and TV shows to the contrary, Grady's experience has been that those bonds tend to be a lot looser and come apart a lot more easily than those in what he thinks of as the normal world. There's no point in arguing with Gina now, though. Who cares about the trespassing or unlawful entry or whatever the charge could have been? And what is he going to do? Lecture her on the importance of nurturing friendships? Keeping up relationships? When he's done such a generally crappy job of it himself? Move on, Grady.

"So you let yourself in."

Gina nods. "Yeah. Of course. I waited until the woman from next door left, and…" She stops. She isn't eating. She's just looking down at her hands, the right one holding the burger, the left one the Coke. She puts down the food and turns to him.

"I knew something was wrong right away. Because Missy has great taste. She's really particular. I knew her apartment would be all neat and pretty like it always was. But it smelled terrible."

There weren't any lights on, and it was starting to get dark. Gina found the switch that controlled a lamp and looked around. The living room was empty. The attached kitchen was empty. She went down the hall and looked into the half bath. No one.

She could hear music playing, very faintly. The door to the bedroom was closed. She opened it and went in. There was a bedside lamp on. The room was empty. The music was louder, and the smell was worse. The door to the adjoining bathroom was closed. And there was no crack of light under it.

She walked over to the door, put her hand on the knob, and turned. "I was scared, Uncle Jack. I had a really bad feeling."

The door swung open. The music was loud. The stench was horrible. Gina found the wall switch, turned the light on—and started screaming.

"Detective Moreno said she was in the tub."

Gina nods. Tears are starting again.

"I couldn't even tell it was Missy. It was just this…thing."

Grady knows what the body would have looked like if it had been in the water long enough to smell. It would be bloated, discolored. Hideous. Even hardened crime scene investigators have trouble with corpses like that.

"I threw up, Uncle Jack. All over the bathroom floor. And then I backed out of there, away from that…"

"But you didn't run." His niece has guts. He has to give her credit for that. "I'm proud of you, Gina."

His niece's face changes for a moment.

"I was going to. I wanted to. But I knew I couldn't. I closed the bathroom door behind me and the door to the bedroom, too. I don't know why. I'd seen the wall phone in the kitchen, and I used it to call 911. They told me to stay where I was. So I did. But not in Missy's apartment. I went back out on the landing. Even out there, I could still smell the…the…" Gina breaks down again.

Grady waits. "Take your time," he says. Just like she's a witness he's questioning, he scolds himself. He wants to hand her a tissue (even though that's also standard procedure), but he doesn't have one. He does have an extra napkin that came with his burger, though. It's clean, so he puts it in her hand. He knows he should reach out, touch his niece reassuringly, but things between them aren't so simple right now, and somehow he just can't. Besides, she's clearly getting support from one or more of her favorite chemicals.

After a moment, she blows her nose on the napkin and continues. "I could smell the body out there, just a lot less strong. I can't believe I didn't notice it before when I was going to wait there for her. But at least I didn't have to look at..."

"And you took something."

Grady sees momentary alarm.

Gina shakes her head. "No. I didn't. I didn't take anything."

"C'mon. I know you. You were upset so you swallowed something. Let's call it 'self-medication.'"

He thinks he sees a look of what could almost be relief pass over her face, but she doesn't say anything. He needs to know, and the soft-pedal approach isn't working.

"Don't kid me, Gina. The cops could tell you were high. Hell, anyone could tell you were high. And they searched you, didn't they?"

Gina nods silently.

"Why do you think they did that?"

Gina shakes her head. An innocent. Like she really has no clue.

"What did you take?" Grady has to know what he's dealing with here. It doesn't seem too serious—at least in the context of Gina's history, but he still needs the information.

"Just a couple of pills."

Grady looks the "What?" at her.

"Vicodin. All I had on me. I was really upset. Do you blame me?"

Does he blame her? How many times has it been: I've had a shitty day, I need a drink. I've earned a celebration, I need a drink. I can't sleep, I need a drink...

No. Right at this moment, he doesn't blame her at all.

\#

Gina was dozing almost before she'd swallowed the last bite of her burger. Grady pulls the car into his building's underground parking, helps her out. She leans on him heavily all the way to the elevator and slumps in a corner for the quick trip up, but she manages the hundred or so feet from the elevator to his door almost on her own.

As soon as he gets her into his apartment, he parks her on the couch. "Stay there," he says, "I'll only be a minute."

He makes a quick trip to the john. Then he gathers up a pillow and blanket—for himself. He's going to give her his bed. No choice.

He carries the bedding into the living room. And sees Gina curled up on the couch, sound asleep. He tucks the pillow under her head, spreads the blanket over her. She doesn't move.

12

Braydon Malone, twenty-five years old, born St. Clair Shores, Michigan. Graduated South Lake High School middle of his class. One hitch U.S. Army. Two years a local cop, uniformed, back in his hometown. Blonde, blue. Height five-eleven. Weight 170. No arrests. Parents, two younger sisters, one fiancé. No children. No obvious strong religious feelings or political preferences. Hobbies: basketball, video games. The usual social media presence, no nudity, nothing inflammatory, no harassment incoming or outgoing. Postings since Malone's death all typical: We love you, Braydon. We will miss you forever, Braydon. May God heal your wounds. May you rest in Jesus's hands...

A file that told Rachel nothing, or at least nothing helpful. And her call was coming through.

"Gil?"

"Hi, Rach."

"What you got for me?"

"Not much."

"So nobody's saying nothing."

"You got it."

"Do you get the sense they're clamming up?"

"I can't tell. Nobody's acting squirrely. Nobody's avoiding me, or being overly friendly. Nobody's refusing to talk or talking too much. But, of course, I don't know them."

A given. Tell me something useful, Gil. "So there may be nothing."

"Yeah, well, the cause of suicide and the act don't always track."

Gil's right. People's motives for suicide can appear trivial to the outside world. So if you ascribe this suicide to that kind of disordered thinking... We mark the case closed, move on. And based on what they've learned so far, this wouldn't be a surprising conclusion. But her gut says this would be wrong, or at least premature. "Absolutely true. The act of suicide is almost always irrational by definition. But with this clean-cut all-American boy..."

"The cleanest."

"There's no history of PTSD, no indication of substance abuse. Right?"

"Right."

"So we need to keep digging. Just in case." She clicks through the file again. "Fill me in on Malone's immediate environment."

There are about a dozen guys billeted together, Gil says, in, "let's call it 'the house.' The numbers vary a bit as people come and go from tours. But the max is twelve. There's a core group, seven, eight guys who are pretty tight. People are in and out of Baghdad on different schedules, so the makeup of the group shifts somewhat."

"Leader?"

"Hartman Pickett."

"Hartman?"

"Southern. They like using family names that way. He's a former Ranger."

"Age?"

"Thirty-three. Hard core body builder. Hasn't spent any real time stateside since he was eighteen.

"So he's the alpha dog." There always is one. And that dog's rule isn't always benign.

"Yeah. But it seems pretty harmless. They all look up to him, even the couple of guys who are older than he is, but it's not nearly as much monkey-see, monkey-do as it could be."

"So it's the typical partying together up on the roof, telling each other how they have each other's backs, nicknames, surfing the web, swapping war stories."

"There's some swagger, but for this much testosterone…"

"You've seen worse."

Gil has. "Malone was apparently the nerd in the bunch. He was mainstream enough to be part of the core group but deep into computers. He helped everybody with their tech problems and spent a lot of time with his nose in a screen. But he was affable and even if he wasn't as much into body building or partying as some of the rest of them, he was still recognized as one of the boys. He had a third-grade sense of humor, liked knock-knock jokes, so they called him Goofy."

"So we've got the core group. What about the four or five other guys in the house? The ones who aren't part of the band of brothers?"

"Again, the dynamic doesn't seem too bad. They're not shunned. They're just not part of the group. Some of it seems to be age differences, some of it just personalities—there's a loner or two. A lot of it is just different interests."

"Geezer?"

"Not part of the in-crowd."

Older. Less inclined to video games. Not into social media. Set apart.

So why would Malone say, "Geezer will take care of it"?

Take care of what?

She decides to push Gil on his sense of things. "Should we break them up?"

"Maybe." She hears hesitation in his voice, but she knows it's only because Gil hates to be noncommittal. They both know her question is premature.

She acknowledges that. "But not yet, huh. If this is nothing, we've disbanded a cohesive unit."

"And damaged morale."

"And if it is something, we've spread the poison. And there's time. If they needed to get their stories straight, they've already done that. So…next steps."

"Are you on the move?" Gil's words let her know they're on the same page.

She closes the file. "Yup."

13

By ten a.m., Grady has showered and shaved. He isn't sure what the occasion calls for, so he's turned to the interview outfit he bought to wear to his meeting about the contractor job. Even though that wasn't much more than a year ago, it feels like way back when. The pants are looser but still fit well enough. The blue dress shirt with a faint woven stripe looks good. It's been in his closet since he unpacked it yesterday, and the wrinkles have pretty much hung out. Which is fortunate since he doesn't own an iron. Now the questions. Tie or no tie? Sport coat? He decides tie no, sport coat yes.

The night before, just as he was finally falling asleep again after getting Gina settled, he heard a "ding." It took him a couple of drowsy moments to realize that it was his phone. When he looked at the screen, he realized it was already early morning. And he had a text. From Rachel Greene.

His first reaction was surprise bordering on shock. What was an FBI agent doing texting him?

> In Tucson on biz. Hoping u r around.
> Would love to get together and catch up.

He couldn't blow her off. And he didn't want to. He owed her way too much. It wasn't as if his social calendar was crowded. And it might be, if not fun, interesting to see her again.

But "catch up"? Was she assuming that he'd be in Tucson because he didn't get the job, never went to Iraq?

Or had she kept track of him? And, if so, why?

Don't be paranoid, he told himself. She "sponsored" him, she wants to see how he's doing, confirm to herself that she didn't make a bad call. Women have egos, too. No big deal. She'd be in and out of his life in ten minutes.

He texted back.

Nice to hear from u. How about coffee? 10 or 11am?

The answer came seconds later:

Hope I didn't wake u. Still running on D.C. time

Just realized how early it is here. Sorry!
Can't do am coffee.
How about lunch? 2pm? U pick the place.

Lunch? So much for that ten minutes. After a moment, he replied:

Sounds good. Will pick place and text info later.

\#

Rachel's back from the hotel gym and just out of the shower when her phone rings. It's Gil. Unscheduled. She slides to accept the call, then puts the phone on speaker while she dries off and pulls on her clothes.

"What's up? Fill me in."

"I've been playing it low-key. Routine investigation of a death in theater. You know the drill. And everybody's been on their best behavior. 'So tragic.' 'Senseless.' 'Know it wasn't an accident, but can't help thinking that it must have been.' 'Maybe he snapped.

People do.' They're making up reasons, filling in the blank of why he died."

"A natural instinct." She slides her top on over her head, steps into her skirt.

"Maybe. But I've been seeing some interesting body language. Some of them are visibly tense. Some are a little too obviously relaxed."

"Everybody?"

"No. Just the guys in the core group. The other men have reacted pretty much the way I'd expect them to. Surprise. Shock. At a loss to understand."

"It's pretty subtle stuff, reading body language. Easy to get it wrong." As the crucial first days after Malone's suicide have passed and Gil still seems to be drilling a dry hole, she's becoming less and less convinced there's any "there" there in this investigation.

"I agree. But, Rach, we've found something."

She lets him fill her in as she puts on makeup, glides a comb through damp hair. Pull it up? Back? No, let it hang, straight and shiny.

"I'm on my way to the meet. Lunch." She adds a silver chain around her neck.

"Rach?"

She listens while she shoves her feet into black pumps, stows her laptop in her briefcase, settles the long strap on her shoulder.

On her way out the door, she makes another quick call, gives instructions. Just before she disconnects, she confirms: "I'll make that lunch a long one."

#

Grady had decided to use what was left of the morning and the early afternoon to finish up his shopping: more towels, dishes, pots and pans, a set of glasses, mugs, silverware, cooking implements, hot pads, dish soap, laundry detergent, another set of sheets, a better pillow. But by the time he's halfway through the list, the sun is high in the sky, and he's flagging.

He didn't get what anyone would call a good night's sleep. Not with the trip to the police station to rescue his disaster of a niece and then with her passed out on his living room couch. Okay, she was asleep. But homeless. And using. Just a couple of Vicodin, my ass.

First, there were her threats about turning lives upside down to regain custody of her baby. And now this latest mess. It was after five (and after the texts with Rachel Greene) before he finally dropped off.

As he turns from the store parking lot onto the main road, he spots a Starbuck's on the corner. The mom-and-pop diners and ordinary old coffee shops that have dotted Tucson all his life are disappearing. There are still a few around, but even those are starting to "rebrand" themselves and charge big bucks for a slug of caffeine.

When the chirpy kid with five large rings in his left ear and a smaller one through a nostril is finally ready to make his life better by taking his order, Grady points at the size he wants, grunts "Coffee, black." And lays down more money than any simple cup of the stuff should cost.

Because he got to sleep so damned late, he didn't get as early a start as he meant to that morning. Once he was moving, he did the usual things: made coffee, poured himself a bowl of Cheerios, ate it sitting at the kitchen counter. Gina was still sacked out on the couch, but he didn't bother trying to be quiet. He even thought about turning on the TV to catch the news. If it disturbed Gina, that would be just too damn bad. This was his place. Then he remembered: he still hadn't bought a TV.

Gina didn't stir. She was still breathing: he could see the blanket covering her move up and down.

When he was ready to leave, he thought about what the fuck he should do—and couldn't come up with a good solution. In the end, he wrote a note and propped it up against his empty coffee mug.

Out on business. No spare key so stay in the apartment.

Back by five or so. Help yourself to food.

The line about no spare key was a lie. He'd been given two full sets when he moved in: two keys for the security door down at street level, two keys to his mailbox, and two keys to his own front door. But he wasn't about to invite his niece that deeply into his life—a life that he was finally managing to get in order.

The level in his cup is getting low. He considers getting a refill, decides no. Way too pricey.

Should he call home? It's not that he fears Gina won't help herself to the cereal, peanut butter, and few other staples that are around. No, he's afraid that she'll make herself at home with a vengeance. He pictures wet towels on the bedroom carpet, strawberry jam smeared across the couch, music turned up so loud that his neighbors call the management, or the cops. And it's not like he can do anything if she's not okay, or if she doesn't answer, or if she's already turned his living room into a shooting gallery. But he should check on her. He pulls out his phone, then realizes he can't call the apartment. All he has is his cell, which is right here in his hand. He doesn't yet have a landline.

He takes the last swallow of his coffee, tosses the cup in a nearby bin, and moves on with his day.

His list seems endless. He'd hoped to go back to his place and unload before meeting Rachel for lunch, but suddenly it's one-thirty.

14

He's a few minutes early, which is a relief. He'd been afraid he'd be late, which would have been rude—and stupid. He tells himself there's no reason to be nervous about this lunch. She means what she says, that she just wants to catch up. But he doesn't believe it.

He'd had a hell of a time figuring out where they should eat. He figured she'd be used to upscale Washington eateries. What did he know but burritos, burger joints, and low-end steakhouses? Then he recalled a place he'd met Jill for lunch a few years back.

The restaurant, Tohono Chul, is still as nice as he remembers, casual, but classy. He waits at the hostess stand for Rachel. And he's surprised at what a pleasure it is to see her walk in the door. Hers is an urban look. No one would ever mistake her for a Tucsonan. She's in her usual black, but it's a skirt suit this time, tailored with accents of silver zippers—down the front of the jacket, across two pockets. Her legs are sheathed in sheer black, her heels are high. He approves.

She pulls off her sunglasses. "Bright out there," she says to the hostess. Then she sees Grady. "Hello!" she says offering her hand. "Good to see you."

As they're seated, Rachel removes her jacket. Her arms are bare, and her white top is lower cut than he can imagine the FBI is comfortable with. Breaking the dress code? Or just staying cool?

"I'm roasting," she says. "So this is fall in the desert."

"Yup. We're getting out our parkas and long johns."

They both flip through the menu. Grady wonders if he should pick up the check. And he realizes that he actually can if it seems appropriate. Until his current gig, he wouldn't have dreamed of getting in a position where he had to pay for himself at any place pricier than Mickey D's, let alone spring for his companion's meal. The lunch with Jill all those years back had been her treat, a thank you for a favor he'd done her.

"This place is great," Rachel says. "I'm surprised it's so empty. I'd have thought they'd have a good clientele."

Grady looks around. Except for a table of four working out the math for splitting their check and a couple who's just finishing their post-lunch coffee, he and Rachel are the only patrons. It makes sense to him, though. "This is Tucson," he says.

Rachel apparently notices him looking at his watch. "Oh," she says. "Different cultures. I always forget. Back in D.C., one-thirty is considered standard lunch time, and two is still busy."

"Out here, we're hungry by eleven. If you and I wait much longer to order, we risk running right into Early Bird dinner."

Grady chooses a steak sandwich and fries. He expects Rachel to go for a salad. She looks like a woman who subsists on rabbit food. Instead, she opts for pulled pork on a roll, slaw, and red potatoes. He should have noticed her biceps and realized that she's feeding lean muscle.

"Nice of you to look me up," he says.

"I was going to be in the neighborhood, and I found our meetings memorable."

He can't imagine why, and attempts to cover. "Because I'm from Tucson. I get that a lot."

"No. Because you were memorable. Think about it. How many people can make it for months on the run from the F.B.I. *and* local law enforcement all across the West, then identify and catch the real perp, and come up washed clean, innocent as a new-born babe. Hell, how many people can simply survive all that? You're a rarity, Mr. Grady."

"Call me Grady."

"Not Jack?"

"Only my ex-wife calls me Jack. With anyone else, I wouldn't know who they were talking to."

"Okay. Grady. And it's Rachel. Not Ms. Greene."

"Rachel. How'd you know I was back in town?"

A shrug. "Lucky guess. I figured you'd be about due for one of your thirty-day breaks."

Lucky guess, my ass. Even if she'd made the assumption that he'd been hired, there was no way she could have known up front how long it would take him to get the gig, when his training would be complete, when his first tour would start, let alone that he was still at it. No, she checked it out. But why?

He might be a rarity. But he wasn't the kind of treasure that someone would collect. And he didn't think he'd aroused any particular sexual interest in her when they met, let alone the kind of lust that would lead her to reach out to him more than a year later.

He's too old to play this game.

The food arrives. He waits until the server has left, stays silent while his affable FBI agent chooses a packet of sweetener, watches quietly as she slides the paper off a straw and uses it to stir the sweetener into her lemonade. Then he speaks.

"You knew how to reach me because you already had the number of my cell. I haven't changed it since we met in Detroit.

"You might have followed up with your contact to find out whether I was hired. I can see that. And it's possible that the contact mentioned a timeframe when I was likely to make it to Baghdad. But that would have been a rough guess on his part. I had to be scheduled for training, which meant joining a class on a particular start date. Fact is, I had almost six weeks to fill between the moment I learned I had the gig and the date I reported to their facility in North Carolina. And, yes, all tours for the kind of duty I've been pulling are three months with thirty days off, minimum, between tours. But I might have washed out in training. I might have not completed my first tour, or quit after one, or two. And under any scenario, I might have decided not to come back to Tucson. After everything that happened before I took that gig, there wasn't much left for me here."

"Mr. Grady, Grady, I…"

"No, Ms. Greene—excuse me—Rachel, you used the resources available to you to find out where I was. And I suspect you made a trip to our lovely city specifically to see me. The question is why."

He's managed to shake her, if only slightly.

It takes only a moment for her to regain control. She purses her lips around her straw, takes a slow sip of the lemonade. "Hmm. Well, I was going to get to that. You can't blame me for the white lie. If I had the history that you have and suddenly learned that an FBI agent I'd had dealings with was in town to see me, I might, well, freak out. You're good at running. I didn't want you to do it again."

"Those were extraordinary circumstances."

"Yes."

"Running would never have been my preference. And I wouldn't have done it now."

"You're sure?" She's smiling.

Grady's stern demeanor cracks. He shrugs. And they both laugh.

"So, Rachel, what do you need?"

"There is—was—a contractor named Braydon Malone. Billeted with you."

"Sure. I know Bray." Then it registers. She said "was." And he doesn't think Rachel Greene picks her words carelessly. "Or I *did* know Bray. What happened?"

"Suicide. Gun shot."

71

"Shit! Stupid kid."

"No one knows why." She's answered his question before he's asked it.

Grady's shocked and sad, but can't figure out what the hell this has to do with him. He waits. Explaining this is on her.

They're almost done eating, and the place is empty. Turns out, it closes down between lunch and dinner (something he didn't realize when he made the reservation), and the girl at the hostess station is tapping her foot and glaring at them. He waves for the check.

"You know what," he says, "let's take a walk."

Tohono Chul is a café in a garden, with acres of grounds spread out behind the restaurant's rear patio. They take a path back among the cactus. This isn't a popular activity on a hot September Tuesday in Tucson, and the only sounds are the occasional chirping of birds.

"You're wondering what this has to do with you," Rachel begins.

No shit, thinks Grady. But he doesn't say it aloud.

"Malone was in good health physically and, as far as we know, mentally. He was close to his family, in love with his fiancé, and looking forward to their upcoming marriage—the plan was one more tour after this one and then tie the knot and settle down. He got along well with the others billeted in the house. In fact, as we understand it, he was one of what might be called the 'in crowd.' Does that correspond with what you observed about him?"

"Yes."

"Were you close? Or, should I say, how close were you?"

What is she getting at? "Not close at all. We talked a few times. We liked some of the same music. I kept that quiet since he was young enough to want to fit in and it wasn't the kind of stuff that his buddies were listening to. We had some of the same views. He wasn't a braggart. He wasn't macho. He wasn't a genius, but he was smart enough. Helped me out with my computer more than once when I was having trouble using the damn thing to call the States or getting my email to work. I'm a technological Neanderthal so I can't rate his skills. But he seemed to have extensive knowledge. I probably spent more time with him than with most of what you're calling the 'in-crowd,' but it wasn't very much."

"You had meals together."

"We all did."

"What about working together?"

"Sometimes we found ourselves on the same detail. But it didn't happen a lot. Our schedules—the times when we were both in-country—were kind of out of sync. And that core group you were talking about liked to stick together."

"Didn't you have a rotation?"

"Sure. Whoever was up, went. But there was swapping, and Malone was one of the guys who'd do that when possible to go out with his buddies. I tended to end up with the others who were odd men out, and Malone tended to work with pals."

They're on a graveled path that's an offshoot from the main walk. Tall, spiny plants with small orange flowers at the end of long branches fill the spaces on both sides of them.

"I've never seen anything like that before," Rachel says.

"Ocotillo," Grady tells her. "It's all over the place here."

"Odd but pretty," she says. She reaches out a hand. He catches her arm, pulling it back. "Careful," he says pointing out the thorns that project from the whip-like spines, "our vegetation has a nasty habit of defending itself."

She moves slightly away from the edge of the path, toward him. "When was the last time you were teamed with Malone?"

"Hmm. I don't have all this in my head. I know it was a while ago. Back in June, I think, right at the beginning of my latest tour. And the times before that would have been in the spring. Late March, April. But you know all this. Better than I do."

Rachel ignores his comment. "And those were routine assignments?"

"Just escort duty from Baghdad International, as far as I remember. We did it all the time. We did it so often that you got so you almost had to remind yourself to be just a little terrified."

"Just a little terrified?"

"A reasonable amount of well-grounded fear keeps the adrenalin flowing, the senses alert, and the man alive."

"But those were all routine trips?"

"Incident-free. But, again, you already know all this." Maybe he should have let her stick her hand into the ocotillo.

It helps a little that Rachel nods this time, acknowledging that what he says is true. "Did you participate in any assignments that weren't 'incident-free'?"

"On my second tour, I was in a convoy between Baghdad and Fallujah that ran into an IED. The vehicle ahead of the one I was in was blown up, two guys were killed, another one lost a leg. Our driver managed to swerve to the side, just missing the wreck. The man next to me bumped his head."

"Was Malone along on that assignment?"

"Not that I recall. In fact, I'm not sure he'd arrived in Baghdad yet." He stops, touches her elbow, turns her toward him. "I'm right, aren't I? He wasn't in-theater."

Rachel ignores the question. She's neither confirming nor denying. SOP, he thinks to himself, although a good investigator sometimes gives a little info to get a lot, and she's no slouch at this. She was smart enough to let him pull her back from the ocotillo earlier (and not just because of the thorns) and she let him turn her now, didn't shake off his hand either time—which he's convinced would have been her normal reaction, almost a reflex. Building a rapport with the individual you're questioning never hurts.

And she's smart enough to give it a rest, at least for a moment. They're both facing forward and walking again before she asks, "Anything else?"

"A few minor fire-fights. They shot first." That was one of the regulations under which he and all the other armed contractors functioned. They could open fire only in defense. There were times when this was not just frustrating, but stupid—to the point of endangering their lives and the lives of those they were escorting. But that line was what it was, and he'd never crossed it himself or seen anyone else cross it. He wants to confirm, subtly he hopes, that he— and everyone he ever worked a detail with—followed the rules.

"The first incident, there were two insurgent fatalities and one of our guys was wounded. Not too bad. He was evac'd to Germany and then, I guess, sent home. The second time, nobody shot anybody as far as we could tell. We weren't hurt, and we didn't think they were either. The third, it was snipers from a roof-top. Some of our guys thought we winged one of them, but they all faded away." But, fuck it, she knows all this. Or she can get the info—if she doesn't already have it. "I think we were firing at smoke. I'm not sure we even accurately homed in on where they were shooting from."

"We were okay on each one," he adds. "We operated by the book. It's all in the record."

"Was Malone along on any of those?"

"No. And if you're asking why I'm so sure of that, it's not that I have the best memory in the world. But certain things, like those times when you think you might die, tend to stick in the mind. And, as I pointed out, Ms. Greene," he says, using her last name on purpose, fuck the friendly 'Rachel', "it's all in the record."

Instead of answering, she runs a hand across her forehead. "I'm getting way too hot. How about you?"

He's more acclimated to desert temperatures than she is, and it's only about ninety. But even he's wishing he had a hat and a bottle of water.

"Are we done?" he asks her.

"Sorry. Just getting started."

"I'm confused. You're talking about Iraq. I thought you guys were strictly domestic."

"Well, that's what people think. But not strictly. Not for a long time. We do more and more in cooperation with other agencies and other governments. Lots of counterterrorism stuff. And we actually have a presence in embassies around the world. In this case…" Her voice trails off. He gets the idea. She'll tell him only what she wants to, but he has to answer her questions.

He can't believe he's going through this crap again. He's back to visualizing her impaled on cactus. Even though he'd decided when he first saw her text that it would be stupid to blow her off, he's pissed enough now to seriously consider it. Would he lose his job?

Technically, he shouldn't. She's not his employer. In reality, who knows? But he has a hunk of money in the bank, and he should be able to find something else to do with his time, especially with his recent experience added to his resume. He doesn't have to take this.

"We'll get to it," she says. "You have to hang in here."

"Am I being officially questioned?"

"Not at this point. But…"

The power in this situation is all on her side. The whole thing stinks. She went to a lot of trouble to talk to him in an informal, non-official setting, though. Whatever's going on, he needs to keep it that way. As long as he can.

They could go to the parking lot, climb into his truck, and blast the A/C. But Grady has no intention of sitting in a parked vehicle having a lengthy conversation, and he can tell Rachel Greene doesn't either. No matter how harmless it would be, they're both conditioned to be inconspicuous. It would go against all their instincts.

He comes up with another neutral venue.

"There's a coffeeshop. It's part of an old chain, not hip. Dying, in fact. Nobody goes there anymore except people so old they couldn't hear us from two feet away." He gives her the name and location. She can put it into her GPS. "I'll meet you there in twenty minutes. If you get there before I do, I'll know you've been speeding."

15

The place is just as sparsely populated as Grady has predicted. "Don't get the coffee," he says. "It'll trash your taste buds and eat your stomach lining." They both order iced tea, and Rachel adds a piece of apple pie. "To share," she says to his amazement—and annoyance. She must get how little he wants to share anything, even this town, with her right now.

He has nothing to say, waits for her to begin. Once she's completed what seems to be the ritual stirring of a packet of Nutrasweet into her iced tea, she does.

"You're right, of course," she says. "We do know all that, everything that's on record. We're looking for something else, and I..."

"You were trying to check me out. You wanted to see if I'd stray from the record. Or if I'd parrot it too closely. Either way you'd know you couldn't trust me."

"Yes."

"So did I pass?"

"What do you think?" But she smiles.

Then she's serious again. "Malone left a note. Well, a video. It wasn't up onscreen when he pulled the trigger. My colleagues scooped up his laptop and found it. Doing a routine check."

"A suicide in theater."

"Right. Always has to be checked out."

Grady expects Rachel to plow ahead with whatever she has to tell him. Instead, she pauses. He's surprised, but there it is: a chink in her armor.

After a moment, she continues. "Most of the video was what you'd expect. But right at the end, he said something odd."

Grady waits.

"He implied there was a strong reason for his suicide. And he referenced you."

"Me?"

"You."

Greene pulls a laptop out of her briefcase. Grady recognizes the military cast to the hardware. It will be hardened against shock and, probably more important these days, cyber-intrusion. She opens the laptop, fires it up. While they wait for it to boot, she takes a forkful of pie.

"A little too much sugar," she says taking another bite. "But not bad."

Grady takes her word for it.

"Okay," she says, setting the fork back on her plate. "We're live." She plugs in a set of earbuds, hits a few keys, and turns the laptop around to face him. Malone's face is frozen on the screen. The guy looks as if he's in agony. Grady puts in the earbuds and clicks the arrow to play. The video is hard to watch and even harder to listen to. What a generation. Recording yourself so that the people who loved you watch you live your last few moments before you kill yourself. And—even worse—no matter how many times they view the video, are helpless to reach through time to stop you.

The first part of the video is the usual: professions of love, apologies, removing blame, explaining only, "I can't go on." Terribly sad, but standard stuff. In his years as a detective, Grady saw enough suicide notes to realize how alike we all are when it comes to this individually tragic moment. Everyone thinks their situation is unique, that no one else has ever felt the level of pain they're feeling. But true mental illness aside, we are all the same in this kind of extremis.

Why is Rachel showing him this? From what she's said, he was in the air on his way home when Malone did the deed. He didn't have a clue the kid was contemplating such an act. He's not family; he was barely a friend.

Rachel reaches over and hits pause. "It's the next part," she says.

Grady clicks on the arrow again. And is stunned and puzzled by what he hears.

> Mom and Dad, you raised me right. And I let you down. I disgraced you. I can't live with it. The other guys, they can. But I can't. And I'm such a fucking coward I can't do anything about it either. I can't go through all that. So I'm leaving it to Geezer to take care of it. I'm counting on him. He'll do the right thing. I'm sorry.

"What is he talking about?"

"That's what we need to know. We know that you're 'Geezer.'"

Grady nods. "Could have been worse. Could have been 'Gramps.'"

"I looked it up. It's kind of a cross between old guy and fuddy-duddy."

"That's me."

She closes the laptop. "You don't have any idea what it is that you're supposed to take care of?"

"None."

"He didn't share any sensitive information, entrust you with any item for safekeeping?"

"He taught me how to do something he called 'clearing my cache' on my laptop. It sounded vaguely obscene to me, but the thing did work better. I shared an Ornette Coleman recording with him.

That's jazz." The look on her face says she knew that—maybe. "It's a classic, but an obscure one."

"He didn't talk about his troubles, problems with his girlfriend, run-ins or issues with any of the other guys in the house?"

"Not once. At least that I remember. I'm not much good as an amateur shrink. Most people catch on to that pretty quickly."

He waits while she tucks the laptop back in the briefcase, stows the case under the table.

"Look, Rachel, you and I got the same implications out of what Malone said. He was part of something that he didn't feel he could live with any longer. Whatever occurred was nasty, against regulations, maybe even flat-out illegal. Others were involved. Due to the timing, I assume it happened in theater. Which means sometime during the past six months since Malone only arrived there for the first time in late March. And my guess is that he didn't live with it all that long, so it was fairly recent, during this tour, which means within the last seven weeks. Maybe I didn't notice he was acting squirrely, but what about his pals? How did he seem to them?"

"No one observed anything unusual about his demeanor or his behavior."

"Or no one's admitting it. Which means…"

"They knew about it. Or they were involved."

"And you don't know what *it* is."

Rachel has just about finished her pie. She takes a sip of iced tea and nods. "We don't."

"And you're worried that whatever it is will come to light and cause a shit storm with the Iraqis and the American press."

"We've had too many scandals already. Abu Ghraib in 2004. Not finding the WMDs."

Grady remembered when that conclusion—that there were no weapons of mass destruction, America's rationale for the invasion—became unavoidable. Then-President George W. Bush expressed his "disappointment." But anyone with any brains knew it was a hell of a lot more than that.

"Those things, well…" Rachel's using her straw to play with the ice cubes in her glass. She's not looking at Grady.

He finishes her thought. "We looked like crap in the eyes of the world."

She stops stirring the cubes, looks him in the eye. "Yes. It's getting harder and harder to hold the coalition together. Okay, the original operation was almost eighty-five percent American and fifteen percent British and fucking little from any other country. It still matters that we're not out on this limb all on our own."

"We were the ones who climbed into the tree."

Rachel gives a grudging nod. "We need to find out what happened—if anything. Malone could have had some sort of psychotic break. It does happen, especially with young men. Whatever 'Geezer' is supposed to 'take care of' could have been just some hellish fantasy cooked up by a mind that was coming unhinged. But we need to know. We need to uncover whatever it is. If it's bad, we put it out there ourselves. We own up to it, identify everyone involved, very publicly bring them back to the States, and prosecute."

"Something the Iraqi authorities can't do."

"Right. Just like our troops, contractors don't fall under their authority."

She's telling Grady something he already knows. But he agrees with what she says next and isn't sorry she says it. "I know some people think that's appalling, but I think it's right. Who would go there if they could trip over some local law and end up in an Iraqi prison?"

Damn few. No matter how great the money, Grady wouldn't have even thought about taking his current gig without that assurance—that he would be legally safe. He doesn't always trust U.S. authorities, and he trusts foreign ones even less.

He takes them back to the reason they're talking: Malone's suicide. "Malone intended the video for his family. Did it ever get to them?" If it did, the rumor mill would be buzzing. Even though Grady's not on "social media," he might have heard something—if he'd bothered to check his email. He'd gotten in the habit of doing this semi-regularly while he was in Iraq, but he hasn't even thought about it since he left Baghdad. He'll need to take care of that.

"Of course. We sent them the video right away."

"But edited. Without the last section."

"Yes, we clipped it."

Rachel Greene is a smart, interesting woman. And attractive. Under other circumstances... But she's not local, and except for thirty days every fourth month neither is he, and the outcome of her current investigation sounds messy. If something comes to light, having lived in the same house with whatever contractors were involved is already too close for his idea of comfort.

He understands why she needed to talk to him, but he figures their conversation, and his involvement in some undefined mess, ends here.

"Look," she says. "These things we talked about. That's why we need to get out in front of this. Deal with it head-on."

"You have a real problem," he says. "I get it."

He tips up his glass and drains the last of his iced tea, taking his time, showing that he, too, can be in control.

"Sorry I can't help," he adds, calling for the check.

16

Grady sets down the boxes he's carrying and digs out his keys. He thinks, not for the first time, that there was something to be said for his old place out in the desert. It may have been a dump, but he could drive his truck right up to the door, unload anything from a few sacks of groceries to a refrigerator. None of this hauling stuff through a parking garage, up an elevator, and down a hall. He puts the key in the lock, turns it, and pushes down on the handle. No dice. He turns the key the other way, pushes on the handle, and the door opens. It wasn't locked.

Gina.

Shit.

The blankets are in a ball at the end of the couch. A bowl of soggy Cheerios sits in a pool of milk on the kitchen island next to a large butcher knife and a pizza box holding one greasy slice with the pepperoni picked off. His only large towel is a wet heap on the bathroom floor, and his tube of toothpaste, without its cap, rests in the sink. But the place is empty. She's gone.

Did she leave the door unlocked to spite him? More likely, she's planning on coming back. She managed to get into the building before, buzzed enough apartments, or talked a resident into it, or followed somebody in. No big mystery there. She probably figured she'd do it again, then just waltz into his place through the open door.

Shit. There's an old saying that you can't choose your family. If he could have, he would have done a better job.

Back in the kitchen, he dumps the Cheerios into the garbage disposal and sets the bowl in the sink. The milk on the counter has run over the edge and dripped down the front of the lower cabinets, making a puddle on the floor. He wets a corner of the only kitchen towel that's available (the new ones are still in a bag in the back of his truck) and wipes the wood.

He reaches for paper towels to mop up the liquid on the floor and notices a footprint in the milk. He cusses at himself, tosses the kitchen towel on the floor near the stove, pulls off his shoes, and dumps them on top of the towel. Then he bends and uses a paper towel to sop up the milk, wets another paper towel and wipes the floor.

He washes the knife, the only decent one he owns, and puts it back in its slot in the block that sits on the island. Using a ten-inch butcher knife to cut left-over pizza. What was she thinking? Okay, there are only a couple of other knives. (The knife block was his mother's, and most of the slots are empty.) But the other knives are smaller, more suited to the job.

Having Gina around is like living with an overgrown toddler. He's never stopped missing his sister, Frannie, but he's glad she can't see what her daughter has become.

He reaches for a mug thinking he'll reheat some of the morning's leftover coffee. But the pot's empty—and the note he left for Gina is stuck underneath. He pulls it out. To his message to her explaining about the key and asking her to stay in the apartment, Gina has added:

Gone to find out what really happened to Missy.
Then I'm going to get my baby back. Whether you help me or not.

P.S. No spare key? What a liar!! They always give you two.
You just don't want me to have one.

P.P.S. You should get a TV!

Shit. She shows up after disappearing for almost two years and thinks she can just turn his life upside down, and wreck Mattie's.

What is he supposed to do? He said he'd kill her rather than let her take Mattie, but she must have known he didn't mean it. Did he? How far is he really willing to go?

He's freaked about that whole thing. Can't deny it.

But he's not worried about Gina looking into Missy's death. Whatever she does, she does. And he doesn't see how it can be much.

He thinks back to his conversation with the detective, Moreno. Just before they left the station, as he was waiting for Gina to use the restroom, he asked Moreno again for his take on how likely they were to need to speak with his niece again. He was concerned that Gina would take off before the investigation was complete and end up on the wrong side of the law.

Maybe because Grady had once been one of them, maybe just because it was late and he'd caught a shitty case that didn't matter, the detective laid it out for him: he was ninety-nine percent sure they wouldn't need Gina again. "It won't be official until we get the M.E.'s report," Moreno said, "but we know what happened. We knew her. She might have called himself an escort, but she was just a higher-priced working girl. There was a bottle of pills—oxy—on the bathroom counter. And she'd been drinking, had her glass and bottle of wine right there by the tub. She took some oxy—with alcohol, climbed into the water, added some more alcohol, drowned. Not the first to go that way. Won't be the last."

So it's okay. There's nothing to find. Even Gina can't get into any trouble.

But Mattie… That's different.

Who will she go to? Will she tell them some sob story about her baby being snatched from her arms? And does it really matter if she does? No one will listen to Gina, will they?

He needs to bounce this off somebody. Ally. She's always clearheaded; her thinking always makes sense. But this mess involves Mattie. It's a threat to his well-being. For Ally, that strikes at the core of family, where she's most vulnerable.

So Jill. He'll call Jill. She sent him the text about Gina, already knows that Gina's in touch. He picks up his phone, pushes the buttons. But all he gets is voicemail. He doesn't bother with a message. She'll see the missed call and get back to him. Or not.

He changes into jeans and a t-shirt, stuffs his feet into a pair of Keds, stows his phone in his back pocket, and makes the three trips it takes to retrieve the rest of his new stuff from the truck.

He has no illusions about the judicial system, especially where the rights of a birth mother to have access to (and thoroughly damage) her child are concerned. If she can keep it together enough, it's possible that Gina can find a lawyer who will take her case and make a real stink. He can't let Ally and Mattie be dragged through the courts. He has to find a way to defuse Gina.

And he can't do that if he doesn't stay in touch with her. He has to talk some sense into her, get her to see reason.

He'll wait in the apartment, cross his fingers that she'll show up at some point before morning to get some sleep. That takes care of tonight. And then? He'll figure that out later.

He reminds himself that he should check his email. He boots up his laptop and logs on. His Inbox contains a bunch of junk and three messages. One's from Ally with attached snapshots of Mattie. The other two are from a couple of the guys he works with, ones he's friendly with (if not friends). The first says: "Did you hear? Malone offed himself. Stupid fuck. Take care of yourself, bro." The other says: "Goofy shot himself. Fucker's dead. Shit. Screw some real live pussy for me."

He steps out on his balcony, opens a fresh pack of cigarettes, and lights up. No one's ever old enough to die, but, still, Malone was way too young. "Death is permanent, you asshole!" he wants to scream at the kid. He stands there facing the building across the way, the street below, but seeing Malone in one of the common rooms at the house helping him straighten out his computer, watching the kid's face as he hears John Coltrane for the first time. "We'll take it slow," he was thinking, enjoying the challenge of introducing this guy raised on hip-hop to jazz, "first the ballads, then the harder stuff."

Shit is right.

He lights a second cigarette off the butt of the first, watches a small SUV cruise the block looking for a place to park, sees it pull up to the only empty spot, watches the driver maneuver, back in once, pull out, back in again. It's tight, but he's got it. Two couples climb out and head east, toward the new trendy restaurants on Congress. He can't hear their words from here, but they're laughing, having fun.

Malone's gone. And there's nothing Grady can do about it.

#

He refocuses on getting settled, unpacks the boxes and bags he brought in, stows the new towels in his bathroom, finds a drawer for the cooking utensils he bought. It's after eight before he realizes how hungry he is.

He orders a pizza with mushrooms and sausage, adding a side salad as a concession to health. He makes the pizza a large, thinking he'll save half for Gina, get any conversation they have off on a more positive note. ("Did you think you could bribe me with pepperoni, Uncle Jack?" "No, Gina, it's just the closest I can come to crack.")

His cell rings only once all evening. It's getting close to midnight, he's listening to Lester Young and dozing when it goes off. He grabs it, but it's a wrong number.

He doesn't expect to sleep, but lack of shut-eye the previous night, a long day on his feet, and more than half a large pizza (he did save three good-sized pieces for Gina) send him right out. He's sleeping hard when the phone wakes him.

He fumbles for it on the nightstand, knocks it to the floor, curses himself for not already having a regular goddamn phone, and scrambles to answer the call before it goes to voicemail. He expects to hear Gina's voice. Who else would call him at (he glances at the screen of the phone) three a.m.?

But it's Jill.

"Jack," she says. "I just got a call from University Medical Center's ER. It's about Gina. She's there, and they say she's badly hurt."

Gina? Why would anyone call Jill about Gina?

"She's unconscious now. But before she passed out, she gave me as her next of kin."

Huh?

"I'm on my way," Grady says, grabbing his pants off a chair.

His loafers are still in the kitchen. When he flicks on the under-cabinet lights, the ones angled out at the room, their illumination falls across the floor in a way that reveals all the dust, dirt, and imperfections on the surface of the tile. He can see faint dull patches. It almost looks like someone walking from the kitchen side of the island around to the living room side and then toward the front door left a faint, almost invisible trail.

Gina again. Or him. Did he step in the spilled milk on his initial trip, before he spotted the mess? He picks up the shoes, flips them over to make sure the bottoms are dry. But, of course, they would be. They've been sitting on the kitchen towel for hours. And who knows what he's tracked in and out of here with all the boxes and packages? And this is the desert. All that dust. You can never get it all.

Those—whatever they are—could have been there since two minutes after the floor was mopped. Which would have been before he moved in.

Get a grip, Grady. He can't believe he's worrying about the damn floor, especially right now. You're not running on all cylinders, he tells himself. He grabs his keys and heads out.

17

Grady's standing helpless at Gina's bedside, staring down at his niece—her head wrapped in bandages, tube down her throat, IVs in her arms, attached to a monitor counting out her heartbeats—when Jill arrives. "Wait!" she'd said on the phone just as he was about to push end on the call. "If Gina's not able to give permission, they may not let you make any decisions, or even talk to you. I'll meet you there."

Has Jill has gotten herself down to UMC in the middle of the night because she really thinks the hospital might not deal with him on Gina's care? Or is she concerned for him and his state of mind? Grady doesn't know. And it doesn't matter. He's just glad she's here.

She gives him a quick hug and looks the question at him.

"I don't know anything," he says. "They brought me back here and said someone would come talk to me."

"And no one has."

"Not yet."

A nurse comes by, fools with an IV line going into Gina's left arm, eyes the display on the monitor.

"Did she OD?" Grady asks.

The nurse shakes her head. "Is there a history?"

"Yes." You could say so. A long and extensive one.

"Well," the nurse says, "Not that we can test for everything, but she came in close to sober. Just a little codeine in her. Not much more than some of the rest of us on a bad day." She smiles, apparently to make sure they know that was a joke.

"So why is she…?" he begins, but the nurse cuts him off.

"Look," she says, her expression communicating that maybe she's already said too much, "you really need to talk to the doctor. She'll be with you shortly."

Shortly is apparently different in hospital time than it is for the rest of the world. It's five a.m. before a fortyish, tired-looking woman in scrubs appears in the doorway.

"I'm Dr. Reid." She holds out her hand. First Grady shakes it, then Jill.

"Jack Grady," he says. "I'm her uncle."

"Jill Whitehurst. I'm, um, a friend."

"Oh. Right. She designated you as next of kin. Let's see." She flips through papers on a clipboard. "She was found unconscious in an alley down near Speedway and Hayes." Grady knows the area. Everybody refers to it as "where the Salvation Army used to be." It was bad when Sally Ann was located there. Now it's worse.

There's a buzz from the pocket of the Doctor's coat. "Sorry," she says. She pulls out a cell phone, hits a button, stows the phone back in her pocket, turns her attention back to the clipboard. "Somebody called 911. The patient was still out when she came in but revived at one point when we were working on her. That's when she gave us your name." This is addressed to Jill. "Apparently, one of our nurses found your card in her pocket and asked her if we should call you. She said yes, you were her next of kin." She looks pointedly at Grady. "Her *only* next of kin. The only identification on her was an expired state ID card that listed an address on Camino Naranja." Grady's mother's address. Sold months ago.

"She has two fractured ribs and some bad bruises, not serious. But she has a subdural hematoma. A bleeding in her brain. That's why she lost consciousness, and we're keeping her that way for now. A layman would call it a 'medically induced coma.' We think the bleeding may stop on its own. And we're monitoring the pressure on her brain. If it rises any more, we may need to do surgery to relieve it."

"And then?" Grady understands only part of what the doctor has said, but he asks anyway.

"Then we'll see."

It occurs to him that in his old job with the TPD, there's the question he would have asked first. And that he's only thinking of it now. He guesses that's the difference between being a cop and a family member. "What happened? Was she hit by a car?" That seems the only situation Gina could have found herself in that would have caused such extensive injuries.

"She was beaten. We contacted the police. This is a matter for them. No sign of sexual assault, by the way."

At least there's that.

Still, this is a matter for the police.

So where are they?

"Two detectives were here earlier, I understand. But she was unconscious, I wasn't available, and you hadn't arrived yet. They told the charge nurse they'd be back."

The doctor turns to the papers on her clipboard. Maybe she needs to refer to the information that's written there; maybe she just finds it more comfortable to look at the details of Gina's medical condition than at worried loved ones. "We'll be admitting her to the ICU," she says. "They're getting a bed ready."

Later, Grady realizes that before leaving the room the doctor asked if they had any questions. She must have. They always do, don't they?

But the big question that he had—and that he did ask early on— was, "Will she be okay?"

And that wasn't one the doctor would (or could?) answer. She mouthed some platitude, a phrase she must have been taught in medical school: "We're doing everything we can."

So when she left the room, Grady asked Jill, who was standing in for the entire medical profession at the moment, "Will she be okay?"

Jill didn't answer either. She just said, "She's in the right place. They're taking good care of her."

"She could die," he said to Jill. "That's what the doctor meant. She could die."

Unlike the doctor, Jill did look at him. She looked him straight in the eye and nodded slightly. "Yes."

#

There's only one chair in the curtained cubicle. Grady drags in another one. Then he goes looking for coffee. The pickings are slim. The cafeteria doesn't open for another hour, and when he takes a tentative sip on his way back to Gina's bedside, he discovers that the coffee from the vending machine is almost worse than no coffee at all.

Now, he and Jill sit, watching Gina's chest go up and down, staring at the monitors, hearing the beeps. The paper cups of coffee grow cold in their hands. They wait for the ICU bed. They don't talk.

He doesn't know what Jill's thinking. And he doesn't know how to ask. He can't seem to even open his mouth to thank her for sitting here with him. He does know what he's thinking, though: three questions that repeat themselves over and over in his mind.

Who did this?

Why?

And where the fuck are those two detectives?

Grady knows damn well they aren't out looking for the perp. Gina was found in a bad area, one of the worst in Tucson. And nothing about her suggests she's what they'd think of as an upstanding citizen.

They probably assume it was a drug deal gone bad, scum beating scum. And they might be right, except that Gina isn't scum. Grady remembers how the twelve-year-old Gina missed her dead parents, how she always loved her grandma, how she struggled against addiction from the time she was in her teens. Okay, so she mostly lost, so she found the pull of substances that promised escape irresistible. That made her pitiful and erratic. Hard to deal with. Unreliable. Never to be counted on.

But not a bad person. Her core is good—even when it comes to her insistence that she can and will regain parental rights to her baby son. She's deluding herself. And he can't believe she realizes the full implications of what she's talking about and the damage she could do.

Grady finds the number for the TPD and makes the call. He's put through to a desk jockey. He introduces himself, explains why he's calling. Finally, he's transferred to one of the detectives who caught the case.

makes sure that the man he's talking to, a Detective Bachman, knows that he's not a civilian, that he was once one of them.

Which gets him nowhere.

"The victim is still unconscious, right? The doc isn't available. And I'm going off shift." The man is a jerk. "Leave me your name and your phone number. I'll get back to you when we have something." Bachman's eating as he talks. Grady can hear him chewing.

Fuck him. And fuck this polite routine. "Did you ever hear of paging someone—like the fucking doctor?" He tells the man to get his butt over here now, threatens to call his superiors.

As soon as he disconnects, he regrets letting his dinosaur brain take over. The outrage may get Bachman moving—for now. But it's also likely to put the asshole's back up. He'll slow-walk the case even more than he would have otherwise. Shit.

He's still kicking himself when some piece of machinery attached to Gina blats. The nurses have been in and out, but he and

Jill are alone with Gina when the alarm sounds. He runs to the nurses' station, but the woman who was at Gina's bedside before is already on her way. She turns the alarm off, and checks everything Gina's connected to. They ask if Gina's okay, but the nurse doesn't answer. He doesn't like the look on her face.

Dr. Reid arrives in a rush, and he and Jill are sent to the hallway. They stand there helpless. Moments later, the nurses are rolling Gina's bed down the corridor. The elevator doors open, and she's pushed on. Grady starts to run toward the elevator, but Jill pulls him back. "It's Dr. Reid," she says.

He turns, and is face to face with the doctor. She explains what they're going to do. He doesn't understand all the words, but he gets the bottom line: emergency surgery on Gina's brain. It's "what we were afraid of."

They sit in the surgical waiting room. There must be lots of scheduled early morning procedures; the place is nearly full. People have come prepared with books, newspapers, hand-held video games. One woman is knitting something long and tubular out of bright yellow yarn. A TV in the corner inflicts a twenty-four-hour cable news channel on them all. The audio is too low to be clearly understood, and there are no subtitles. Jill pretends to read a magazine. Grady just sits.

He knows who the man is the moment he walks into the space. Bullet-headed, big, just starting to run to fat, wearing clothing that's both cheap and ill-cared-for, Detective Bachman is a cop out of Central Casting, a walking visual cliché.

Grady stands as the detective approaches. He tries to make the look on his face as neutral as possible. "Mr. Grady," Bachman says, making the correct assumption. "They told me I'd find you here."

"Where's your partner?"

"Tied up. I'm what you got."

Grady pockets the beeper the hospital's given him so that he and Jill can go to the restroom or pace the halls and still be notified when there's news about Gina. Jill stays in the waiting room. Grady walks

Bachman to the cafeteria, which is finally open. Cops, and Grady, always think and talk better over coffee.

They fill cups out of an urn and make their way through the breakfast crowd to a vacant table. "Tell me," Grady says. "Start at the beginning and don't leave anything out."

Bachman flips through a small spiral-bound notebook. "She was found in the alley between Hayes and Cordia." He looks at Grady. "Rough part of town." He glances at the notebook again. "She's a user, huh?"

It's not really a question. Grady nods, knowing that Bachman is basing his conclusion on the location and time of day. Young white woman, bad neighborhood, middle of the night equals druggie or hooker. He supposes he should be grateful (or surprised) that the detective isn't also assuming the latter.

Bachman's no longer bothering to look at his notebook. "Maybe she tried to rip a dealer off, somehow got her hands on the stuff and couldn't pay. Or she had some, the guy wanted it, and she wouldn't share."

Now the man's making up stories. No matter how often Grady did that himself when he was a cop, he can't let it happen here. A scenario spun out of air and bias early on in an investigation all too often becomes a narrative etched in stone. He has to head this off.

"But there was nothing on her when they found her." He's guessing, hoping he's right.

A shrug from Bachman. "Well, nothing by the time the squad car arrived. They checked her out, called an ambulance, it brought her here."

"Any witnesses?"

"Not to the act itself. That we know of. Hell, there could have been a crowd that watched the whole thing for all anyone in that shithole is going to tell us. Oh, there were gawkers hanging around at the end of the alley. That's how we finally found her. But the assholes ran as the car pulled up. She was on the ground next to a dumpster, all by herself."

"Just lying there? Unconscious?"

A nod. Bachman takes a swig of coffee and makes a face. "This tastes like shit."

Grady agrees. Cops—and former cops—can always bond over bad coffee. They're experts on the subject.

"How's she doing?" Bachman becoming human.

"Emergency surgery. Not good."

"Too bad. You're her uncle, huh?"

It's Grady's turn to nod. "I'm pretty much all she's got. Both her parents are dead. Killed in a crash when she was just a kid."

"Whew. Tough." In spite of what he just said about the coffee, Bachman is still working on it. He takes another swallow, his face registering his continued distaste. "So that's what did it to her, huh."

Grady doesn't bother acknowledging the detective's shot at psychoanalysis. "How'd you find her?"

"911 call. We think the caller was the victim herself. The 911 operator could hear her screaming 'Help.' Nothing else, though. Just screams. Then the phone cut off. We triangulated on the cell tower, got close. But it still took us a while to locate her. And no phone around when we got there."

Gina with a cell phone? Where'd she get the money? He answers his own question immediately. He'd tucked some spare cash in a kitchen drawer. He doesn't have to look to know that it's gone.

The detective pours the rest of the coffee down his throat, makes another face, and stands up. "So we'll be back when she wakes up."

If she wakes up, Grady thinks, in spite of himself. "You going to talk to the doctor? Take my niece's clothes for evidence?"

Another shrug. "Yeah. All that stuff."

"You're going to work this, right?"

Bachman's moment of common humanity has clearly passed. "Sure. But I don't know what good it will do. One druggie, probably another druggie. You've been on the job. You know how it is."

She's not a "druggie," she's Gina! He wants to slug the guy, to shove his smug look down his throat and let him eat those big white teeth. But all that will do is get him locked up—and physically damaged either before or after the arrest (or both).

He forces his face into something that he hopes resembles a smile and extends his hand. They shake.

"Take care," Bachman says, walking away.

Go to hell, Grady thinks. Go to fucking hell.

18

Rachel double-clicks, then enters the password she's been given. The spreadsheet opens. There are approximately thirty rows of data in six columns with the headings:

<u>ID</u>   <u>Date</u>   <u>Type</u>   <u>Where</u>   <u>Who</u>   <u>Notes</u>

It's a log. But of what? "Tell me what I'm looking at, Gil."

"It's an unofficial record of the assignments Malone participated in during his time in Iraq. In chron order. The entries covering the period from the beginning of his last tour until he died are grouped at the bottom.

"Once we caught on to what the file was, we began comparing it with official records. The 'ID' column is the mission designation. 'Date' is self-explanatory. 'Type'—sec/p or sec/e—we're interpreting as security-persons and security-equipment. 'Where' is location. BI would be Baghdad International—a run escorting arriving or departing personnel or equipment. ML is Mosul, we believe. And so on. 'Who' is the initials of the men who were on the detail. 'Notes' had us stumped for a while—it doesn't correspond to anything in the official record."

Rachel focuses on the "Notes" column. Most of the entries are simply "UL." But several are "UL – good." A handful are "UL – bad." A few simply contain an "X." And two are "equip mal." Not exactly intuitive. "It looks like a code."

"That's what we thought. But then we found information on Malone's laptop about an Internet site he was using. Turns out UL is an abbreviation for 'upload.'"

An upload. Shit. "Of what?"

"We got lucky there. Malone used a password manager on his laptop, so no hacking needed. We were able to find the site, log in, take a look. He was uploading videos."

Huh?

"In late May, after he'd been in theater about two months, he began recording every assignment he went on. He also recorded scenes around the house. Lots of guys do that, shoot video of their buddies. It's replaced taking snapshots for his generation. So that's normal. The rest of it, though—recording the assignments—wasn't the usual."

"Did other people have access to the videos he uploaded to that site?"

"No."

"Any signs of distribution? Or downloading?"

"No."

So Malone was recording and storing but wasn't sharing. Rachel sees where this is going. "He was an aspiring filmmaker." With big dreams. No settling for YouTube postings for him. "He was planning to put together his own documentary on Iraq. First-hand experience, cinéma-vérité."

"Looks like it."

"Umm. He's videoing all these assignments. Did he have permission to do that?" And did he need permission? Rachel isn't sure. Her best guess is that it probably depended on the nature of the detail. Some would be sensitive to the point of secrecy; some not so much.

"He didn't. This activity had no official sanction at all."

"And that's why his buddies didn't mention it when you asked about hobbies." And if they were covering this, what else were they covering? "I assume you went back and talked to them again?"

"We re-interviewed them. Briefly. Keeping it as low-key as possible. You know the drill. We buried our questions about Malone's videos among all kinds of other questions."

"Which still made them suspicious as hell."

"Well, at least damned uncomfortable."

"Couldn't be helped. What'd you learn?"

"Only the in-crowd was fully aware that Malone was videoing missions, or, at least, doing it so regularly. Remember, they tended to buddy-up on assignments, not just in the house. He was discreet, wore a small body-camera that he left turned on. It's not like the days when you had to stick a camcorder in someone's face. This thing was small, and everyone got used to it. Didn't think much about it, they say. When we compare Malone's log with the official one, we can see that he knew when to stow the thing, or even leave it at home. He was bending, if not breaking, the rules with all the filming, but he never did it if he knew that the detail would be secret or even borderline sensitive. It looks like that's a line he was careful not to cross. Those assignments weren't logged in the spreadsheet."

Rachel reflects, not for the first time, that technology enables today's warfare, but technology also complicates it immensely. Any eleven-year-old today knows more about computers than Rachel knew in college. She and Gil and their ilk use sophisticated technology in their investigations all the time, but she'll never have a tenth the comfort level with it that the kids do. Still, she's aware enough to recognize how embedded technology is in the lives of Malone's generation and the extent to which they take it for granted. And she can project that knowledge into this situation. "So Malone shot his 'documentary' consistently—and discreetly. And because what he did and how he did it were always the same, it became background noise."

Gil is silent. Rachel may not be stating facts, but they both know she's describing an underlying reality. It's a talent she's always had, one that can often illuminate an investigation. Her male colleagues might ascribe it to the fact that she's a woman, and she might secretly agree that her brain works somewhat differently from theirs, and is certainly more subtle. But they would never dare say that aloud, and this amuses her.

She moves on. "I assume you've been looking at the videos."

"Yes."

"And?"

"So far, absolutely nothing. It's some of the dullest footage you've ever seen. Badly shot, muddy audio. Even for an independent project, it's a reach to think he could ever do anything with it."

"Hmm."

"Looks like he was a naïve kid with outsize ambitions."

Rachel's surprised to hear Gil sum up Malone this way. He's normally nothing like a bleeding heart. A certain ability to read people (and make educated guesses at their thoughts) is an asset in what they do, but empathy is only a tool, and sympathy is never helpful. Even if you can't help feeling it, it's always bad form to share it with a colleague. And in this case, it's irrelevant. Gil must still be jet-lagged.

She decides to ignore his comment. "I'm wondering what this has to do with Malone's suicide. If anything." Something is tickling at the back of her mind, but it's not quite accessible yet. She brings the conversation back to the immediate topic: Gil's team's analysis of the log. "Was there an uploaded video for every row in the log?"

"Unless there was an 'X' in the 'Notes' column. Comparing this file with the official information, we're guessing an 'X' meant Malone misjudged the nature of the assignment, realized it was more sensitive than he'd thought, and stowed the camera. Just didn't record."

"What about the two marked 'equip mal'?"

"No videos on the site for those."

"So you're thinking that before an assignment began, Malone would enter data in all the columns except 'Notes.' Then, if he didn't record, he entered an 'X.' And if he did record and upload, UL indicated he'd done that. If the video was especially compelling, he added 'good.' And when he entered 'bad'?"

"It appears to be related to the quality of the image. Like I said, none of it is what I'd call professional quality. There are a lot of underlit and over-lit scenes, muddy sound, jerky motion."

"Well, he was wearing the camera. That would severely limit control."

"Yup. But some were worse than others. When it was especially lousy, he added the word 'bad.'"

One downside of Malone's generation's comfort with technology was sometimes a lack of focus on anything other than the technical aspects of things. Maybe he was incapable of aesthetic judgments. Or maybe he simply thought they'd be premature. For her purposes, it doesn't matter. But she does need to confirm what she's hearing. "No relationship to content? How the mission went? Anything like that?"

"Not that we can tell."

"And 'equip mal'?" The meaning of the abbreviation seems obvious, but she needs to make sure that Gil's analysis agrees.

"Just what it says. The equipment malfunctioned."

"So he omitted secret or especially sensitive missions from the spreadsheet entirely, but entered at least some info on all the others."

"It appears so."

She sees the picture: what Malone was doing, how he was doing it, how he was tracking his progress. If the project had anything to do with his suicide, there might be indications of that in the log in spite of his shorthand and the rote nature of his entries. "What about the recent assignments? The ones within a week or ten days of his death?"

"There were seven in that timeframe, on September 7, 8, 10, 11, 13, 14, and 16. The first two, as you can see, were uploaded with no additional notation. Just 'UL.' The third was an equipment malfunction. The fourth was uploaded, marked 'UL.'"

Rachel articulates the conclusion she's sure Gil has already reached. "At that point, he was still following his routine."

"Apparently. The final one has all the info except for the last column. That's blank. No notation at all."

No answers yet, not much even in the way of guideposts. Time to push Gil for specifics. "And that last detail—let's call it 'mission seven'—was?"

"An escort. Picking up a diplomat at Baghdad international and escorting him to the Green Zone."

"And nothing went wrong? Nothing happened out of the ordinary?"

"Nothing at all."

"That's confirmed?"

"Confirmed."

Gil's done his homework. Rachel takes a leap, but a small one. And she wouldn't be surprised if Gil's gotten there before her. "So if Malone didn't video the last assignment that he logged and didn't enter the reason—or videoed it but didn't upload, he wasn't behaving normally. He was decompensating at that point, heading toward suicide."

"That's a logical assumption."

"And the mission before that: 'mission six?'"

"Just as routine. Another VIP, another airport run."

"And he uploaded. So he was still functioning." Keeping it together in the eyes of the outside world in spite of the shit storm growing inside him. Rachel knows all about putting up that kind of front. It's a skill she was forced to develop early on. She focuses on the second 'equipment malfunction' in the group of entries. The ID doesn't mean much to her. But the rest of the data…

Date	Type	Where	Who	Notes
2018-9-13	sec/e	RFB	TA, KP, LS, MC, JG, HP, JM, BM	equip mal

"This one's interesting. "What about 'mission five?'"

"Let me see." She hears Gil's keyboard clicking. Then he's back. "That was escorting kitchen equipment from the Green Zone to a temporary Marine base northwest of the city."

"So out of Baghdad, a little less routine."

"Yes."

"But nothing happened?" She's starting to see the picture here, she thinks. And she'll bet...

"Well, there was one thing. There were two escort vehicles, but when they reached the Marine base, one of them was having mechanical problems. It stayed behind, with its crew. That base isn't a permanent set-up but it's a lot more than an outpost. It has repair capabilities."

"You said one escort vehicle and its crew stayed behind. And the other one?"

"Started back to base."

Rachel hears a hint of surprise in Gil's voice, like he still finds himself amazed at the ways trained, supposedly intelligent people find to fuck up. She, herself, got over that years ago.

"Which broke protocol." She didn't even need to say it. Any contractor involved in this kind of security detail knows that no escort vehicle rolls alone. Ever. There are always a minimum of two, providing front and rear security, and depending upon the nature of the convoy, often others interspersed in the middle.

"But..."

Rachel finishes his sentence. "They made it home safely. So no one cared."

"Right."

"And other than that?" C'mon, Gil, give me a little more to go on.

"We have no indication that anything happened."

Rachel takes another, closer look at the file. "Hmmm. These initials, of the men who were on that detail with Malone. Translate please."

"They started out with eight men in two vehicles, four and four. The first three sets of initials are the men who stayed at the Marine base with the vehicle that broke down. The fourth, Michael Carter, switched to the vehicle that Malone was riding in."

Another violation of protocol. Those fucking cowboys.

Gil's continuing to list names. "The others in that vehicle on the way back were Jesus Garcia, Hartman Pickett…"

"The Alpha Dog. Interesting. Who else?"

"Jason McFarin."

So. Carter, Garcia, Pickett, McFarin—and, of course, Malone. She has a hunch. "All from the in-crowd?"

"Yes."

And she's right. Shit. All buddies, rolling along at high speed, no restrictions on that for them, in an armored vehicle in a war zone where they aren't allowed to be the aggressors but are still (out of necessity) heavily armed and pumped up on fear, adrenalin, their natural testosterone, and, very possibly, steroids. Everyone knows that these guys are big on muscles and not much worried about side effects. "So they're on an assignment out in the middle of nowhere—if I'm remembering my Iraqi geography correctly."

"You are."

"How long were they out?" She'd put money on what this answer will be.

"Let me see. I need to open another file for that." Rachel hears keys clicking again, then: "Six hours."

"And the assignment involved?"

"Just the escort duty. They didn't even have to wait for the equipment to be unloaded from the truck. The truckdriver was staying at the delivery point, at least overnight."

Rachel does the math in her head. Two hours out. A break, maybe a meal at the Marine base. Give it an hour. A few minutes, maybe fifteen or twenty, discussing the problematic truck and what to do about it. She figures the missing time, netting it out at thirty to forty-five minutes. "Why were they out so long?" If her thinking is right, Gil won't have an answer to this.

"Weather? More mechanical problems?"

She has an awful feeling she's got it. And it's worse than she expected. If she's right, this is a potential bombshell.

She's not ready to discuss it yet so she instructs Gil to do something she knows he'll do anyway. "Check on all that." Then she moves on. "What about Malone's camera?"

She isn't surprised by the answer.

Gil says they finally found it in the kid's footlocker, under a pile of clothes. They'd already gone through his belongings, discreetly, then left them to be packed up and sent to his next of kin. They did the second search after they found out about the recordings.

The Iraqi woman who cleaned the house said she'd found the camera under Malone's bed a couple of days after he died, knew it was his, and stowed it in the locker. ('Where it belonged,' she told them in Arabic.) But, Gil says, his guy who did the initial search is good. And he swears it wasn't there, that the floor under the bed was clear.

"The camera had a memory card," Rachel prompts.

"Right."

"And I assume it contained nothing."

"Nada."

So someone checked that camera to make sure that either the contents of the memory card were innocuous or that it was empty. Then that individual put the camera under the bed to be found by the cleaner. He—and it was a "he" since the house was populated entirely by men except for the cooking and cleaning crew—he decided that was less suspicious than having the camera or the card permanently disappear, especially since it was clear that Gil's people had learned about Malone's project. Maybe Malone deleted the contents of the card himself. It's even possible that he cleared the camera's memory routinely: record, upload, erase, reuse... But it's at least as likely that somebody else did it.

And the magical disappearance and reappearance make this point almost moot. Whether the memory card contained anything or not at the time it went missing from Malone's footlocker, someone in that house was taking no chances.

19

As Grady closes the door to his apartment behind them, Jill goes straight to the kitchen area. "How about some real coffee?" she says, and he can hear the effort she's making to sound upbeat. She pulls the glass carafe out of the maker and dumps the dregs of yesterday's brew down the drain.

He heads for the bathroom, pees, washes his hands—and then finds himself just standing there, still holding the towel, looking at himself in the mirror but not seeing.

Gina went into surgery just before six a.m. It was after eleven before a short, slight woman in scrubs with a mask hanging around her neck and a surgical cap covering her hair appeared in front of them and introduced herself as Gina's neurosurgeon. Gina was alive. That was the good news. But the surgeon couldn't say when she would wake up, or if she would wake up. They could see Gina as soon as she was settled in the ICU. But there would be nothing for them to do. "I'd advise you to go home, get some sleep," the surgeon said. Grady gathered she was telling them that, at best, this was going to be a long haul.

There was more medical talk, there were long technical terms, and maybe Jill absorbed it, but Grady didn't. "She's alive!" his brain cheered. But then it added, "For now."

In spite of what the doctor had said, they made their way to the ICU and hovered over Gina's bed. His niece was unconscious, but she didn't look like she was sleeping. She barely looked like a person. A machine was breathing for her. Machines were monitoring her. Tubes were going in and coming out.

He and Jill paced there for hours. Once Grady thought he saw the flutter of an eyelid, and Jill ran for the nurse. But it was a false alarm.

Finally, the nurses shooed them out.

Early that morning, Jill had cancelled her appointments for the day. And she'd continued to insist on sticking with him. "You shouldn't be alone," she said when he objected to her turning her life upside down this way. "But you're not staying here. You're going home for a few hours. I'm the semi-objective party in this situation, and I say you get some rest. Gina doesn't need you right now. She's being well taken care of. But she'll need you later."

He hangs the towel on a hook and walks into the bedroom. The bed covers are just as he left them when he sprang up in response to Jill's three a.m. phone call. The blanket he covered Gina with when she fell asleep on his couch is still in a heap on the dresser. The pillow she used rests on top. He sees—or imagines he sees—the imprint of her head. All of that is less than thirty-six hours in the past, but it seems an eon ago.

Suddenly, he's crying. He's sitting on the bed and crying.

He's barely aware of Jill entering the room. Then she's next to him, with her arms around him, and he's continuing to cry. Then he's lying on the unmade bed, sobbing, and Jill is still holding him, stroking his forehead, whispering, "Sssh. I know. I know."

#

Jill's spooning her ex-husband. He's asleep; she can feel his slow, regular breathing. Whatever comes next, this rest is what he needs. And what comes next may be heartbreaking. It's not that he's the most together guy in the world. He's deserved some of the crap he's gone through. But not all. And not this. Sometimes he just can't seem to catch a break.

And Gina. What a struggle her life has been. Not that she's ever made smart choices. As far as Jill knows, the only good decision Gina has made since she was a young girl was giving up her baby. And from what Jack says, she's trying to get him back. How many lives will that screw up?

As she lies with her body pressed against her ex-husband's for the first time since…since so many years ago, she realizes that it's not just Jack who's worn out. She's bone tired. It's not so much the hours she and Jack spent at the hospital, it's everything else that's going on in her life. She's tired of worrying, tired of trying to change, or at least delay, what she's more and more convinced is inevitable: the break-up of her marriage. She's exhausted physically and emotionally. When she said Jack shouldn't be alone right now, what she partly meant was that she shouldn't be alone.

So she lies there, hoping she'll fall asleep, too. If she can just relax…

But within minutes she can tell that's not going to happen. Too much adrenaline. When she was younger, she was a weeper. Under anything close to her current circumstances, she would have sobbed her way into sleep. Now, she's either too grown-up or too… Numb? Is that it?

And lately there's been so damn much that deserves crying over. She doesn't think she's hardened. Or stoic. She feels. But the tears never come. The hours become days become weeks, and she just rides the tight surface of her pain.

She leaves the bed as gently as she can. She's still fully dressed except for her shoes, and she picks them up, carries them out of the room, closes the door quietly behind her.

The kitchen's a mess. She discards the left-over pizza, sets the box aside for recycling. She decides Jack has too few dishes to leave any in the dishwasher or to bother loading and running it, so she finds dishwashing liquid and runs hot water into one bay of the sink. By the time she's dried the dishes and found places for them in the cupboards, she's feeling better, more centered. She makes that fresh pot of coffee she talked about when they walked in the door—before she heard Jack crying—and wipes down the counters until the granite gleams.

She realizes she's found her way back to her comfort zone, taking care of others. She's fixed what she can, which isn't much. And managed to avoid her own problems for a little while.

The plant she brought Jack as a housewarming gift only three days earlier is looking a little sad. She gives it some water and moves it along the counter closer to the sunny door wall. Then she pours herself a mug of the newly brewed coffee and stands sipping it, looking out at the street below.

She sees a couple, young, college kids maybe. The girl takes a short-cut across the street, mid-block. The guy follows, puts his arm around her, gives her a quick kiss. The girl is blond, her hair long and straight. The wind tosses it, and the girl reaches up, pushes it out of her eyes. Something about her, maybe the motion, reminds Jill of Sophie. Her daughter is a great kid headed for a good college. No problems there. But who knows, even at eighteen, what it will do to her if—no, face it, Jill, *when* her parents split.

How did I get here, she thinks, two marriages down? She misses the way her family was a year ago, two years ago—so solid—before things began to go wrong. And realizes she doesn't even know when, or how, that happened.

She goes back into the bedroom, climbs onto the bed, curls herself around her ex-husband's sleeping form. The air conditioning has chilled the room, but Jack's body is warm. She closes her eyes, slows her breathing, and begins counting back from five hundred by sevens. It's a trick she's relied on for years on those rare nights when sleep eludes her. But it's not working now. She's in the three hundreds and still awake...

Grady's lost somewhere. First it's dark and twisty, but then it's warm, and it's a place where nothing bad has ever happened. He wants to stay here a long, long time. The air turns golden, and there's a pile, a hill—almost a mountain, of all kinds of things: windows and baby carriages and Gina's doll from when she was five. He's about to examine the hill, maybe pull some things out of it, look at them more closely, when something kicks him out of the dream. He lies there still half seeing that mountain, feeling the emotional echo, only gradually aware that there's another body on his bed. He slowly realizes that it's Jill. And she's spooning him, as much as a smaller, slender person can cradle a taller, bulkier one.

He turns toward her. Her eyes are closed, her breathing slow and steady.

Still half asleep, he kisses her, not thinking of the consequences, not thinking at all.

To his surprise, she kisses him back.

He draws her to him, and they're embracing. Then he's kissing her hair, her forehead, her eyes, her nose, her mouth again, moving down her body...

And it's good. Bed was never one of their problems.

It's better than any part of his life has been in longer than he can remember.

20

Rachel's sitting on the room's only upholstered chair, her feet up on the ottoman. This is a voice-only call, which is just as well. Her laptop camera would show her wrapped in the white hotel robe, her hair pulled up in a messy knot. Not exactly professional, so not the best idea, even though she wouldn't really care. At this point in her career, she's comfortable letting her performance speak for itself, especially with someone who reports to her.

She long ago developed a way of dealing with hotel rooms: no digging through a suitcase, always unpack; take advantage of whatever creature comforts the venue has to offer—a well-equipped gym, a decent shower, a comfy robe, room service. Grab whatever down time is available to you. Stay away from the hotel bar unless you're lonely and looking for a hookup. (And stick to your rules: don't get lonely; don't hook up.) But do whatever else it takes to unwind. If that means a late breakfast and a video call when you're fresh out of the shower, so be it.

She recaps where she and Gil left off in the middle of the night, summing up what they have. A mission that took a crew, including Malone, out into the boonies, that took longer than it should have—and that, according to Malone's log, wasn't recorded because he had an equipment malfunction. Malone's subsequent behavior. His suicide, and the statement in his farewell video that Geezer would take care of something he himself didn't have the balls to face. And, of course, the missing and miraculously found camera.

She's had hours to mull over what they know so far. She even managed to catch a little sleep. Now, she's ready to take her thinking to the next stage, to articulate the situation she's convinced they're faced with.

She knows her conclusions will hit Gil in the gut—God knows they did that to her—but reality is what it is.

So she lays it out.

"I think something happened on that assignment, something against regs, probably illegal from the moment it began, and, I'm guessing, violent. And, in spite of what his log says, I think Malone recorded it."

She hears a muttered "Fuck" from Gil, ignores it, and continues.

"Then they covered it up. Everybody who'd been on that detail agreed not to talk about it. And if it was the kind of incident I think it was, you can be sure that any locals that they interacted with are dead. They wouldn't have left anyone alive who could have contradicted their version of events, whatever those events were."

She registers Gil's sharp intake of breath even though he covers almost instantly with a throat clearing and pours herself another cup of coffee from the carafe on the side table, giving her words a moment to sink in before she goes on.

"They're back at the ranch. Whatever happened is done. They've sworn some kind of brotherly oath to clam up forever. It's over with. And then someone realizes that Malone was wearing his damn camera. And he'd videoed the whole thing. So Pickett—I'd bet on it being Pickett since he's the alpha dog—went to Malone, and Malone assured him he'd erased the recording. Gone. No evidence. And after Malone died, Pickett or one of his minions scooped up the camera and made sure."

"They're home safe."

"Right. The filmmaker has offed himself, no indigenous personnel are left to speak up, everyone else involved is tight. So nothing happened. But here's the thing, Gil. Everything we know says Malone was putting himself through hell because of what happened. The guilt destroyed him. I don't think Malone did erase that recording. I don't think his conscience would let him. And I think that before he died, he gave that video to Geezer."

"Shit."

Shit is right.

"So what does Geezer say?"

"He describes his relationship with Malone as something between an acquaintance and a friend. I'm not sure he's the type to share his intimate thoughts, and if he were going to, I can't see him picking a kid like Malone. And I can't imagine him on the receiving end either, encouraging Malone to pour his heart out. In fact, I'd bet he's one of those guys who never 'shares' with other men."

"Got it. If he's going to open up, it's going to be with…"

"A woman." Why do you think I'm the one on the ground here in Tucson, Gil? She thinks it, but doesn't say it.

"So…"

"I showed him Malone's farewell message."

"And?"

"He claimed to have no clue what Malone was talking about."

"You had a team do a search, right?"

"They went into his apartment yesterday afternoon while I was schmoozing him over lunch."

"And they didn't find anything?"

"Not a thing. They didn't know about Malone's little project at that point, of course, so they had no idea what they were looking for. But any DVDs, thumb drives, or other electronic devices would have been items of big-time interest just by default. They didn't find any of that, not even a DVD of the guy's favorite movie. The man doesn't even own a CD. He's strictly vinyl."

"Sounds like he's not exactly tech-savvy."

116

"I think that may be an understatement. He does have a laptop, though. And from what he said, the guy he turned to when the magic wasn't working was Malone."

Gil takes the logical next step. "So Malone had access to Geezer's laptop. That's got to be it. The video is on Geezer's laptop."

Rachel agrees. She fills him in. The laptop was sitting on the kitchen counter, right out in the open, and the password was a joke. Her guys cloned the computer on the spot, no problem. "The techies checked in with me about an hour ago. No luck so far, but they're still looking through it. Maybe a hidden file, they say."

"Look, Rach, maybe we're spinning stories out of thin air here. Could still be there's nothing to find." She can hear the hope in Gil's voice, and she knows what he's thinking. The tech guys are damned good. And they've had a good eighteen hours to go through the laptop. If they haven't found anything by now... And truth is, the lead tech she spoke with didn't sound all that optimistic. From what he said, they were done except for running forensics on the hard drive to recover any deleted files, but finding the video there seemed like a long shot.

She chooses not to share this with Gil. Caution is said to be wise, and it's sometimes warranted. But she hasn't gotten to where she is by being afraid to make a leap. She surprised that Gil is. She's willing to go out on a limb here, and it doesn't feel like much of a risk. Especially since the downside of not looking hard enough and therefore not finding something that does turn out to exist is huge. She exerts her authority without shutting Gil down: "I don't believe that. And neither do you. Remember when I said Geezer claimed to have no clue what Malone was talking about?"

Gil's known her a long time, and she's not surprised that he knows where she's going from here. But she's a bit surprised at his incredulity. "You believe him!"

"I do. And if Malone wasn't blowing smoke in that heartfelt goodbye—and he'd have to be one twisted fucker to do that—I think Geezer does have the video. Thing is, he doesn't know it."

21

There's a phone ringing. Grady reaches out, fumbles around, comes up empty. The room is dark. Did he somehow knock his cell off the nightstand? He hits the button on the bedside lamp, scours the floor for it.

The ringing stops. And he realizes the sound was coming from the other room.

It feels late. He can tell he's been out for hours. Gina is in the ICU.

Still groggy, he stumbles to the bathroom, pees, splashes water on his face, pulls on some clothes, heads for the kitchen.

There's his cell sitting on the counter, and Jill taking a mug of coffee out of the microwave. She's fully dressed, all her corners neat and tucked in as usual. Did he dream that they...? No, that was real. "It wasn't the hospital," she says. "I wouldn't normally answer your phone, but..."

"Thanks."

"I called the ICU nurses' station just a little while ago. There's no change." She hands him the full mug, pours another one for herself, sticks it in the microwave, hits a button.

Shit. "She could die," he says. "Her mind's not there, and her body's just barely hanging on." He's known death was a possibility since before Gina was rolled into surgery. He even said it out loud, but until now he's not sure he believed it.

He takes his coffee, walks over to the window wall, slides it open, steps onto the balcony, looks down on the street below. Streetlights. Trash cans. Empty. So much for the revival of downtown Tucson. He leans on the railing, pulls out a cigarette, and lights up. He knows Jill hates his smoking, but at this moment, he just can't find it in himself to care.

Jill walks out, stands beside him. "I know it's hard," she says. "But Gina's made it through a lot, and she's still alive. You have to have hope." She woke up about a half-hour before, left the bedroom as silently as she could. Now she's spouting platitudes. Pathetic. But it's all she has.

Jack grunts dismissively. "I don't care what they say. You and I both know the longer this goes on, the worse it has to be."

Jill can't think of anything comforting to say, and it doesn't help that her mind is spinning. Gina's situation is overwhelming for Jack. Of course, that's all he can think about. It's understandable, even appropriate.

But a few hours ago, they had sex for the first time since their marriage fell apart. After they made love, they lay there, not speaking, his arm around her, her head resting on his chest. Then they both fell asleep, Jill first.

So they didn't talk about it then, and it looks like they're not going to talk about it now. She knows the circumstances are dreadful, but even so... Does Jack plan to ignore it?

"Now what?" Jill says. She's broaching a topic, but she's not sure which one.

Jack takes a swig of his coffee, doesn't answer her. "Still cold," he says, "goddamnit!" And Jill knows the anger isn't directed at the coffee; it's directed at the situation.

She reaches out a hand, lays it on his arm. So far, it's the only sign that either one of them remembers the physical intimacy of a few hours before. "It's okay. I get it. If it were someone I loved…"

"But it wouldn't be, would it? The people in your life aren't addicts. They don't do stupid, risky things that get them beaten up and left in alleys."

He doesn't even seem to notice that she's touching him.

There are other behaviors that don't involve drugs or dark alleys or even alcohol, Jill thinks, but still cause great pain. They may be more socially acceptable, but aren't they just as risky in their own way?

"Gina could die," Jack says again. "And what I have been doing? Taking a fucking nap."

Jill doesn't remind him that he needed the sleep, that he wouldn't have been good for anything without it—and that there's nothing he can do anyway. She also doesn't remind him that he did more than sleep.

"And the guy who beat her, may have killed her," Jack says. "He's going to get away with it."

"But the police…"

"She's a junkie, Jill. She's white and they've got me breathing down their necks, so they'll at least go through the motions. If she were black… Hell, if she were Hispanic. Either way they wouldn't do shit. Not that they'll put much effort in anyway. No. This will be an unsolved that they won't lose any sleep over. They won't even miss a coffee break."

Did he used to be this skeptical about the police? Not when she first knew him. Back then, he and his fellow detectives were, if not saving the world, at least (in his view) bringing criminals to justice and closure to victims. As time went on, he began talking more and more like what she's hearing today. And when she'd say he was being cynical, he'd tell her he was just being realistic, that this was how things were. No use fooling yourself.

And suddenly her mind is back on the topic of her marriage. It's over, no matter what spin Charlie wants to try to put on it. Fini. Dead. Kaput.

Just being realistic.

When she surfaces from her own thoughts, Jack is talking about that "fucking poor excuse for a detective who had to be dragged back to the hospital and then was so damn dismissive." He's still staring straight ahead, glaring at nothing. It's as if he's put all his sadness, apprehension, worry—even the pain of everything he's been through with Gina over the years—into his outrage at the beating and the weak law enforcement response.

"I have to take care of this myself," he says. "I have to find the guy who did it."

"So you're going to do the job the police can't."

"Won't. And, yes, I am." There's cold fury in his voice.

She regretted her words as soon as they were out of her mouth. She was being judgmental. And snippy. Some of the worst traits Jack accused her of toward the end of their marriage. The things she tended to say never made a situation any better then, and they haven't now. She can see he's still seething.

But she's never known how to stop trying. "Okay," she says, "I get how you feel. But slow down for a minute and think about it. You don't have their resources. You don't have any evidence. You don't have any idea how this happened or why."

He shakes off her hand, still on his arm, stubs out his cigarette, and carries his mug back inside to the kitchen counter.

Jill follows him into the kitchen. Automatically, she picks up his mug and puts it in the dishwasher, then curses herself. He'll think she's compulsive (another tendency he hated), and sometimes she is.

He gathers up his phone and his keys. "If I hear anything from the hospital, I'll let you know." He pats his right rear pocket. "I need my wallet."

"Let me know? What are you talking about?" She calls after him as he goes into the bedroom to retrieve the wallet from his other pants. She barely knows Gina, but Jack's been part of her life for a long time. And now, under the circumstances... "I'm going back to the ICU. It's the least I can..."

Jack's back in the room. He cuts her off as if he's reminding her the two of them split more than twenty years ago. "Doesn't your family need you?" He gathers up his keys again.

There's a pause. Maybe he's letting it sink in that she's not his family, maybe he's not remembering what she said on Sunday about Charlie.

Does he think that she and Charlie are still together and that she was just casually cheating on him, scratching some kind of mindless itch? She can't tell. But he should know her better than that. Today was important, at least for her.

Maybe.

Then Jack says, "What about Sophie?"

"Sophie's eighteen, Jack. She's a senior in high school. She can tie her own shoes, cook a meal, even drive. She'll be fine." Jill woke her daughter on her way out the door to the hospital in the early hours of the morning to let her know what was happening. Later, they exchanged texts. Sophie was going to her friend Caitlin's house for dinner and would spend the night. "Not a problem, Mom," Sophie had reassured her.

Jack hasn't asked about her practice, maybe because he heard her on the phone first thing in the morning when she called her office and instructed Paige to cancel all her appointments for the day. What he didn't hear was another call she made later (he'd gone to grab snacks for them from the vending machine), when she spoke to Paige again and told her to cancel everything for the rest of the week. And, on second thought, also for the following Monday. Who knew how long this would take?

And he hasn't asked specifically about Charlie. Maybe he really didn't get what she said on Sunday just as the elevator doors were closing. And she knows now isn't the time, and maybe he doesn't want to talk about it, at least right now, but she goes on anyway. "I know I said…what I said…about Charlie. When I was here on Sunday. I hadn't told anybody before then, even said it out loud."

Now that she's letting it out, she can't seem to stop herself. "Charlie's in Denver. A new job. A new city. Oh, he's still back and forth some. He was home for two days three weeks ago. But he's moving on."

"Doesn't he want you to…"

"Be with him? Relocate? He says he does. But…"

But?

"I don't think he means it." She hopes she looks calmer than she feels. She feels as if she's holding in a dam that could break at any moment. "So you see, I don't have a lot of 'family' to worry about right now."

"Fuck, fuck, fuck. I always thought you and Charlie… Jesus. I didn't forget what you said on Sunday, but I didn't think… And I thought we…you and I… Look, I don't understand why we … And I get that it's a big deal, but…"

For a moment, she thinks he's going to reach out, take her in his arms, comfort them both. But he doesn't.

"Oh shit, Jill. I can't do this now. You can stay here if you want, or you can go. But I have things to do."

He doesn't mean to be cold, she tells herself. He's just upset, and he's being clear. She needs to be just as clear. "I told you. I'm going back to the hospital."

He's almost to the door when she spots his phone. When Jack left the room to get his wallet, he set his cell down. She picks it up off the stool where he laid it and hands it to him. "Here." And that reminds her. "Oh. That phone call. The one that woke you up. It was someone named Rachel. I told her you weren't available and offered to take a message, but just she said she'll call back."

"Huh." Just a grunt. No thanks for telling him. Not even common courtesy. What's that about? The message? Or her?

Stop it, Jill, she orders herself. You've had no business inserting your problems into the middle of Jack's crisis with Gina and making more trouble by sleeping with him.

All of this is so unlike her. None of it is sensible, or even kind.

She knows she shouldn't push it again, but seeing him rush off like this... "Jack? Where are you going to start? And why now? There's nothing you can do tonight."

But he's already on his way out. The door closes behind him.

Grady knows he isn't being fair to Jill. Shit. He's falling short now, as he fell short so many times years ago. What happened that afternoon was momentous for him, but he was telling the truth when he said he couldn't deal with it now. He can't talk about it, doesn't dare even think about it.

He can't wait for the elevator. He pushes open the door to the stairs leading down to the street.

"There's nothing you can do tonight." Jill's last words as he finally got the hell out of that apartment. He knows she couldn't be more wrong about that. Night is when Gina's people come alive.

22

The only place he can start is the scene of the crime. Cliched though that is, and severely limiting because it doesn't take into account anything that led up to Gina's beating, it's all he has. Gina has no home to search for clues. No workplace, friends, or acquaintances that he's aware of other than the dead Missy. She doesn't even have any possessions here in town, at least not anywhere he knows about. Everything she had was with her in her backpack. And she didn't leave anything at Grady's, not a change of underwear, a toothbrush, even a stray sock. He has no idea where she was staying even a week ago at this time. He only knows it wasn't in Tucson.

He should have asked her: Where have you been? What have you been doing for the last twenty months? How have you survived? (Although he's not sure he wants to be enlightened on that.)

The contents of that backpack and whatever she had in her pockets might conceivably be of some help. But he can't get his hands on them. The cops confiscated them during their first visit to the ER before he even got there. They're evidence, a part of the investigation. But they'll be treated routinely, at best. They won't get the kind of aggressive attention that they would if Gina were some upstanding member of the middle class. Or if the detectives had a suspect to match trace evidence to. Unfortunately, cursory is the word.

Grady envisions her backpack and blood-stained clothes reaching their ultimate destination: a box on a shelf, labeled and filed, but as good as lost for all the help they'll be. What a fucking waste. Not that he could do anything with a lot of it himself. He's not in a position to test the blood on the clothes she was wearing or identify any anomalous fibers. But there might have been something that would at least point him in the right direction.

He considers whether to park near the alley where Gina was found or some distance away and decides to slot the pickup into a space as close to the scene as he can find. His truck will be visible, but that shouldn't be a problem. He's still driving the old Ford F-150 that he bought from a friend of Ally's. There's nothing spit-shined about it. It's a workingman's truck, plain and proud, and he likes it for that. He's thought about getting something newer. He'd promised himself for years that he'd do that if he ever had the money. But now that he can afford it, it doesn't seem to matter all that much. The pickup runs well, it's dependable, and he and that truck have history. It's been less than two years since it helped save his life and his freedom.

And the pickup is inconspicuous. His own appearance and bearing may or may not still shout cop to certain segments of the population, but at least the truck won't. He hopes it will help tag him as just another civilian. That they'll think he's in this druggy neighborhood looking to buy.

To canvass the area, which is what he plans to do, he really needs a photo of Gina, and he doesn't have one. Or, rather, he doesn't have one that's anywhere close to recent. There is a snapshot of her in his billfold. (The guys in Iraq made fun of him for that, for carrying photos of the people he loves in his wallet in one of those old-fashioned plastic multi-pocketed inserts. So he's a fossil. Who cares?) But that photo is too old. It's Gina at fifteen, at her birthday dinner when she was having a good day and he and her grandma had managed to take her to a fancy restaurant, with none of her increasingly dubious friends involved. There may be a better picture in the albums he's just retrieved from storage, but he hasn't had a chance to look through those yet. He'll have to make do with a verbal description.

But right now, there's no one to talk to anyway. It's too early. Dark. And late. But not late enough. No action yet.

He decides to take advantage of the empty streets to get a close look at the spot where Gina was found. He grabs a flashlight from the glove box.

There's a streetlight on the corner half a block down from the entrance to the alley, but nothing casting any light into the passageway itself. Grady can make out the shapes of several dumpsters and what may be a pile of flattened cardboard boxes.

He takes a few steps into the gloom before he flicks on the flashlight. Discretion is always a good idea even when it's unlikely you're being observed. A cop rule.

The alley is a dead-end and so narrow that Grady's surprised trash trucks can pull in and then back out without taking a bin or two with them. On the left, several beat-up metal doors provide rear access from the bar and convenience store that face the parallel street. Each door has a dumpster parked nearby. There's a light fixture over each door, but the bulbs are smashed or missing. The people who hang out around here apparently do what it takes to make sure this slot between buildings stays dark. And he was correct about the pile: flattened, bundled boxes ready for recycling. The right side is a wall of blank brick, the eyeless flank of an old, deep building facing the perpendicular street.

He decides to start his search at the far end and work backwards toward the street. It's almost certainly overkill, examining the entire alley. And he doesn't know what he's hoping to find anyway. But it's procedure, and it's in his bones: you do the basic grunt work of detecting, and you do it without preconceived ideas. Most of the time, it doesn't pay off. But when it does…

The alley ends at a high wooden fence. The area in front of the fence has attracted the kind of litter that becomes permanent and breeds additional crap. Broken glass, splintered boards, the twisted frame of a bicycle, an old mattress, heavily stained. It's in a spot too dangerous to be a bed for even the most desperate homeless person, but makes a perfect cushion to rest on while shooting up, or hastily servicing a client when you don't have access to a room by the hour or the backseat of a car.

He steps on discarded fast food wrappers, smells spoiled meat, urine, vomit. He knows there are—or have been and will be—rats. If he wants to sort through all this crap piece by piece, he'll need gloves, which will mean a trip back to the truck.

He picks up a several-foot-long piece of one-by that's lying a few feet away. He'll start with a visual scan, do a good job of inspecting areas with his flashlight, using the wood to move items and dig into piles as necessary. Then he'll decide whether a more detailed search makes any sense.

If he ever doubted whether the mattress was a favorite outdoor shooting gallery, the debris dispels those doubts. There are bloody tie-off rags, needles. His stick hooks a ragged pair of jockey shorts, shoves aside soda cans, beer bottles, chicken bones.

The futility of it hits him. He's not going to find anything. And he's not going to find anything because there's nothing to find. Gina's in a hospital bed, unconscious, and he's out here making himself feel better by pretending to be doing something. You're fooling yourself, Grady, his inner voice tells him. But he keeps going, and the inner voice answers itself: I can only do what I know how to do. And this is what I know how to do.

He moves back up the alley to the entrance. The street is still deserted. Time to check the dumpsters. He lifts the lid of dumpster number one and looks in. Nothing but trash. And every bit of it looks like it belongs. Nothing out of place. He looks around the dumpster, under it, behind it, pokes with his stick at a small mound of empty beer cans. A rat skitters away.

He follows the same procedure with dumpster number two, with the same results.

As he lifts the lid of dumpster number three, he's already thinking about next steps: where to hang out until the streets wake up and the neighborhood becomes a bazaar of vice and sin, how to approach its late-night population: the addicts, small-time dealers, working girls. The kids and disillusioned immigrants behind the counter at the convenience store, the jaded and cynical bartenders. He looks inside and shines his flashlight over the contents. The usual crap. He checks the area in front of the dumpster, the right side, the left. He shines his light underneath. What's that? Way at the back…

He thinks he sees… It's a small, rectangular object. Light glints off it.

Probably nothing. But could it be…?

The dumpster is tight against the wall of the building. He won't fit behind it. He gets as close as he can at the back and reaches in with the stick. It touches the target. He pulls the piece of wood back and then adjusts, inserting it again, trying to place it so that it will make contact with the far side of the thing. Then he'll slide it toward him. It's working, he's got it, he's got it—and the stick bangs against the metal back of the dumpster. The object goes sliding into the far corner. He gets the stick under as far as he can, maneuvers it into the corner. No luck. He can touch the target but can't move it. It's stuck.

He's going to have to get down on the ground and reach in from the front. And the asphalt is filthy. He's no clean freak, but this… He needs something to lie down on.

The cardboard. He uses his pocketknife to cut the plastic twine holding the bundled cardboard sheets together and, with a silent apology to whoever will curse him and have to redo the work, pulls out two good-sized pieces. He lays the sheets on the ground in front of the dumpster and lowers himself onto them. He lies there on his stomach and moves forward enough to insert his head under the dumpster. It's awkward to the point of pain, but he manages to get the flashlight pointed in the right direction. Then he stretches his right arm, hand grasping the stick. He can just reach his target… But it won't budge, and the damn flashlight keeps wanting to move. He can hardly see. Maybe he'll have to leave, come back with some kind of device. Barbeque tongs?

"What the fuck?" The voice startles him so much he almost bangs his head. It's a woman, young by the sound of her, and definitely street. "You okay down there?"

He is, and he isn't. He's lying on the cardboard so he's not rolling around in filth, but he's not getting anywhere. Then it occurs to him.

He slides back on the cardboard, stands up. She is young, a hard-lived twenty-five or so, he guesses, and (yes!) she is small. "I dropped something," he says, "and it slid under there. Can you help me get it back?"

She looks skeptical. She's dressed for work: black satin shorts, spike heels, a low-cut halter top, a shiny red patent handbag. "I need to pee," she says, disappearing behind the next dumpster in. He hears a stream of urine hitting the pavement.

He catches her on her way back out to the street. "You're small," he says. "You can fit under there." She looks horrified. "You won't get dirty," he reassures her. "I'll put down more cardboard."

"What's it worth?" she asks.

He pulls out his billfold, holds out a twenty. She shakes her head. He takes out another bill, same denomination. He can see her considering, assessing how much cash is in that wallet and how high he'll go. "This is it," he says. "This is what it's worth to me."

She takes the bills, tucks them into the red purse. He slides more cardboard under the dumpster. "There," he says.

She seems to consider handing him the purse, then wraps the strap of the bag around her left wrist and drops to the cardboard. She has to scrunch into the space, snakelike, not even able to use her elbows like a marine. It's a tight fit. She slowly makes her way under the dumpster. Then she stops. "If I get dirty…"

"You won't."

"If I do…"

He gives up. "Another twenty."

She's under the dumpster, only sticking out from the knees down. Grady's crouching, shining the light into the darkness. He sees the item, spotlights it. "There," he says. "On your right."

She stretches out her arm, can't reach it.

He re-aims the light. She stretches again.

She's got it.

She scrunches her way back out. He reaches down, takes the object from her.

It's a cell phone, one of the new "smart" ones that he's read about but never seen, in a case that was once a shiny silver, now smeared with dirt. He's been assuming that the phone Gina used to call 911 was a cheap burner. Could this be hers? How much of his spare cash did Gina steal?

"Huh," the girl says. "That really yours?"

She watches as he looks at the flat glass front panel of the phone. The screen warns him: Low Battery. He pushes the one big button below the screen, sees "Slide to Unlock," and mentally crosses his fingers. Don't let Gina have thought to password-protect this thing. Don't let Gina have…

She didn't. For a moment, he's lost in what he's learned to call "the interface." Then he clicks the icon that looks like a phone receiver, finds his way to "Recents." And there it is, an outgoing call at 2:08 a.m. 911.

The screen goes black. Dead.

He stows the phone in his pocket, can't do anymore until he gets it charged. The girl is still standing there looking at him. He waits for her to turn and walk away, but she points to a smear of grease on her arm, holds out her hand.

He pulls out another twenty but hangs onto it. "There's one more thing."

Her expression says she's been expecting it. What else would a middle-aged white guy who's not a cop be doing in this neighborhood at night?

"No. Not that. I just need some information."

Now, she's wary. He sees her thinking maybe he's a cop after all.

"The girl who was beaten up here last night? Do you know about that?"

She shrugs. "Some." Still wary.

"Her name is Gina. She's my niece. And she's in the hospital. Unconscious."

The girl makes a little noise of sympathy. "Sorry."

"I'm hoping somebody saw something, heard something."

The girl shakes her head. "I wasn't here last night."

Grady hands her the bill, tucks his wallet back in his pocket. She looks at him. Considering? She's a girl working the streets. Maybe she realizes that this time it was Gina, but next time it might be her, because she apparently makes a decision in his favor. "Like I said, I wasn't here last night. But I know people who were."

#

Three hours later, he's made no further progress.

The problem might be the generic nature of his description: female, white, twenty-eight years old, 5' 7" maybe 110 pounds, brown hair, brown eyes. If Gina has any tattoos, he's never seen them. If she has any other identifying marks, they weren't visible two days ago. He doesn't even know what she was wearing when she was attacked.

He considers going to the hospital, taking a photo of her, and coming back. But in her current state, his niece is barely recognizable even to him, so there's no point in that. Or he could go back to his apartment, dig through his mom's photo albums, see what he can find. But it makes sense to do all that he can while he's here. He decides that a picture of Gina at fifteen is better than no picture at all, pulls the snapshot out of his wallet, starts showing it around—and finally gets somewhere.

Yes, Gina was there last night. Several people agree on that. And no one recalls seeing her hanging around before, although one girl thinks she remembers her from "a long time ago," but isn't sure. So whatever Gina was doing with her time between whenever she hit town late Sunday and last night, it didn't involve the nightlife on this particular street.

This tells Grady nothing he doesn't already know: Gina was around here for an undefined period of time before the attack. She was found in the alley around the corner. She was located by the 911 call with the screams for help, and he found the phone she made the call from under a dumpster only feet away, so she wasn't moved after she was beaten.

He's thinking maybe he should pack it in for the night. Get Gina's cell phone charged. See what that tells him, start again tomorrow.

Then there's a shift change at the convenience store. The late-night guy, skinny, late teens, with a straggly goatee, remembers not just that he saw Gina but that she bought a Diet Coke. "Yeah," he says. "That's her. She wanted a Cherry Diet Coke. I told her we don't carry it. I don't even think they make it anymore."

"How'd she look?"

"Okay, I guess. But a lot older than that picture. And kind of skanky. No offense." No offense taken, Grady assures him. "Mainly, she looked tired," the clerk goes on. "Real tired."

"Was she high?"

The clerk shrugs. "Nah." Then he considers. "Well...I dunno. So many people around here are high I don't pay much attention. So maybe a little."

This jibes with the tox screen done by the ER.

"She was looking at the magazines," the clerk adds. "My boss don't like that, people flipping through them without buying, and I shouldn't have let her 'cause she had a backpack and, well, you know…But she wasn't hurting anyone. And she wasn't working. She wasn't dressed like a hooker if you know what I mean. And she didn't look like any dealer I ever saw. Not a lot of women doing that, at least around here. And them that are, they're hard. A lot harder than your girl. So she wasn't going to get us in no trouble. And she didn't seem like she was going to steal anything. And, like I said, she seemed real tired. So I just let her."

Grady gives the kid a calculated smile, an approval of his humanity. Then he prompts: "So she stood there, drinking her Diet Coke, looking at the magazines."

"Yeah. Like she was killing time. Like maybe she didn't have anywhere to go. That happens here."

"And then?"

They're interrupted by a customer, some older homeless guy buying a single can of malt liquor.

Grady waits while the kid rings up the purchase. Then he gets them back on the topic. "She was looking at the magazines and…"

"She just left."

"Was she using her phone? Did she maybe get a call?"

The clerk considers. "Don't think so. But there were a few people in and out. I coulda been busy. She had a phone. She laid it on the counter when she took the money out of her pocket to pay for the diet soda. I noticed it because it was one of those cool new ones. Really slick. But I never heard it ring."

"What time was it when she left?"

"I dunno. Late but not that late. Maybe around two?"

Grady's back outside, showing the picture around again with renewed hope. But the street has been humming for a couple of hours, and he's already talked to just about everybody.

Then he spots a newcomer, a girl with bleached blond hair tipped in pink who looks too young to be out this late let alone hooking (as if anyone is old enough for that). She's decked out in seventies-ish thigh-high platform boots and a top that would reveal a lot of cleavage if she had any to reveal. She says her name is Kitten, and she laughs at the photo. "Whew," she says. "How old is this thing?"

Grady allows that it was taken a while back. "You saw her? Last night?"

"Yeah. But she looked like she coulda been my mother."

Grady wonders how old Kitten is, how old her mother is. If the girl is eighteen (and he'd bet she's still a year or two away from that birthday), her mother could be as young as mid-thirties. If Kitten's sixteen, add sixteen and sixteen. Thirty-two, thirty-three. Gina's not quite there yet, but late twenties is genuinely old in this girl's eyes.

"She was asking about a friend of hers, Missy. I didn't know her. So I figured, she's old, Missy's probably old. And I took her to Libby."

Grady figures Libby also is "old." "Is Libby here?"

"She got a client. But she'll be back any sec."

Any sec is twenty minutes. And Kitten was right: Libby is "old." Pushing forty is Grady's semi-educated guess. And she catches whatever remaining whiff of cop he's putting out.

"You're TPD," she says.

"Used to be. Long time ago."

"Huh." Grady hears the "I'll bet" in her tone. He shows her the photo. "This girl is my niece. She was talking to you last night."

"Nah. I saw Kitten bringing her over, but I had to split. Work 'intervened.'"

"You never spoke?"

"Not a word."

He lays it on the line. "She was beaten last night. Found in the alley around the corner."

"I heard about that." It's a bare acknowledgement.

"It was bad. Really bad. She could die."

The woman shakes her head. "Shit." But there's no feeling behind the word. She says it as if she's commenting on a remote act of God, an unfortunate but unavoidable event.

Grady chooses his next words carefully. "Look, she's my sister's kid. I need to get the asshole who did this."

He can see he's hit the mark with Libby. Family, she gets. Revenge, she gets.

She nods. "What do you need?"

"Her friend Missy died the day before. It was an accident, but Gina, my niece, didn't want to believe that. I think she was playing detective. And I think Missy was in the life."

The woman looks around, maybe checking to see that she's not missing potential business. Or making sure that she's not spotted by her pimp wasting time talking to Grady. Once she's scanned the area, she takes advantage of the break in her night to light up a cigarette. Grady pulls out his own pack. He's happy to keep her company if it will keep her talking.

She takes a long drag and blows out smoke. "I used to know Missy. She didn't work the street long. Had the looks and the class to go upscale. Got herself a book and a good set of johns."

"She was a call girl."

"Yup. Did real well, I heard. But she didn't hang out with people like me anymore." Another long drag. "She died, huh? Too bad."

"Did Gina talk to you last night, maybe about Missy?"

The woman shakes her head. "No. Like I said, I had to split. Never even said 'Hi.'" She regards the growing ash at the end of her cigarette, tips it onto the pavement. "But I was here when the cops found your niece. A bunch of us heard the screams."

And what did they do about it? Libby gives him a weary look up from under hooded eyes, a look that says I wasn't born yesterday and neither were you, a look that says you've got to be kidding. Nothing. They did nothing.

"We just figured some bitch was having it out with her man."

Or some girl was being "beat on" by her pimp. And no one wanted to get in the middle of that.

"A couple of the girls, the dumb new ones, did run over there, to the alley. I don't know what they thought they could do."

"Who? Are they around?"

"One of them is. Kitten. The one sent you to me."

Kitten denies it at first, then confesses. "They told me I shouldn't get involved," she says. "So I didn't, like, mention it when you asked me before." She and Shawna, her best friend on the job, heard the screams and ran to the mouth of the alley. The screams had stopped.

It was black back in there, but they thought they saw—for just a moment—what looked like a man with something in his hand hitting something that was down by his feet. Maybe he saw them watching. He charged out of the darkness, almost knocked them down, raced off past them.

They could see a still form on the ground, back by one of the dumpsters. They were too scared of getting in trouble themselves to go into the alley, and were still talking about what to do when they heard the police siren. The cops were coming. Some of the other girls came over to see what was going on, but she and Shawna beat it.

An eye witness. Fuck!

"What did he look like?"

"I dunno. It was so fast."

"Tall? Short?"

"Tall. Thin."

"White? Black?"

"White, I think. But he was covered up, except for his hands."

"Covered up?"

"You know. Jeans, a hoodie."

Kitty and her friend never saw his face, or even his hair. Shit. Nothing here for an identikit. But still... He knows that by the time the patrol car pulled up, Kitty and her friend were gone, but he asks anyway. "Did you tell the cops this?"

"Yeah. Right. As if."

Grady keeps probing, does all he can to prod her memory without pushing her away. But no matter how he tries, that's all Kitten will say.

He finally decides that's all she's got.

23

Grady stands on the balcony off his living room smoking a cigarette and working on cold coffee—at least his tenth cup of the day. He's waiting for Rachel Greene. He ignored her calls for hours, but she was persistent. When he finally answered, she insisted she had to talk to him. Today. In person. She'd come to him.

So it was the hospital or the apartment. He felt a little guilty deciding on the apartment because it meant leaving the hospital, but he had no interest in telling Ms. Greene about the situation with Gina. It wasn't just that talking about it was pretty much guaranteed to make him feel worse, not better—or even that Rachel Greene was someone he barely knew. It was that she was an FBI agent, a Fed first, last and always. Bottom line: no one with any brains shares anything with a Fed unless they absolutely have to.

He isn't looking forward to this meeting, but he's glad to be away from Gina's bedside. He and Jill spent the morning just sitting there. Every once in a while, one of them would leave to use the bathroom or to get another cup of bad coffee. Their conversation was almost nonexistent: a few words here, a few words there. None of it meaningful.

A couple of times during those long hours, he thought about bringing up their situation. To ask her what it meant. But he'd shut her down earlier. And maybe she hadn't brought it up since then because she'd decided it was just a one-time thing, a mistake she doesn't want to repeat, or even revisit. If he called her on it, she'd be forced to tell him that. And he'd be devastated. With Gina lying there somewhere between life and death, he just…couldn't.

The nurse on the day shift, a largish woman wearing a scrub top with pink and blue teddy bears printed on the fabric at such acute angles they seemed to be in danger of flying off into space kept telling them to "have faith." He'd heard her humming some peppy little tune a couple of times while she was checking Gina's vital signs and making small adjustments to the ventilator. And he had to step on his adrenalin and zipper his mouth. It didn't mean she was uncaring, he reminded himself. She was entitled to her own happy life outside of this room. And she probably wasn't even aware she was, figuratively speaking, whistling while she worked. But somehow the humming still struck him as insensitive, even callous. It seemed heartless—or maybe unfair—for her to be going about her business so cheerfully.

After he made the appointment with Rachel Greene, not saying a word about it to Jill, he had to get himself out of the hospital. He could see that Jill was exhausted. He told her he was wiped out too, insisted they both needed a break. The nurse in the pink and blue teddy bears backed him up, and he realized he wasn't angry at her, he was angry at the situation.

In the end, Jill didn't fight him. But as they were leaving, she made it clear that she was going with him to his place again and that she assumed that they'd both come back to the hospital later. He didn't get it. What was going on with her? From what he could see, she was going AWOL on her life for an entire second day, and he didn't understand how she could do that—or why she would. He still didn't bring up her marriage or their recent intimacy, but he did ask her about her patients, her daughter.

She waved him off. "I'm handling it. Don't worry." That was all she said.

Even though he maneuvered them out of the hospital because he needed time for his meeting, it was a fact that they were both short of sleep.

It was nearly three a.m. the night before when Grady finally returned to his apartment from his trip to the alley where Gina was attacked. He unloaded his pockets including the cell phone that was Gina's onto the dresser, called the ICU nurses' station and learned that there was no change in his niece's condition and that Jill was still there dozing in a chair. He decided there was nothing more he could do until morning, fell into bed, and managed to get a couple of hours of broken sleep before dragging himself back to the hospital.

Now, Jill's asleep in his bedroom, and Gina's cell is still in there, charging. Jill has one of the fancy new "smart phones" herself. When they arrived at his building, she brought the charger from her car up to the apartment with her. After his meeting, he'll go through Gina's phone.

And about his semi-friendly visiting FBI agent. What the hell does she want? The FBI must not have enough real crimes on its plate if it can spend so much time, money, and energy on a minor mystery in a suicide note. "A few follow-up questions," she'd said when he pushed her on it during their brief conversation.

She'd reached him at the hospital. He'd noticed that the rules on using cell phones had eased up a lot over the past few years. It used to be that just having them turned on was verboten anywhere on the premises. Now people were yakking in hallways, waiting areas, everywhere. He wondered if anyone else missed the quiet.

He and Jill both kept their ringers off when they were in with Gina, but when he felt his phone vibrate in his pocket for the fourth time, he pulled it out, answered the call, and excused himself. He left the room, made his way out of the ICU and talked with Rachel down the hall from the main waiting area.

When he returned, Jill asked what to her must have been the logical question: "Was it about Gina? Have the police found something?"

He managed not to laugh in her face. He'd already explained that the cops weren't going to do shit about Gina's assault, that if she died and it became a murder case, they'd do a little more, but still not all that much. He didn't bother going into this with her again, and he sure didn't see the point of sharing anything about Malone's suicide and the FBI's interest in it. He just said the call was business.

"About your contracting job?" she asked.

He nodded. Close enough. Not quite a lie.

"So you're still going back. To Iraq, I mean."

Of course, he was. He'd never had any intention of not returning. Did she think he'd changed his mind in the past four days? He could see doing two, three, even more tours, he told her.

He supposed she was looking at the situation with Gina, thinking it might make a difference in his plans. It wouldn't. Gina would be okay. Or she'd be dead. He refused to consider any outcome that might leave her alive but diminished in some horrible way.

Or did Jill's "still going back" refer to what might have been a change in his relationship with her? No matter how surprised he'd been by what happened between them, he was afraid even to hope that it meant something for the future. And, whatever happened, he had to earn a living.

He'd been mildly surprised that Jill hadn't pushed him on the Iraq thing the first time it came up, when she came by on Sunday to welcome him back and see the apartment. So he shouldn't have expected that she'd let it go now. And she didn't.

When he didn't elaborate, she asked. "Why, Jack? Why are you going back there?"

Why? What else do you think I'm going to do, my highly educated, professionally successful, affluent ex-wife? How hot do you think the market is for middle-aged ex-cops who left the force under a cloud? He shouldn't need to say all this. She should know it.

But apparently he needed to state the obvious. "Because the money's good, and parts of the job manage not to be boring."

There are the other reasons he doesn't mention, reasons he's only begun to acknowledge to himself. The losses: his mother, his childhood home, his crappy yet perfect place out in the desert, the romantic part of his relationship with Ally, and, not least, his dog. Rather than ask him why he was going, she should be asking him why he would want to hang around. And if he should hang around because of her, she should say so. The fact that she hadn't, that it wasn't the first thing out of her mouth… That told him a lot.

He could see she had more to say on the topic, and he was pretty sure that he was about to hear a speech on the foolishness of putting himself in danger when he didn't have to. She might even have used the word "stupid." But at that moment the nurse came into the room for more checking of vital signs, more fine-tuning of equipment. And, to Grady's relief in some ways and disappointment in others, they never got back to it.

His cell rings. It's the downstairs door. Rachel Greene. He buzzes her in, steps out into the hall, meets her as she comes off the elevator.

She's dressed down, in slim black pants and black flats, sporting a high ponytail and a red t-shirt. He's never seen her in color before. The red does good things for her dark hair and olive skin.

There's no briefcase today, just a small shoulder bag worn cross-body, big city style. And she's clutching a Starbuck's carryout tray. "Since I'm imposing on you," she says, "I thought the least I could do was supply some good coffee." She unloads two tall cups onto the kitchen counter, lifts a small bag off the tray and takes out two pastries. "Scones." She takes the lid off her cup of coffee, brings it to her lips, and looks around. "Huh," she says. "Nice place. Much more urban than I would have expected."

"Don't let appearances fool you," Grady says. "Tucson will always be a cow town." He takes a swallow of coffee, a bite of scone. It's the best thing he's had all day.

They settle on the couch. "I'm still moving in," he says, kicking himself for stating the obvious.

"Huh," she says with a smile, glancing around at the boxes, the empty shelves. "I never would have guessed."

He has to admit that he doesn't dislike her. She's okay to be around—for a Fed. And she's easy on the eyes. He wonders if she's been flirting, tells himself that's not possible. And she made it clear on the phone that whatever it is, it's urgent. She's not here for a social call.

The bedroom door opens, and Jill wanders sleepily into the room heading for the refrigerator. She's wearing one of Grady's t-shirts, which is just long enough to cover the essentials. Her hair is tousled, her legs bare. "Oh!" she says, flustered. "I didn't know you had company."

There's a moment of awkward silence. Grady recovers first. "Rachel Greene," he says, "Jill Whitehurst." To Jill, he explains, "Business. Routine stuff about my next tour." He still sees no reason to share any information about what Rachel is really doing here.

"Nice to meet you," Rachel says. To Grady's eyes, she looks amused.

"You, too." Then to Grady: "Just needed a cold drink." She grabs a bottle of water from the refrigerator, disappears back into the bedroom.

Rachel had been flirting. It wasn't a honey trap. She's never used herself for bait in that way and she never will. She finds Jack Grady attractive. He's a big guy, not quite handsome but undeniably good-looking in a very masculine way that appeals to her. So, she was thinking, why not have a little fun? And if getting up close and personal also allowed her to check him out a bit more on the whole Malone mess, that would be a plus.

But now. Scratch that plan. The woman who stepped out of his bedroom half-dressed was one of those tall, thin, blond types that some men go nuts for.

It's not that Rachel's afraid of the competition. She could have him if she wanted him. But why bother? She'll be out of this burb in a day or two anyway. The hell with it.

24

Grady watches Jill leave the room. He thought she was asleep. When they returned from the hospital, she wanted a nap, which seemed like a good idea to him. His plan was that she'd fall asleep, and he'd sit around and wait for Rachel. He was making no assumptions about the two of them, either what had happened between them or what might happen in the future, but when Jill handed him a pillow and a throw pulled off the bed, telling him that he needed some rest, too, their hands touched, and the next thing he knew they were in the bed together again, making love.

Jill fell asleep. He drifted off, then shook himself awake to deal with his appointment. He remembers when Jill used to wear his t-shirts as improvised nightgowns or around the house in the morning, cooking breakfast, her hair adorably mussed. Seeing her that way again, it's like…

He brings himself back to the present.

"So," he says, "what can I do for you, Agent Greene?"

"Rachel. We already established that."

She's right. They did. He nods, indicating that he's heard her and that he gets that she wants them to continue on a less formal basis. But he doesn't say anything, reserving the right (at least in his mind) to revert to a form of address that recognizes the power imbalance between them. If this causes her any discomfort, she doesn't show it. But then he wouldn't expect her to.

She starts by making it clear that this meeting is hers and she's setting the agenda—as if there were any doubt.

"It's about Malone's suicide," she says. "As I explained on the phone, we have a few follow-up questions."

Whatever they are, he's unlikely to have the answers. He's already told her all he knows. But it's important to indicate willingness, to be cooperative. "Okay." He takes another sip of coffee. He still thinks it's over-priced, but it is good.

He can tell she's ready to get down to business. She's ignoring her coffee and her scone, and her shoulders are straighter. She's stiffer. Here we go.

"Our investigation has uncovered some new information."

Okay.

"We're now almost certain that there was an…incident…"

An incident. Related to Malone's suicide. He'd gone a long way down this path with her before, when she showed him Malone's videoed suicide note. Now, given the venue, the possible players, the availability of weapons and excess of testosterone…

Whatever game she's playing, it's time to show her that he still has his investigatory chops. "I assume you're talking about an interaction between U.S. personnel, contractors in this case, and the indigenous population, also known as the citizens of Iraq. I assume that the interaction was unauthorized and/or irregular. And that it involved casualties."

She's silent, and he knows he's right on target.

So he makes it explicit: "It's an 'incident' that some might call an atrocity."

Rachel sets down her coffee cup and brings her hands to her forehead. She looks as if she wants to bury her face in them, maybe rub out a headache, turn away from the whole situation. Then her hands find a purpose—tightening the ponytail, and the moment's passed. When she speaks, she's straight and stiff again, and her voice is as level and factual as always. "Atrocity. That's a strong word. We don't know. We're still putting the pieces together. Right now, everything is circumstantial. We have a good idea of when the incident happened. We even have what we believe is an accurate list of which contractors were involved. But we can only make an educated guess at the general nature of what it was."

"And you believe this 'incident' is somehow related to Malone's suicide?"

"Yes and no. We think it—whatever *it* was—happened on a routine detail on a particular date, a date within the past few weeks. And that it involved Malone, the others who were on that assignment, and—as you surmised—Iraqi nationals."

He's starting to see why she's so hot about this thing. The situation in Iraq isn't as explosive as it was a few years ago, but there's still huge anger at Americans on the part of many Iraqis who weren't part of Saddam's machine and aren't involved in the insurgency.

And if some of the troops have a bad reputation, the reputation of contractors is worse. They're accused of routinely driving at high speed on the wrong side of the road, using gunfire to warn oncoming cars away, running them off the road, ramming the ones that don't move aside quickly enough. They've been rumored to have actually run over more than one civilian vehicle, crushing the car and its occupants. When they do drive in the "right" lane, they're said to strafe the road behind them with automatic weapons fire to force vehicles to keep their distance. Back in 2007, contractors were accused of shooting directly at a car that didn't get out of their way fast enough. That turned into a firefight that the Iraqis say killed twenty civilians, including the people who were in the car, a mother and father and their small child.

All this—and any number of smaller flare-ups where troops—or contractors—didn't observe protocol, or were reputed to be trigger-happy, or even just insensitive, has done major damage to the war effort and put every American in Iraq at even greater risk.

He takes the logical next step. "Sounds like there's a cover-up."

"Yes. We have reason to believe there is. But we don't have enough information to push the men we think were involved."

What the hell? She'll push him but not them? Stay cool, he tells himself, and don't jump to conclusions. After all, who is he to question the workings of our national law enforcement agency? He'd have to be nuts to give her too much of a hard time.

That doesn't mean he has to be totally goddamn passive, though. Time to ask the key question. Let's get to it, Ms. Greene. "What does this have to do with me?"

"We believe there's a recording."

"Of the incident?"

She nods.

A coverup. A recording. What the…??

"Audio?"

She gives him a look.

"Video?"

She nods.

He confirms what he's heard. "There's a 'tape' of this…whatever it was."

"Yes. We think so. And we think that Malone gave it to you."

To him? What the fuck? Buying time, he brings his coffee to his mouth, takes a slow drink, then sets the cup down. When he speaks, he concentrates on making sure his voice is calm and his words are clear. He doesn't want to give Rachel Greene any reason to misunderstand his reply. "When I left Baghdad, Malone wasn't around. He gave me nothing. Not even a handshake as I walked out the door."

"Hmm," she says. "Maybe you don't know he 'gave' it to you. He could have slipped something into your duffels, or your backpack. Whatever you were traveling with."

Shit. He focuses on keeping his temper under control, his voice from rising. "I've unpacked," he says. "And everything I unpacked was mine."

Rachel stands up, takes a slow circuit around the room, sits back down on the couch. "You might have missed something."

"I didn't."

She's silent a moment. When she speaks, her tone is conciliatory, almost as if she's simply making a suggestion. "Isn't it possible? After all, you had no reason to think anything 'extra' was in your luggage. We—all of us—tend to only see what we expect to see."

From his years as a cop, he knows this is true. But it sure as hell doesn't apply in this case.

Now, he's the one on his feet. He gestures at the room, opens his arms to indicate the balcony, the half bath, the bedroom, the full extent of his space. "Feel free to look," he says, even though this goes against every instinct he possesses. His rational mind tells him he has nothing to hide. His gut tells him to stonewall. He goes with rationality. "Bring in a team. Search the place."

She's good at her job, but he still catches the momentary look that crosses her face.

"You already did."

She nods.

"And my laptop?" Her face gives him the answer. "That, too, huh?"

What the fuck? Did they have a warrant? If so, they never served it. But maybe they weren't worried about that. Why not? He's no expert on federal law enforcement, but this doesn't seem right... "I'm a patriot. Of sorts. And not a bad guy. You could have asked. Nicely."

"I know," she says. He has the impression she's slightly embarrassed, maybe even a little ashamed. At what she's done? Or at being caught? She reaches out a hand. For a moment, he thinks she wants to touch him, perhaps reassure him, but he's six feet away and she'd have to get up and come over to him, and maybe it wasn't her intention anyway, because she pulls the hand back, rests it on her thigh.

"Maybe we should have asked," she continues (although her tone doesn't convince Grady that she means it). "But we were still flying blind at that point. We had a pretty good idea there was something, but we didn't know who or when, let alone what..."

"And you still don't," he says. "The 'what.'"

She ignores the interruption. "At that point, we didn't know the timing or who was involved. We thought it was possible that you might have been implicated in whatever caused so much guilt for Malone. And that he believed that, like him, you had a conscience and that—unlike him—you had the guts to be a whistleblower. We also thought it was possible that he was wrong. That you were 'loyal' to your buddies, or too scared, or simply apathetic..."

"And why'd you change your mind?"

"A sense of you..."

He must look skeptical because, before she continues, she owns up. "Okay. I did get a sense of you. But that kind of thing doesn't count for much in my business. We have to stick to facts. And if we're right about the timeframe, you weren't present for the actual incident. You were in Baghdad but not on that detail. And you weren't tight with the men who were. Our conclusion: it's unlikely that you've been involved in the cover-up."

"Unlikely?"

"Highly. Verging on certainty."

Although he should feel vindicated, he finds he's shaken by her unwillingness to rely on her own judgment about his character. It's as if she can't help looking at the world through a filter of deep cynicism. Which probably shouldn't surprise him, but it does. A little.

Or is her approach "trust, but verify"? Hard to object too strongly to that.

Verify. Okay. He takes her points one by one. "I wasn't present for whatever happened. I wasn't aware of any incident of the sort you're talking about. And no matter what my sympathies might have been, those who were involved had no reason to involve me in a cover-up. I wasn't needed. We call that logical reasoning, Ms. Greene. So much for a 'sense of me.'"

He's taken them back to formality and let himself sound cold, and almost as angry as he feels. He knows he shouldn't have said the last part, though; it wasn't smart, but he couldn't help himself. Maybe he feels like she's been playing him, wanting him to think that she somehow has seen into his soul and judged him a good and honest man. And that's crap.

Rachel doesn't flinch. She looks him straight in the eye, her face giving away nothing. It's almost as if she's acknowledging, I am who I am. We are who we are.

He may not like it, but he has to deal with the reality, that he's somehow assumed to be party to a situation—no, call it what it is, a crime—that he knows nothing about. He's lived a complicated life, and he hasn't always been wholly innocent, but when it comes to this mess he is. Shit.

"And what do you think now?" he asks her.

"That Malone believed you'd find the recording, recognize it for what it was, and do the right thing. He thought you were one of the good guys."

One of the good guys. Huh. That and $2.99 wouldn't even buy him a cup of Rachel's fancy coffee. Time to get to his own bottom line. "So where does that leave us?"

"I was hoping you could tell me."

"It would be electronic, this recording, wouldn't it?"

"A thumb drive, a disk, a file on your laptop."

"But I don't have a thumb drive—hell, I barely know what that is. I don't do DVDs or even CDs."

"We noticed."

"And you've checked out my laptop a lot more thoroughly than I ever could."

"Yes."

"So what the fuck makes you still think I might have this recording in my possession?"

"Well, there are some remaining possibilities. Did you stay with a friend when you first returned to Tucson?"

"No."

"Do you have a second home?"

"Right." Like they don't know all about him and his finances.

"That was a stupid question. Sorry. How about a storage unit?"

"Yes. And I've been making trips to and from it since I got back to Tucson. But only to take things out. I haven't put anything in."

"Would you mind if we…"

"Hell, no. But it wouldn't matter if I did, would it? You'd search it anyway."

She doesn't acknowledge the truth of that, but they both know he's right.

Grady writes the name and address of the storage facility on a piece of paper, hands it to Rachel, and then watches as she enters the information into her phone. It occurs to him, not for the first time, that he truly is a dinosaur. He removes the storage key from his ring and gives it to her. If he needs to get into his locker before she returns it, he'll dig out the spare.

"Thanks," she says. She brings her cup to her mouth and tips it up, emptying it. She gets to her feet.

They're done.

Grady's impressed that, even in this sensitive situation, she actually drank all of her pricey coffee—and ate her scone, that the refreshments she brought weren't just a prop—or if they were primarily that, she had the good sense to take advantage of them. He trails her to the kitchen area. "So you're at a standstill."

"Pretty much."

"You're waiting for a PR nightmare that may never happen, or that could explode at any moment."

"Yup."

"And you can't get in front of it, just put it out there, call the bad actors to account, because you don't really know what 'it' is. And if it blows up, comes out some other way, the U.S. will look like shit. We'll look like we can't keep our people under control and won't even own up to their misdeeds. Again."

Rachel doesn't reply.

She retrieves her handbag from the kitchen counter and slings the strap over one shoulder and under the other arm, across her body.

"You probably don't need to wear it that way in Tucson," Grady says. "Downside, we're not some hip urban center. Upside, not a lot of purse snatchers here."

Rachel shrugs. "Habit."

"About the search," he says as walks her out. "I'm not the most organized guy, but I'd like to still be able to find things when you're done."

She smiles, even gives him a little wave. "No worries," she says. "We know how to be neat."

25

That's it. He's been interviewed twice. His apartment has been searched. Rachel's people will pick through his storage unit. They'll check out the interior of his truck, if they haven't already. They won't find anything, because there's nothing to find. And with that, any theoretical connection he might have to the incident in Iraq, or to its aftermath, will be at an end. Finished.

Rachel Greene has a tough problem, one he doubts she'll be able to crack. All she can do is wait for things to blow sky high. He can almost empathize. She doesn't seem a bad sort. And if he knew her better, and if the Feds hadn't jumped the gun with that stupid investigation of him a couple of years back, he might actually be more sympathetic. As it is, he has his own problems.

It's now Thursday afternoon heading toward evening. His last full night's sleep was Sunday, which feels like the distant past. Sacking out on the couch for an hour or two would be the smart thing to do. During his years on the force, he knew plenty of macho detectives who thought it was a badge of honor to work a big case around the clock. He's learned better. Physical exhaustion equals foggy brain equals missteps and errors, many of them stupid, some massively so. Not to mention substance abuse, broken marriages, heart attacks…

But.

Jill's gone back to sleep (after he explained to her that Rachel Greene was here on routine business about his contracting gig—not quite lying to her, but implying that his visitor was connected with his employer—and after they silently made love another time). He's not going to be able to even doze. He was a groggy lump much of the time at the hospital, smacked by emotion, lethargic from all the sitting, oddly lulled by the low lights, the regular soft beeping of the machines, frustrated by—and probably retreating from—his inability to act.

Now he's wired. Maybe it's picturing the Feds pawing through his stored crap. The thought makes him shudder. He'd bet it would have that effect on anyone. Or maybe it's something about his frustration with the TPD and their lack of any real interest in Gina's case, or his confusion about Jill.

Whatever it is, he only has one next step. He needs to look at Gina's phone.

He opens the door to the bedroom as quietly as he can. Jill doesn't stir. He creeps to the dresser and disconnects the phone from the charger. Back in the kitchen area, he settles on a stool at the counter.

He's heard about the interface on these new phones, but it's nearly as foreign to him as Swahili. Or maybe French. He knows the thing has a touchscreen, and he's semi-familiar with terms like "touch" and "slide."

He hits "Home," the same big button he used in that alley when he managed to find the record of his niece's 911 call. And he (finally) manages to "Slide to Unlock." He feels slow-witted and lost. He didn't have any trouble navigating through the phone the night before. Must have been the hyper-acuity that sometimes comes with bursts of adrenalin. One thing's for sure: he doesn't have that now. And the lack of sleep isn't helping.

There are multiple icons on the screen: "Messages," "Email," "Phone," "Contacts." "Settings." Something called "Angry Birds." Another labelled "ToneIt." A few others that don't seem relevant.

He touches "Contacts" and sees an alphabetical list. In the part of the list immediately visible on the screen, most entries are two letters: AK, AM, BZ. He touches "AK," and it opens to a screen with places for the contact's details. The entry has a mobile number and a note, "Talker. No kinks. Needs encouragement." Nothing else.

He spots a left-pointing arrow up at the top of the screen and pokes it. He's back at the main contacts list. He touches the letter "M, which moves him to that point in the alphabet. More initials: "ML," MP." He goes back to the top and scrolls slowly through the entire list. In addition to what he estimates are about sixty of the two-letter entries, there are a handful with names and Tucson addresses, including a doctor, a dentist, and an entry with the note "Landlord."

He clicks the big button again. He's back at the main screen.

After touching a few irrelevant icons ("Tools," which offers him a flashlight and an "iHandy Level" and "Utilities," which include a calculator and a compass), he tries "Dates & Weather" and finds what he's looking for: a calendar. It opens to today's date. There are two entries:

2:00 PM	Hair
8:30 PM	LD – tentative

He manages to navigate back to the previous day. The calendar for Wednesday lists:

12:00 PM	Yoga
2:00-5:00 PM	shopping – new outfit
7:30 PM	HP

Damn.

No way in hell this is Gina's phone.

Say she took some of his spare cash late afternoon on Monday, the first time she was in his apartment—and he can't see how she could have because she was in his sight every moment. She came in, they had the blow-up, she stalked out. But even if she pulled a magic trick and managed to grab some bills, he can't imagine her entering all this information (some of it pretty weird) between Monday evening and when she was attacked at two a.m. or so Wednesday morning. If she took the money when he rescued her from the police station about twenty-four hours earlier than that, she'd have had even less time. And the Gina he knows doesn't have her hair done, do yoga or shop for new outfits.

Another thing. What does one of these new "smart" phones cost? From what he's heard, they're hundreds of dollars. Would the money Gina swiped from him have covered it?

So—did the cell belong to her attacker? Did she somehow wrestle it away from him and manage to push 911? Bone skinny, semi-strung-out Gina?

How likely is that?

He knows already, but still… He navigates back to the main screen and touches "Messages." The bubble at the top is a text from "CB," timestamped Tuesday 3:37 p.m.

On for 10pm usual place. Will text you rm#.

Then, at 9:00 pm:

Rm 473. See u soon.

At 10:30:

R u lost?? Same place. 473.

And at 11:00:

Not like you to miss. Damn! Oh well. Next time.

He touches "Mail." The one at the top is from FlyGurl158@hotmail.com, received on Monday.

Hey babe – Where the hell are u? A no-show for
brunch & now???!!! WTF???

Below that, notice of a new electric bill, a reminder from a dental office that it's time for a cleaning. And on Saturday, from cammie85712@hotmail.com:

Partying tonite at Mary Kate's. Will you make it? 😊
Or are you working 😞?

If he had any doubt, these messages put a stake through its heart. This phone belonged to Gina's dead friend. It's Missy's.

He sets down the phone and walks around the counter, over to the coffeepot on the opposite side of the kitchen. There's only an inch left in the carafe, and that's cooked from sitting so long on the hot plate. He pulls the carafe out so it can cool and digs in the cupboard for the bag of ground coffee.

So…

It's Missy's phone.

Which tells him nothing except that his niece wasn't above stealing from a dead girl whose body was barely cold.

It was Missy's phone that Gina had on her when she was attacked. She used it to call 911 as she was being beaten, and then she dropped it and it was kicked or skidded and ended up under the dumpster.

He checks the kitchen drawer where he's stowed his extra cash. He stuck $500 in twenties at the back behind the can opener and other kitchen miscellany on Saturday, and he hasn't tapped it since. He pulls out the bills and counts. It's all there. Gina didn't take any of it. He feels like crap for assuming…

But maybe she just didn't find the money? That possibility makes him feel less like a suspicious jerk for a split second. Then reason reasserts itself. The cash was barely hidden. If she'd been looking at all, she would have found it.

So she stole from her dead friend instead of from him. Except Gina wouldn't have seen it that way. She'd have taken the cell on impulse. Seeing it there on a counter, or a nightstand. Broke, wanting a phone, telling herself that Missy had no further use for it. Maybe (he hopes) not spotting the cell phone until after she'd made the 911 call from Missy's landline. He hopes even more that the phone wasn't in Missy's handbag, that Gina didn't go looking for it.

He opens the cabinet under the sink and digs through the trash, which is mostly fast food wrappers along with a few pieces of pizza crust, not too gross. And he finds it about halfway down: the note Gina left him. When he came home two days ago to find his door open and Gina gone, he crumpled it in anger and stuffed it in the garbage can under the sink. Now he brushes off the old coffee grounds and tomato sauce and unfolds the piece of paper on the counter.

He's always seen his niece as headstrong, full of life, but also unfocused, scattered, someone who can't sustain an effort for an hour, let alone an entire day. She's never demonstrated the ability to set a goal and work toward it, even in spurts. She's always been sidetracked by the bright and shiny: mostly drugs.

Now he looks at the note again.

> Gone to find out what really happened to Missy.
> Then I'm going to get my baby back. Whether you help me or not.
>
> P.S. No spare key? What a liar!! They always give you two.
> You just don't want me to have one.
>
> P.P.S. You should get a TV!

He inspects the handwriting: strong block letters angled up the page. In some long-ago continuing education seminar, which he mostly dismissed as a crock of shit, he and his law enforcement colleagues had been told (he thinks) that forceful handwriting that moves up the page from left to right signals optimism and drive.

He must have picked up on some of that when he first saw the note, or he wouldn't have been so worried about Gina's resolve to get her baby back. It struck him, even at that first moment, that this mission might be compelling enough to override some of the distractions that always threw her off course.

And his focus on that threat to Ally and Mattie caused him to miss something.

"Then I'm going to get my baby back" was what had hit him, but it was the second line she'd written, the second goal she'd laid out—not the first. He'd been so staggered by the potential for disaster that he hadn't really absorbed the "then" or focused any attention on the rest of the note. There was something else she said she was going to do immediately.

She'd put it right up front:

Gone to find out what really happened to Missy.

Shit.

He washes the crud from the trash can off his hands. Leaving the note on the counter, he turns back to the coffeemaker.

The idea that she could "find out what really happened to Missy" is nuts. Starting with the premise that there's anything to find. He's often been skeptical about the thoroughness of some investigations (he's seen too much from the inside), but the thinking Moreno shared with him made a lot of sense. Grady has no reason to doubt that the conclusion the detective reached about Missy's death is correct. Gina's friend drowned by accident.

He opens the filter basket, pulls out the used filter, dumps it in the garbage, finds a clean one, inserts it, measures in fresh grounds.

So it's settled. Death by misadventure, as they used to say. But—damn it—the whole mess still nags at him. What if the cops are wrong? He hasn't forgotten the powerful attraction of the easy answer that closes a case. He knows how tempting it can be to disregard other potential, but problematic, explanations.

What if the attack on Gina wasn't random or related in some way to a drug buy (or even drug use)? Could she have been playing detective? And could she somehow have gotten dangerously close to the truth?

He fills the carafe with cold water, pours the water into the coffeemaker's reservoir, and clicks the thing on.

He tells himself again that this line of thinking is crazy. You were right the first time, Grady, he assures the part of him that's growing increasingly uneasy. You're seeing connections where they don't exist. Your niece is an addict and a thief. God knows she's stolen before. And your brain isn't to be trusted right now. You're wiped out. You've had too much emotion, too much coffee, too little sleep.

Suddenly he wants, craves, *needs* a tumbler of Scotch. Or Irish whiskey. Vodka. Even bourbon (never his drink). Rocks, no rocks. No glass even. Straight from the bottle. Doesn't matter.

What are the rules for staying sober? Don't get too hungry, too angry, too lonely, too tired.

Sobriety. God, he hates that word. He thinks of it as just not drinking today. With hopes for not drinking tomorrow.

And he won't. Not today. Instead, he'll find something to eat, he'll sleep…

Fuck it.

Focus.

No liquor.

He stands there, listening to the water heat up, watching the brew slowly seep through the filter. The digital clock on the microwave slides through one minute, two, five…

He pulls the carafe out before it's done dripping, ignores the warning beeps, pours himself another cup of coffee, and picks up Missy's phone.

26

Rachel's been pacing. The hotel room is so small that the open area is only ten steps one way, then ten the other, turn and repeat. She tells herself the walking is helping her think, but she knows it's really her body's attempt to burn off some adrenalin. And it isn't working.

It's a relief when the call from Gil comes through.

Everything she does, her job, her life—sometimes, she thinks, her entire being—is focused on getting results. Now, she's stuck. Stuck in an investigation that's going nowhere, stuck in the middle of the goddamn desert in a fucking cow town.

She sits at the desk to take the call. The image on her laptop is jumpy, like a screwed-up cable signal, but Gil's voice is clear. First, they do the hellos. They play the "How hot is it where you are?" game. And Gil wins that one—by a hair. It seems September in Tucson isn't all that bad, at least in comparison to Baghdad.

Then they get to it. She takes the lead, as they both expect. Gil's not her superior. In fact, she outranks him. Even so, she hates having to admit her lack of progress, as if articulating her failure will somehow make it real. But there's no point in trying to put lipstick on a pig. "We've come up dry on Geezer."

Gil doesn't visibly react, but there's a pause and then a long breath. If he's frustrated, he covers it with a neutral "Huh" before asking, "The boys didn't find anything on his computer?"

"Not a damn thing. Not even any decent porn."

She put that out there for comic relief, and Gil rewards her pathetic attempt at humor with a chuckle.

Then she gives him the bullet—in one sentence. There's not much to say.

"Nothing in his apartment, nothing in his truck, and nothing on his computer. A few hours ago, we learned that he does have a storage facility. That was our last hope, but we've been through it with the proverbial fine-tooth comb. Results: zilch."

It hadn't taken long. All the eight-by twelve-foot rectangle held was a lizard skeleton in one corner and a few lonely cardboard cartons, most of them empty. She was surprised at the two boxes of plates, cups, and saucers strewn with pink roses. She turned one over and saw the Royal Doulton symbol on the back. Must have belonged to his dead mother—which explained the ornate cookie jar sitting on his kitchen counter. The apartment was bare even by single-guy-just-moving-in standards. That cookie jar was the only homey touch in the entire place.

She figured Grady didn't feel comfortable using the dishes (not wanting to risk breakage and not being a strewn roses kind of guy—and porcelain dinnerware being of less obvious use to him than a large, sturdy cookie jar) but didn't feel he could get rid of them either. She'd already figured out who the half-naked blond was. Ex-wife. A dentist (of all things). And married. If there was a woman in his life (besides his ex-wife), at some point in the future, there'd be a china cabinet. If people still had china cabinets these days. Not something you could prove by Rachel. In the meantime, she supposed, he'd retrieve the boxes at some point and stick them in a closet.

"That's disappointing," Gil is saying. "But it sounds like what you expected."

"I knew it was a long shot."

"And you're using a tracking device?" The "of course" is implied in his tone.

She confirms that she is, making it sound like she'd never skip such a routine step. But it's a lie. She hasn't done it, hasn't seen the point of electronically trailing Jack Grady's movements around town. Now, though, she realizes that she has no choice.

Her refusal to rely on rote procedures has always been one of her strengths. She prides herself on her reputation as a maverick but a savvy one, not a cowboy who puts the whole ranch at risk by operating too far outside the fence. She's positioned herself as someone who uses her head, who doesn't just check the boxes—and who doesn't overuse resources. But in this case...

Shit. She'll give the order as soon as she gets off this call.

She loathes people who operate on a CYA basis. Is she becoming one?

Now she deflects, underlines the results of her efforts for Gil. "So far, this is a dead end. A big fat zero."

The picture on the laptop has cleared up, and she sees Gil lean back in his chair, hands clasped behind his head, eyes focused on some point on the ceiling. It's his thinking posture. After a long moment, he straightens up and looks in the camera again. "And he's not hiding anything?"

She's not surprised at the question. Gil's never met Jack Grady, and, despite Grady's disbelief when she said that she had gotten a sense of him, it was true that she has. And the sense she's gotten is that in spite of all of the shit that life has piled on him, he just might be that rarity: a decent guy. Anyone will lie with the right motivation, but she doesn't see that happening here. She also believes that Malone was right: that the man has guts, that if the stakes were high enough, he would be perfectly capable of blowing the whistle. He might even feel compelled to do it.

She wouldn't expect Gil to accept any of this as evidence that Grady isn't double-dealing, so there's no point in sharing it. She simply gives him the response he expects, the one that's standard under the circumstances. "I think he's telling us what he knows. But I'm considering whether to have one more go at him."

"Polygraph?"

"Dunno. Maybe." Subjecting Grady to a lie detector test would be a last resort. Her guess is he'd comply, under pressure, but that would be the end of his cooperation. And the end of his usefulness.

"I see," Gil says. "You're taking it 'under advisement.'"

She ignores the edge that has slipped into his tone. She'll give him a pass on it this once. But he better not push it too far. Taking it under advisement, my ass. "I am." Rest assured, Gil. Rest assured.

She turns the discussion around. Time to get caught up on what's going on at Gil's end. And controlling the flow of their conversation is a subtle way to reinforce that she's the boss. She remembers when, not so long ago, she and Gil were at the same level in the organization, seemingly on identical paths. And then she shot past him. They're still colleagues, even buddies. But he's only human. He must resent her on some level. She doesn't want that resentment to lead to sabotage—conscious or unconscious. She's seen too many team leaders, especially women, undermined by jealous subordinates. Thus, her subtle (she hopes) reminders of just who's directing who in this thing.

"How are the boys?" She means the core group in the house in Baghdad, and Gill picks up on it.

"Those assholes," he says in a 'boys will be boys' tone, then adds a shake of his head to show he can hardly believe what unconscious jerks they are. "Nothing new. They're still going out on details, drinking the booze that gets smuggled in, playing video games. Some of them try the online sex thing with their girlfriends back home. When they're not doing any of that, they're competing to see who can deadlift the most weight. One guy almost took out his toes yesterday."

Pathetic. And so fucking typical. It's to Jack Grady's credit, she thinks, that he apparently kept interactions with the group to a friendly minimum.

Next topic. Grady's replacement has just rotated in, but with Malone's death, the crew has still been a man short, offering an opportunity for Gil and his team. Rachel needs to confirm that they've carried out the planned insertion. "Did we get somebody into the house?"

"Yup. Positioned as a short-termer—a replacement for Malone until the right fit is found."

Good. At least one thing is going right. "Has he gotten anything? Any rumblings? Unusual tensions?"

"Not that he's picked up."

"Well, it's early." They both know the insertion is a long shot. It could take months for the boys to open up to him, if ever. And if they don't... Well, everyone agrees that the odds are there's a clock on handling this thing and that the clock is counting down. She redirects the conversation again. "I'm not sure how much more I can do here. It feels like I'm hitting a brick wall."

Gil states the obvious. "It's the only play we've got."

"Tell me about it."

She's ready to wrap the call. She figures she'll spend the next few hours weighing what more she can—or should do—concerning Jack Grady, whether it's important enough that she cover her ass to administer a polygraph to him, or whether just to get the electronic tracker going, monitor it for twenty-four hours or so, and then pack her bags and head for the barn. She's about to tell Gil that unless something demanding stat communication happens in the meantime, she'll talk to him at the same time tomorrow when...

"Oh...one more thing."

Rachel doesn't like the sound of that or the tone in Gil's voice. She wonders if she's about to hear something he doesn't want to tell her. Or is he sandbagging? Saving critical information to mention casually at the end, as a "by the way" post script to their discussion? Is this his way of asserting himself? Subtly shifting the balance of power, if only temporarily? There's a carafe of ice water on the desk. She pours herself a glass, slowly, showing she's not rattled.

"Look," he says, "this is minor." She picks up the unsaid "I hope" in his voice. The picture's gotten screwy again, but she can see him take a deep breath. He's not sandbagging. He didn't want to have to tell her. "It's Pickett."

The alpha dog. In fact...

She flashed on something Gil told her during a previous conversation: "His buddies call him Cujo."

In another context, the nickname would have raised a red flag. But things are different in a war zone, maybe especially in this war zone. No one worries about "aggressive." And the other words that come to mind, "savage," "ferocious," even "bloodthirsty," are traits that simply translate to fearless. They can even be twisted into carrying positive connotations of leadership. Still... Rachel couldn't help but picture razor-sharp teeth, a maw dripping red. It was a nickname to make a more sensitive person shudder.

Gil had chuckled. "Cujo and Geezer. Talk about your mixed metaphors."

She'd already reviewed Hartman Pickett's record, and after that talk with Gil, she went over it again. Nothing of concern in his past other than a bar fight when he was nineteen that resulted in a death. And he wasn't charged with involuntary manslaughter, although that might have been expected. In fact, he wasn't charged at all, which meant he'd been exonerated, or close. And since then, no black marks. His performance evaluations were perhaps not as stellar as she might have expected of a man with his "clear leadership potential" (made official by a box checked off in his file and illustrated by the cadre of bros he instantly gathered around himself in Baghdad), but the only negatives were a couple of notes about a "minor tendency to overreact." These were followed by the usual CYA language, "Pickett has been counseled and seems to have this well under control."

Still, from day one, she'd had the sense that he could be a wild card. "What about him?" She uses a tone intended to bring Gil up short, and it does.

"He went stateside."

What??? Leaving the sandbox off schedule? Her instincts about Pickett were right. "He wasn't due for a break until next month. Who the fuck authorized...?"

"Some paper pusher who didn't know any better."

If she had a dollar for the times some fucking bureaucrat screwed up an op... Fuck! "When?"

"Two days ago."

Calm down, Rachel, she tells herself. After all, how bad can this be? This is the computer age. We're a high-tech organization. We have resources. "Where is he now?"

"Story was he had to go home to Boise. Some sort of family emergency. Routine other than that. He flew out of here, transferred in Kuwait, then again in Germany, landed in Atlanta ..."

Rachel hears Gil's voice trail off. This can't be good. "And?"

"He's not in Idaho. And as far as we can tell, he hasn't been."

Damnit. This is so royally screwed up. "Any idea where he DID go?"

To Gil's credit, he doesn't drag it out, he doesn't make excuses, he simply states the facts. "We had him at Atlanta. Then we lost him."

27

The bar is dark, as bars should be. The place offers alcohol, which—if he weren't sober and committed to staying that way— would be enough for him. But its appeal ends there. The music coming from the sound system is too loud to be background and not loud enough to command the space. The beat is fast, pulsating, but mechanical, without life. The furniture and fixtures are non-descript, worn in a way that makes them look cheap and sticky rather than lived in. God knows what sins bright light would reveal.

The joint is doing business, though. It seems busy for a Thursday night. The youngish crowd looks like the kind of people who come out of high school with modest dreams that don't include college, at least not a four-year one, and a few years down the road find themselves sliding into America's latest underclass. Overweight, tattooed. Bravado hiding deep discouragement. And, he assumes, on some level hugely angry. As he came in, he passed an outdoor smoking patio, which was packed. The patrons here are self-medicating in multiple ways, and he can't blame them.

Holly—FlyGurl158@hotmail.com—stands out. She's mid-twenties, slim and pretty, wearing a halter top, low-slung jeans that reveal a ring in her navel, and scuffed red stilettos. A yellow butterfly decorates her left shoulder. The word "love" flows in curly script down her right arm. Her reddish blond hair is up in a messy ponytail. As he watches, she maneuvers a full tray of beers through the crowd, dodging a smack on her rear from one guy, ignoring a leer from another, and distributes the bottles to three couples crammed into a too-small booth. She grins, shares banter, pats one of the men on the shoulder, picks up bills, makes change from a pocket of her apron— no tabs being run here, not a high-limit credit card in the place.

He intercepts her at the service area of the bar top that runs along the far wall. "I'm going on break," she signals to the guy behind the bar and guides Grady to a corner away from most of the crowd and the worst of the music. She unties her apron and pushes it onto a nearby shelf that supports a collection of dusty beer mugs. "No place to sit," she says, "sorry."

She'd told him on the phone that she'd be working but that she didn't mind taking time to talk with him about Missy. They'd been friends since ninth grade.

And, yes, she confirms to him now, she knew what Missy did for a living. Hooking.

Grady's surprised at her bluntness. This is a young woman who apparently doesn't deal in euphemisms. "She was a call girl as I understand it," he says. "And a high-priced one."

Holly shrugs. "It's the same thing. When you get right down to it, selling your body is selling your body." Missy tried to recruit her a number of times, she says.

"That must have been hard on the friendship."

Holly nods. "It was. I know the money's good. But I didn't like the thought of… I mean, it's—was—her body. And it's not like she was hurting anyone. She'd tell me she'd help me get started. Refer guys. She'd give me tips on, like, how to run it as a business. Then you save up, she said, and you get out. You buy a bar, own it, not wait tables. You buy a house. 'How else,' she would say, 'how else are two white trash girls like us going to make it? Do you want to end up with some asshole who can't earn more than minimum wage? *When* he works. Who thinks he can hit you whenever he gets drunk? You got to use what you have. If you're hot, it's an asset. And you're hot. You got to use it.' She'd even say, 'God would want you to. Jesus would understand.' She knew I was sort of religious."

"So you never...?"

She shakes her head. The pony tail bobbles. "No. It just wasn't me. And Missy was smarter than I am. She knew what she was doing. If it could happen to her..."

"The police say she drowned. Took pills and just slipped under."

Holly shook her head. "Not Missy," she said. "I'm not saying she never did any drugs. But she was one of those people who could take it or leave it—whatever it was. She could smoke two cigarettes on a Saturday night when we were partying and none at all the rest of the week. If she took a hit of something, that would be it. A hit."

One of those people. The rules of physical addiction just didn't seem to apply to them. Grady had known a few, but not many. In his experience, they were rare birds.

"So when Gina contacted you..."

"I was just going on shift so I only had a few minutes. And she... well, it seemed weird. Here was this girl who... No offense, I know you're her uncle, but she looked kind of... used up. Like if she wasn't high on something, she was pretty desperate to be. She seemed like she was hanging on by her fingernails. And she said she was investigating Missy's death. It didn't make sense. I probably wasn't very helpful." Grady can hear the regret in her voice. She takes a deep breath before continuing.

"And, I gotta say, I hadn't seen Missy in a while. Not since the hospital. Our lives weren't going in the same direction. She had money. I didn't. I still live with my mom, but I'm taking classes at Pima."

The local community college. Grady is struck by the contrast between the two friends: one flush with cash from an illegal and dangerous activity, the other waiting tables in a run-of-the-mill joint while doing the hard work of preparing herself for better things. "But you were supposed to see her on Sunday. For brunch."

"Uh huh. My birthday was the week before. And we always celebrated together. Our birthdays were only two days apart. So I'd been thinking about her and feeling bad that it had been so long. I texted her on Thursday… Just a week ago. We made plans, then she didn't show up. Now I know why."

The look on her face says she's astonished by how fast things can change, how someone she'd known what would have seemed like her whole life could go from living to dead—gone for good—just like that. Grady gives her a moment, then pushes on.

"You mentioned not seeing Missy since 'the hospital.'"

"She was in a bad car accident a few months ago. I went to see her in the hospital a couple of times. And I know they were giving her pain meds there, so maybe… People change. But…"

Grady waits. Then he prompts. "It's okay. I want to know what you think."

When Holly speaks again, her voice is lower as if maintaining its normal volume might commit her to a mistake. "I know the police aren't stupid, and it's just an opinion…"

"Go on," he encourages.

"It still doesn't seem like Missy. At least not the Missy I knew."

The cops are wrong and Gina is right? Is that possible? This girl is intelligent, thoughtful, and straight-forward. Grady has to take her assessment seriously.

But the implications are staggering. Gina was nosing around. Could she have she put her nose into the wrong place? Or poked the wrong person? If so…

What Holly's told him doesn't allow him to recreate the connections, if any, from Missy's bathtub to Gina's attacker. But maybe she can send him to someone who knows more. "So you hadn't seem Missy in a while. Is there anyone who might have been in contact with her more recently?"

Holly smiles. "She… Gina was her name? She asked me that. Exactly the same question. I told her there were a couple of girls Missy hung out with. Other 'escorts,' though I don't think they were as successful, if you can call it that. She was kind of the leader of the pack. I never really knew those girls, just had a drink with them a few times when I was with Missy. And that was a while back. I think your niece was going to try to talk to them."

Grady is suddenly proud of Gina's resourcefulness. He's underestimated his niece. "How can I contact them?"

Holly shakes her head. "Like I told your niece—Gina, I just know their names. One's Amber. And the other one is Rocky."

"Rocky?"

"I think because she's always dressed like she's tough. Leather, chains. Missy called it her 'bitch thing,' said it was her 'stock in trade.'"

A "mistress," catnip to the masochists of the world. "Last names?"

Holly shakes her head again. "No idea. The only place I ever saw them was that one bar, and I only went there with Missy."

"And that bar is?"

"Sapphire's."

The bartender is calling her over. Holly picks up her apron. As she wraps the strings around her waist, she pauses. "I did think about doing it," she says. "Missy and I both grew up rough. There was never enough money. That's why I couldn't blame her. And I almost told her a couple of times, 'Sure. Hook me up.'"

"But you didn't."

"No. Still, there but for the grace of…you know…" She shudders.

#

Sapphire's is a very different kind of watering hole, with lighting meant to flatter, a back bar packed with top-shelf liquor, a line-up of craft beers, and a skillfully lettered blackboard touting "artisan" cocktails.

No one's heard of Amber or Rocky, but when Grady flashes a photo of Gina at one of the waitresses, she picks up on it. "Oh, yeah. She was in here a couple of nights ago. I noticed her because..." Her voice trails off.

I know why you noticed her, Grady thinks. You noticed her because she was scuzzy and because if she wasn't strung out right then, she looked like she'd be strung out before the night was over. You only want high-functioning users with platinum cards in here. No junkies.

He slips her a twenty.

"She was asking around, like you. Then she went into the Ladies Room. And my manager told me I had to get her out of here. He thought she was dealing, or soliciting. Although the way she looked..." Her expression says that Gina wasn't classy enough to appeal to their clientele. The word that comes to Grady's mind for her tone of voice is "catty."

He does his best to compose his face in an expression that says "I understand" and follows up. "Did she get anyone to talk to her?"

"When I went into the Ladies Room to tell her that she needed to take her business somewhere else, she was standing with a couple of girls. I was busy, so I just walked up to her and told her she had to move along—now."

"And then?"

"And then she left. She wasn't very nice about it. Called me a fucking cunt."

Grady's almost amused. If it's one thing, Gina has always had, it's spirit. His dad's generation would have called it "moxie."

"Who were the girls?"

"The ones she was talking to?" Shrug. "Not regulars. I didn't know them."

He's at a dead end. Finding out who attacked Gina has always been a long shot. He's not surprised he's hit a wall. He's ready to leave when the waitress adds: "Like I said, I didn't know them. But if you want to talk to them, they're right over there."

She gestures toward a stand-up table in a far corner of the room. Grady sees two young women, both blond, both sleek and shiny. Only the amount of skin showing indicates that they might be in the life. They're both absorbed in flirting with two late-twentyish men wearing suits, which in Tucson means they were either in a wedding party earlier in the day or they're from out of town, here on business. Given that it's a Thursday night, it's a sure bet it's the latter. He wonders if they've yet realized that the gorgeous creatures focusing so much unexpected attention on them are pros.

He thanks the waitress, steps over to the bar, orders himself a club soda on the rocks in an old-fashioned glass with a twist of lemon, and strolls over to a small stand-up table near his targets. He catches the eye of one of the blonds and raises his glass to her. She flicks her gaze back to the man she's been flirting with, then can't resist glancing Grady's way again. He pulls a wad of cash from his pocket, hundreds on top, and fans it—discreetly, but in her eyeline. It takes only moments for the two girls to ditch the guys (he's impressed by how quickly they manage it) and relocate themselves to Grady's table.

The blond who saw him flash the cash, the one with dark eyes that challenge the illusion of her pale-yellow hair, makes the logical assumption. "So you want a threesome?"

No, he tells her, he just wants to talk. The girls exchange a look that says, "That's weird, but we've seen weirder."

He lets himself be amused, assures them it's not like that. Then he pulls out the photo of Gina. "I understand that she was in here two nights ago, and you were talking with her." Their eyes turn hostile. They drove away two perfectly good customers for this guy? And now he's asking them this kind of question? He can see what's going to happen, catches the "Is this a cop?" looks they exchange. They're ready to walk away.

He palms a couple of hundreds and slides them to the girl closest to him. "Share," he says, low enough for his words to be covered by the background noise in the place. He lays the photo on the small table. "This is Gina," he says, as if he's introducing her. They may already know her name, and if they don't, he wants them to. "I'm her uncle, and I'm concerned about her. I need to know what she asked you and what you told her."

What this matched set told Gina was probably nothing. Makeup tips. Info on their dealers. The best place to buy sparkly five-inch stilettos. But he has to try.

He thanks the universe for a healthy bank account and flashes the bills again, making sure the girls remember that there's more cash where the hundreds they just tucked in their bags came from. The blonds nod. Okay.

He waves a waitress over, orders the girls another round, champagne cocktails this time, acknowledging their need to be classy. As soon as the waitress walks away, he puts the conversation in reverse, backs up, introduces himself. "I'm Jack Grady."

The girl farther from him is named "Sheena," or so she says. He has the impression it's her working handle. The other girl, the one with blue eyes that go with the light hair, claims to be "Bethany."

It's Sheena who speaks. "She asked about a friend of ours. Missy." Grady nods to let them know that he knows who this friend is. "She said that the police thought Missy took pills and accidentally drowned while she was taking a bath, but that she didn't believe it."

"Do you?"

Shrugs from both, but more emphatic from Sheena.

He prompts: "Another friend of Missy's told me that Missy didn't do much in the way of drugs. That she could take them or leave them."

Blank looks. Intentional, Grady's sure. The kind they'd give an inquisitive narc.

He palms another couple of c-notes to Bethany, watches as she passes one to Sheena. "Is that true?"

"Sort of." Bethany this time.

From Sheena. "It used to be true."

And Bethany. "Since her accident…" The back and forth seems to come naturally. These girls are a real twin act. But even as he wonders how many threesomes they book in a good week, he prepares himself to hear about the drugs Missy was given in the hospital, and the Sheena/Bethany thoughts on how she'd changed. If he wasn't at a dead end before, sure looks like he is now.

Then Sheena adds, "It wasn't the accident. It was the guy."

The guy? "What guy?"

The waitress approaches with the fresh drinks. Grady takes control, lifting the two flutes from the tray, laying bills on, seriously overtipping. He hands the girls their glasses, and they move in closer to him, crowding around the little table. There's a new looseness in their manner, less caution. They look almost eager to talk.

Bethany begins. "Okay. Well, Missy was in this car accident."

Sheena jumps in. "But she wasn't driving. She was hurt, but she was okay. The girl who was driving was killed."

Bethany's so eager to add to this that she almost interrupts her friend. "And she was high, the girl who was driving. Really high."

"That's why they crashed." Sheena again.

And Bethany. "Her name was Hope, and she had this brother."

"Who blamed Missy."

Both blonds nod, in solemn agreement.

Blamed Missy? For the accident? But Missy wasn't driving.

Grady doesn't even get the words out before Sheena continues. "He started harassing Missy. Calling her all the time, sending her texts."

"Did she report him to the police? Get a restraining order?"

"Are you kidding?" Sheena's on a roll, her emphasis increasing.

"Because she was a call girl?"

Bethany chimes in. "Well, yeah. Missy liked to, as she put it, 'minimize my contact with the authorities.' Besides, he didn't live here in Tucson."

Okay…

"Why was the brother harassing her?"

"He blamed her for Hope's death." Sheena's back.

There's a note of "duh" in her tone. She's said this before, but Grady still doesn't get it.

"For the drugs." From Bethany.

"Hope was just this U of A girl until she met Missy. Then she started using…"

This time it's Grady who interrupts. "Using what?"

Sheen gives him a look that says she can't believe a man his age can be so naïve. "Whatever. And she turned a few tricks. Dropped out of school."

Grady has to make sure he's hearing what he thinks he is. "Hope did? Left school? Turned tricks?"

Both girls nod. Sheena leans in and continues, "I think Missy felt guilty. I think that's really why she didn't go to the police. And she still wasn't using a lot, compared to some people. But she was using a lot more—a lot for Missy."

Bethany clarifies. "She said he was harmless. That he was just sad. And she said she didn't blame him."

Sheena adds the kicker. "And it's not like he was going to show up at her door."

????

Bethany explains. "He lived in Colorado. Denver, I think. That's where Hope was from."

It was a long shot. But Gina would have taken it. He would, too. "Do you know his name?"

Bethany's the one who responds. "His sister, the girl who died, her name was Hope Wendrell. I think his first name was Brian?"

Sheena corrects her. "No. Ben. It was Ben."

And Bethany adds, "She stopped answering after the first few times he called. We kept telling her she should block his number, but…"

Sheena finishes Bethany's thought. "We don't think she did. Like I said, she felt too guilty." Then she gives Grady what appears to be their bottom line. "But that was stupid. What happened to Hope wasn't her fault. People make their own decisions. Nobody rammed those pills down Hope's throat. Or the blow up her nose. Or whatever it was."

Bethany visibly shivers. "God, I hope it wasn't meth. That does such bad things to your skin—and your teeth."

The girls are starting to look around. Grady's money is good, but more would clearly be better. They're getting back to business, prospecting for likely johns.

He brings them back to where he started, asking the question directly. "What do you think happened to Missy? Could she have accidentally drowned? Just drifted off because she'd taken some pills and had some wine and then slipped under the water?"

It's Sheena, clearly the alpha of the pair, who answers first. "Not before the accident. But she was different after that."

Bethany spells it out. "She pretended she was the same, but she was using a lot more. Sometimes, you didn't want to be around her."

"Druggies are messy."

"Messy Missy."

They giggle.

"So, yeah, it could have happened." The alpha Sheena again.

"Or not." Bethany makes her voice heard.

"Yeah. Or not." Sheena sums up.

So Hope's brother harassed Missy, sending texts over and over, calling her repeatedly. Grady confirms his understanding of what he's learned.

"It sounds like I could find this Ben Wendrell's number on Missy's phone—if I had Missy's phone." (Remembering that as far as the world knows, he doesn't.)

"Prob'ly." Sheena.

And Bethany. "Yeah."

28

By the time he pulls out of Sapphire's parking lot, it's late evening. He wonders if Jill's gone back to the hospital. He did his best to let her know that it was fine if she needed or wanted to go home, but he'll bet just about anything that she hasn't. For some reason, she seems determined to watch over Gina. She might even have been upset with him when she woke up alone in his apartment and discovered how many hours she'd spent sleeping instead of sitting at the bedside of a young woman she barely knows (and who has no idea she's there). But she'd been showing the kind of deep exhaustion that comes from a succession of sleepless nights. He just couldn't see waking her.

He did leave her a note.

> Jill – I can't go back to the hospital right now. There's something I need to do that involves Gina. Eat anything you can find. Go back to Gina's room if you want. But if you need to go home, that's okay. I'll catch up with you later.

He found himself writing "Love" without thinking—and scratched it out. Then he realized that what he wanted to write was "I love you" and that the self-protective part of his brain had abbreviated it to one word—a word, it could be argued, that is almost meaningless when used to close a note or a letter.

Dammit! What was going on with them? He wasn't at all sure he liked having these feelings again now. He'd thought he was over them. That he'd moved on. Yes, he and Ally were no longer an item. That ended before she became Mattie's adoptive parent, before Mattie was even born, in fact. But that didn't mean that he had some empty place in him that he needed a romantic interest to fill. Did it?

No. His feelings for Jill had been unchanged since—well, ever since he met her. He loved her, he would always love her. And from the first moment that he heard her say she was leaving Charlie, some long-suppressed part of him had wanted to raise its hand and wave it desperately. Here! Over here! See me. Remember me.

And then she did see him, or something, and they fell into bed together. More than once.

I love you.

Too soon? Or too late?

He crumpled the piece of paper, buried it deep in the trash can under the sink and started fresh. The words were the same, but the sign-off this time was simply "Jack."

A couple of miles down the road from Sapphire's, he pulls into the brightly lit parking lot of a big box store and sits there. After a moment, he turns off the engine.

Before he'd ever looked at the phone he found in the alley under the dumpster, he'd considered the attack on Gina. There were only three possibilities:

1) The attack was random.

2) The attack was drug-related.

3) The attack was specific: the attacker knew who Gina was and wanted her dead.

He'd assumed that either the first possibility (random) or the second (drug-related) was the case, and that the third possibility was the least likely. Now, he starts from the beginning and examines each scenario.

Possibility one. The attack was random, meaningless violence directed against a target of opportunity. He doesn't believe this for a minute. None of the details the cops shared with him suggested a sexual crime, so it wasn't an attempted rape that turned violent. And it sure didn't smell like a robbery gone wrong. Anyone looking at Gina would know she had nothing.

Possibility two. Drug-related is a convenient catch-all term when cops are looking to explain a violent crime. It's as if those two words are a solution in and of themselves. But drug-related means a dispute over territory, merchandise, or money. What could Gina have done to piss off a guy in that business to the point where he tried to beat her to death? A confrontation over territory? No. Merchandise? Possible. Money? Maybe.

If it was her dealer, she could have left town owing him. But it isn't easy to stiff a dealer. They're strictly C.O.D., and even if Gina had somehow managed to skip out on a debt, drug dealers don't build their businesses by killing off their customers. It's not good advertising. And if the guy was a new (to Gina) dealer, what would have led to the beating?

Also, Gina wasn't strung out, no matter how ratty she looked. The convenience store clerk and the hospital's tox screen agree on that.

That brought him to possibility three: the attacker knew who Gina was and had reason to want her dead. But who?

Say it was someone she'd known on the streets. A friend, an ex-lover. Was it a disagreement that got out of hand? Possible, but not probable. That would have been one hell of an argument.

A pimp? Highly doubtful. A pimp may beat up a girl who breaks his rules or rebels, but Gina would hardly have had the chance to get back in business in that kind of "official" way in the little more than forty-eight hours between her return to Tucson and the moment she was found unconscious in the alley. Especially when he nets out the time Gina spent tracking him down and waiting for him outside his apartment, discovering Missy's body, dealing with the cops, sleeping at Grady's, and playing detective. Not to mention that it's not in a pimp's self-interest to demolish the merchandise.

And the attack was vicious but odd. The weapons used in street violence are almost always guns or knives. According to the doctors, Gina's assailant used his fists. The surgeon thought maybe he'd also picked up a piece of wood with nails in it and swung that into her body and, worse, into her head. If so, the perp took it with him. No such improvised weapon was found.

He unlocks the glovebox of the truck, pulls out Missy's phone, gets its call history up on screen.

He's gotten better at navigating through the menus. He already figured out that if he touches the "I" to the right of a call, the screen displays the details: time made, outgoing or incoming, duration. And if the number is already in the phone's contact list, it also shows the contact's name and info.

Gina made only a few calls from the time she scooped up Missy's phone in the very early hours on Tuesday until she was attacked just over twenty-four hours later. Maybe she was concerned about running the battery down, or maybe she was simply focused on her mission.

The calls she made started just after two p.m. on Tuesday. By then, the phone had been in Gina's possession for about fourteen hours. Grady had left her sleeping on the couch at his place that morning—with no idea she had the thing.

There were four calls between that time on Tuesday and the last one, the 911 call made at 2:08 a.m. Wednesday. Before Grady's field trip to Holly's joint and then to Sapphire, he'd already followed up on all of them.

The first two were to "Tiffany" and "Cameron" (cammie85712@hotmail.com). Those were dead ends. They'd heard about Missy's death. They were broken up about it (drugs! drowning! so terrible! such a waste! so sad!). As far as he could tell, neither of them had any useful information. Each remembered talking briefly with Gina, and (he was sure) had said to her exactly what they later said to him.

The third call was to Holly (FlyGurl158@hotmail.com), who led Gina (and him) to Sapphire's and the Sheena/Bethany tag team.

There were nearly eight hours between that call and the fourth one. Grady figures that some of that gap is accounted for by the time Gina spent talking to Holly at the bar where she works and then to the blond tag team at Sapphire's.

That fourth call was made at 10:30 p.m. Tuesday night. Grady had tried the number earlier. It wasn't in Missy's contacts, and caller ID was blocked. When his call went straight to a non-personalized voicemail, he'd hung up.

The area code was 303, not Tucson's 520, so he tentatively chalked it up to Gina taking advantage of having the phone to call someone she'd met on the road over the past months. That call lasted eleven minutes, so whoever it was, Gina and that person had a conversation. This got his attention, but he had no way to follow up on it, and no compelling reason to try. Until now…

Looking back farther in the call history, he sees that 303 number repeated, over and over. All incoming. All missed. And there are none after last Friday. After Missy was dead.

It has to be Ben. Gina called him. And talked with him.

And she learned that Ben was out of state and moved on. Or…

What if Ben wasn't out of state. What if Ben was right here in Tucson? Even Grady knows that with a cell phone, there's no way to know the location of the caller unless you have the resources to track the towers the phone is using. Gina didn't have that capability. And, unfortunately, neither does he.

And if Ben is (or was) here and Gina had guessed that, what was the conversation? Did Gina accuse him of harassing Missy? Did she tell him that Missy was dead? Did she somehow blame him? And if she did, then what? Could he be involved in what happened to her?

It's a crazy long shot. Missy took drugs and then drowned. Just because Gina didn't want to accept it doesn't mean it isn't true.

On the other hand, Gina spoke with Ben. Less than four hours later, Gina was attacked and would have been killed outright if she hadn't managed to call 911 and if the arrival of Kitten and her friend at the end of the alley hadn't scared off her attacker. Correlation isn't causation, but...

There's no point in going back to the police. Any connection he has is way too speculative. But if he can gather more information, point them at the guy: there he is, go pick him up, see what he has to say...

He heads toward mid-town.

29

With most people, you call before you drop by. Or (he guesses) these days, you email or text.

With most people, you don't even think about disturbing them at this time of night.

With Luis, you do. In fact, that's the only time you do. But you better be a very good client, or a close friend. And Grady is lucky enough to be included in that small number. Luis was a childhood pal of Grady's dead sister, Frannie, and somehow the gods of good fortune allowed Grady to inherit the friendship.

He hasn't seen Luis since his second break from the sandbox, when he signed the papers to close the sale of his mother's house and dropped by to repay the loan that, quite literally, saved his life. About two years back, Luis had pulled a wad of cash from a drawer and bankrolled him, no questions asked, when Grady needed to leave town suddenly to avoid a frame-up for the murder of an old girlfriend.

When he handed Luis the roll of bills, Luis eyeballed it and handed back a small stack of hundreds. "Too much, man." Grady tried to convince him that the interest he'd included was minimal, lower than the going rate, but Luis wasn't having any. "I only loan money to friends. And I don' charge my friends. You should know that."

He makes the last turn, pulls over in front of the small one-story adobe where Luis has lived as long as Grady can remember. When he rings the doorbell, he doesn't hear a sound, but clearly there's a signal of some sort way back in the rear of the house, in Luis's workspace. He hears a click as the door unlocks. "Good to see you, man," says a disembodied voice with a slight south-of-the-border lilt. "C'mon in."

Grady makes his way down the hall to the backroom filled with monitors, computer stacks, and other gear that he doesn't begin to understand where Luis spends most of his waking hours. As he comes through the doorway, Luis's wheelchair whirs its way over to him. "Welcome back," Luis says, grasping Grady's arm with his one functioning hand. "What's up?"

The cerebral palsy that twists Luis's body hasn't dimmed his brilliant mind. Grady doesn't know much about technology (his block is almost phobic—he only learns what he's forced to), but he's pretty sure that Luis qualifies as a genius. They're talking mobile phones now, though, and that's a whole different world. He doubts whether even Luis can help him.

"I have a guy's cell phone number," he says, "and I need to find him."

Luis shakes his head. "Not much I can do, man. You know how that works."

Grady doesn't. Not really. "I know you have to somehow track the phone towers."

"If you have the guy's call history, you can work with the provider to see where he made calls from—the closest cell tower. If you want to get him in real time, you can do it. Sometimes. If the equipment is good, and the guy isn't moving too fast—like driving at high speed. And you're lucky."

Shit.

"You got no other way?" Luis asks.

Not that Grady's been able to think of.

"C'mon, man. I know you. You're creative."

Not in this case. And, truth is, Grady doesn't even know if the guy's anywhere near Tucson. If he did kill Missy and attack Gina and he has any brains, he's long gone.

"What do you want with him?"

Grady tells him.

Now it's Luis's turn to be frustrated. "Frannie's daughter? Shit, man. I really wish I could help. Can't you go to the cops?"

"You know Gina's history. And she was found in an alley in a bad part of town. Lots of hookers, drug activity. They won't do crap."

Luis nods. Grady knows he has no illusions about how the system functions for outsiders, or people it decides are losers.

Luis is quiet for a moment. Then, "Go to the kitchen, *hermano*. Bring us back some coffee."

Coffee as comfort? As consolation prize?

Grady makes his way to the small kitchen and pours two mugs of the thick black stuff that Luis keeps cooking all night long.

He returns to the work room, sets one mug down in front of Luis and takes a sip from his own. It burns its way down his throat. Luis laughs. "You gotta give it a minute. Let it cool a skosh or two."

Luis turns to the nearest keyboard. "Tell you what I can do. And it's all I can do." He apparently sees Grady's face because he adds. "Not 'cause of the law. 'Cause of how the technology works."

Grady waits.

"I can get who the phone's billed to. And the billing address. Unless it's a burner. If it is, we're done. You gotta try the cops."

"Okay. Got it. Go."

Grady gives him the number. Then he drinks the sludge in his mug while Luis hits keys, searches screens, hits more keys, searches more screens.

Finally, Luis turns away from his monitors, looks back at Grady. "It's part of a family plan," he says. "Billed to Edward Wendrell, of Denver, Colorado." He points at the address displayed at the screen.

Ben's dad? It's all Grady can do not to jump, scream, do a dance with Luis's wheelchair.

"There are other numbers on that family plan?" he asks.

Luis nods.

"And you got them?"

Another nod.

"Luis," he says, "I think we just got lucky."

30

It's Mrs. Wendrell who answers the phone. But as soon as Grady says, "I'm calling about your son," she hands him off to her husband.

Ed Wendrell's voice reveals his stress. "You have information on Ben?"

Grady acknowledges that he does. It's been a simple matter to contact the Wendrells. He could have tried one of their cell phones, but he chose the old-fashioned route. Once Luis had their address, it took him seconds to look up their home phone number, which is listed. To Grady, this indicates a certain openness that he finds increasingly rare these days. And although he gets the creeping paranoia of many of his fellow citizens, he admires people like the Wendrells, who appear to be hanging on to a neighborly approach to life. Judging by the view of their upscale suburban home that Luis brought up online, though, they likely have never lived in an area where boundaries—of all kinds—aren't generally respected. Odds are Ben's parents have no first-hand experience in the nastier ways of the world, no matter how many crime shows they've seen on TV. What happens from here on is almost guaranteed to be a terrible shock to them.

He takes the gentlest approach he can think of that will still get him the information he needs. "My name is Jack Grady. I'm investigating an incident here in Tucson, Arizona, and I have reason to believe your son may be a witness. We need to speak with him." He's slipped into a vernacular that suggests he's with law enforcement but isn't quite out-and-out misrepresentation. "Is he there?"

"No. No, he's not." Grady hears worry and hope. "What is it? What's happened?"

He alludes to the mysterious rules of law enforcement bureaucracy to deflect the question. "That's all I can tell you at this time. But I assure that any information you can provide will only help us, and your son."

He hears a sharp intake of breath. Then Ben's father says, "Ben disappeared ten days ago." He took his cell phone, the father relates, and he has a credit card on one of their accounts, so he's not without resources. But he's only nineteen and hasn't been answering their calls. "His mother is worried sick. And now you say he's involved in an investigation?"

Grady shades the truth again. "He might be in danger. If we find him, we can protect him." He feels like shit about lying, but he's pretty sure this isn't going to turn out well for the Wendrell family, and any less-than-honest statement he makes will ultimately be a meaningless drop in an ocean of pain.

No response. Ed Wendrell has covered the mouthpiece of the receiver with his hand. Grady can hear a muffled conversation between the man and his wife but can't understand any of the words.

Then Ed comes back on the line. "We believe he's there. In Tucson." Then he says, "I'm putting you on speaker so Joyce can be part of this."

Grady hears the voice of the woman who answered the phone. "We've been frantic. He's supposed to be in school. He's a freshman at the U here in Denver. And when he left… He didn't even tell us he was going. He doesn't have a car. We don't know if he took a bus, or hitchhiked, or… But yesterday a motel charge turned up on our card."

Ed Wendrell explains, "We've been checking it every day online."

And his wife adds, "Thank God he used it. At least we know where he is and that he's alive. We didn't have any idea if he was staying with a friend somewhere or what. But now that we know…"

Grady figures college-boy Ben had been paying cash for a bed and ran out of money. Unless he was incredibly naive or decompensating badly, he must have known that using the card would allow him to be traced. But with his background, he wouldn't have been able to see an alternative, couldn't even consider sleeping rough. He has a moment of feeling sorry for the kid, but most of his sympathy is for Ben's parents.

Ed says, "I'm flying down there first thing tomorrow morning. Joyce is staying here in case he comes home."

Ben's mother gives her child the benefit of her loving doubt. "We don't know why he left, but kids sometimes have a hard time their first semester in college, and what with his sister…"

Ed clarifies. "She died in a car crash a few months ago."

Ben's mom again. "They were close, and…" Grady can hear in her voice how hard she's trying not to break down. "He's all we have."

Grady "takes" their cell phone numbers, which he has already, and gives them his. He tells them he'll be in touch. Which is, or is not, a lie. No way to know at this point.

Just before they end the call, Ed asks, "You're the expert. What do you think? Should I still come?"

All Grady knows of the man is his voice and the few words they've exchanged. And he's surprised at the question. It's another indication of Wendrell's faith in the system, giving someone he believes is a cop the power to decide how involved he gets in finding his own son.

Grady considers. It's possible that Ed Wendrell will swoop into town and make contact with Ben before Grady can find him. If he gets an idea of just how much trouble his son may be in, he might spirit him away, out of the Tucson area and into the protection of as solid a barricade of lawyers as he can afford. On balance, though, he doesn't think so. And maybe Wendrell can help, either by clearing his son's name or helping bring him to justice in the least traumatic way possible.

"Yes," he says. "You should come."

31

Jill wakes up dazed and disoriented. She's curled up on a bed in a strange room. Someone has thrown a light blanket over her. A nightlight in an adjoining bathroom glints on a shiny countertop, a large mirror. The space doesn't feel lived in. Is she in a hotel?

Then she remembers. It's Jack's apartment. She hasn't yet been able to think of it as "his place." It's too bare, too sterile. Not like him at all.

He convinced her to leave the hospital, observed that she looked exhausted. And she gave in, even though she didn't believe she was that tired. But the bedside clock tells her she's slept more than eight hours, slept like someone who's recovering from an illness (she's perfectly healthy) or is running away from something.

Which she isn't. But...

She's naked under the blanket. She and Jack have had sex. More than once.

And it's been so good.

She isn't sure what it means to her. And she has no idea what it means to him. Except... Unless something has changed—and she hasn't picked up on anything like that—he loves her. He always has. Is she taking advantage of that?

She's always been so careful not to encourage those feelings. And now...

Put that aside for a minute. How does *she* feel?

She cares about Jack. No question. But there's too much going on. She isn't ready to think about what's next.

And right now, he needs her. This thing with Gina...

Maybe she's overthinking it. Maybe it's just sex, for both of them. What's wrong with that? She's always been so structured, so strict with herself. Doesn't she deserve a break?

It'll be okay.

Sophie can stay another night or two at Caitlin's house.

Charlie is...gone.

There's her practice. What about it? Why should she continue to put up with people who can't be bothered to floss, who complain that the office is too hot or too cold, her location is inconvenient, the parking lot is too tight, and their insurance doesn't cover enough of the bill?

She's been at all this—marriage, child, practice—a long time. Too long?

Her mind is spinning again. She thinks of herself as clear-headed. Goal-oriented, self-directed. A together person. But lately, not so much.

She shoves aside thoughts of why and what's next and all the usual responsibilities of her life. It barely helps. For the past two days, she's had one simple goal: sit at Gina's side until Gina wakes up. And now she's gone and screwed that up. Not good. The self she's spent her life building is competent, in control.

So: deal with it. Get back to the hospital.

She scrambles off the bed and into the bathroom, pees, hits the light switch. Blinding. She waits a moment for her eyes to adjust and searches the vanity for a tooth brush. No spares. Only Jack's, with splayed bristles that say it needed replacing months ago. She carries a travel toothbrush in her handbag, but she's in too much of a hurry to dig that out right now. She squirts some toothpaste onto her finger, rubs it across her teeth and gums, rinses, spits. Ugh. A dirty mouth. She promises herself that she'll brush later at the hospital.

She runs a comb through her hair, checks herself in the mirror. Not too bad. Thank God for jeans and knits. She looks a little rumpled, but that's pretty much the way all the ICU visitors look.

She makes her way to the great room. As she grabs her handbag, her eye falls on Grady's note. She's annoyed by "Go back to Gina's room if you want." And the suggestion she should just go home if she likes. As if what she's doing isn't important. As if she's a creature of whim. As if nothing's happened between them. He should know her better than that.

As she takes the elevator down to the parking area, she thinks about calling him, but she's too irritated. Anyway, she tells herself, he's probably back in Gina's room by now. There's no time on the note.

Isn't that just like Jack.

#

Grady's sitting in his truck watching the door of unit 107. Ben Wendrell's chosen a place in motel row on Miracle Mile north of downtown. This stretch of highway and the adjacent roads welcomed visitors to Tucson back in the days before freeways. The buildings are quaint, one-story "motor courts," now crumbling. Decades-old signs still proclaim "Heated and Cooled," and some vintage neon survives. But the tourists moved on more than forty years ago, and although Grady has read about artists and preservationists beginning to spark a revival, the general area is still seedy at best, dangerous at worst.

The Moonlight Motel is even more of a dump than its neighbors. He's sure that in paying with a valid credit card, Ben labeled himself with a big, bright "does not belong here" sign. The kid is lucky he hasn't been robbed. Or worse.

Surveilling isn't a problem. The parking lot is so badly lit that hiding in the shadows is no challenge at all. You could almost camp out in one of the potholes.

And getting the number of Ben's room number was easy. He just phoned the Moonlight's office whining that a Ben Wendrell had ordered a pizza and the idiot taking the order didn't write down the room number and now here he was trying to deliver the thing and about to get dinged for handing over cold food… And the night manager caved, maybe just to shut Grady up, or because he didn't give a shit about the privacy of his guests. Most likely the latter.

But now the length of this stake-out is becoming an issue. He's almost out of cigarettes, he drank the last of his take-out coffee more than an hour ago, and the kid hasn't showed.

He's seen prostitutes and their johns come and go. He's seen a drug deal go down behind a muscle car over by the outdoor stairway leading to the second floor. He's even seen a genuine delivery of pizza.

What he hasn't seen is any activity in or around unit 107. No lights going on, no curtains shifting.

Shortly after he settled in, he got out of the truck, intercepted a hooker as she was leaving and paid her twenty bucks to go knock on Ben's door. If anyone answered, she was to pretend she was there to service a client and had the wrong room. He tried to suggest dialog, something like, "Hi, baby, I'm Crystal, and I'm here to…" But the woman cut him off with, "I don't know what kind of stupid, bad-movie-world you think I live in. Don't tell me my business. I know my damn business." Then she gave him a look that made him think that he needed to reassure her that she wasn't setting up the occupant of room 107 for a robbery, a hit, or an arrest, so he did. "I'm a private detective," he said. "It's a kid who's run off. His parents are trying to find him." She just nodded and took the twenty, but as she walked away, he heard her mutter something that sounded like, "Detective my ass. Just a goddamn dick."

He watched her knock, wait, lean close to the door and, apparently speak some soft words, likely coaxing, reassuring, while (he hoped) not breaking her cover, then knock again. She waited, pivoted toward where Grady was parked, and gave a shrug before teetering her way across the parking lot back toward the street.

So he's all but positive that Ben isn't in there. He looks at his watch. After two a.m. If Ben's not here, where could he be? Out partying? Some people deal with stress that way, but from everything Grady's learned, that doesn't seem likely here. Finding some other poor wretch of a strung-out girl to beat up? This is a middle-class college kid, off the rails maybe, but not a thug. Or—mission accomplished—is he on a bus or riding hitchhiker shotgun in a semi heading back to his folks in Denver?

Maybe.

But what was Ben's mission? Originally, it had something to do with Missy. To talk with her? To punish her? To make the people who loved her suffer as he and his parents are suffering?

Nothing to do with Gina.

But then Gina got involved. And pushed him. And maybe threatened.

And if, as Grady has come to believe, Ben was the one who attacked her...

The attack was ferocious, could have been impulsive. Maybe whatever Gina had to say about Missy, about her death, triggered a blind rage. Ben had to silence Gina, whatever it took. And when he saw the two hookers standing at the entrance to the alley, the spell was broken. He fled.

So the act was an uncomplicated frenzy, nothing more.

Maybe.

Maybe even if there was some planning involved, he gave little or no thought to the consequences.

Then. When everything was happening and his anger was red hot.

But now?

Gina can't talk, but does Ben know that? What's his need now?

Grady curses himself for being an idiot. He picks up his phone, starts the truck, and roars his way out of the parking lot onto the road.

#

Jill has never liked parking garages, especially in the middle of the night. She doesn't care how many cameras she sees, or whether there's a security guard (who's probably nodding off in some closet of an office) assigned to wander the tiers. And hospital parking structures are no different. But at least this one's above-ground.

She finds a spot on the second level and jogs down the stairs. She feels better as soon as her feet hit the brightly-lit sidewalk. Most of the hospital's doors are secured this time of night, and it's a hike to the main entrance. Visiting hours are over, but she's headed to the ICU, which is different. Everyone understands what that means.

Up in the unit, once she's buzzed in, the only thing that has changed since she left earlier that day is the nurse working at a computer at the central desk. Jill recognizes her from the night before. "Hi," she says softly as she walks by, not wanting to break the woman's focus, but the nurse looks up, smiles at her.

"Pretty quiet," Jill says.

The nurse gives a little nod, but Jill knows she's thinking of how in an ICU that can change at any moment. "So far, so good," she says. "I'm getting caught up on paperwork."

"How's she doing," Jill asks.

The nurse taps a few keys, looks at her screen. "No change. But Mary's in with her right now. She can tell you more."

The interior drapes are closed on Gina's glassed-in room, and the only illumination is a task light that a nurse, who must be Mary, is using to check settings, adjust machines. She mouths an inaudible "Hi" as Jill enters. Jill finds her chair, the one she's spent hours in over the past couple of days. Someone's moved it back to the far wall. She drags it over to the bedside, sits, watches as Mary draws several vials of Gina's blood.

Mary finishes, inserts the vials in a carrier, then beckons Jill, guides her to a corner of the room away from Gina's bed where she repeats what the nurse at the desk has already said. There's been no change in Gina's condition. She adds a few details: what tests they've run, how there's been no deterioration, which is good, but no improvement (which is bad, although Mary doesn't say so).

As Mary leaves, Jill's struck again by how soft-spoken everyone is. Gina's in a coma. It's unlikely she can hear anything. But all the hospital personnel behave as if her rest, and her peace of mind, are not to be disturbed. As if calm and quiet and soft lighting are healing (and, she assumes, that normal noises and even minor disruptions could do damage).

And Gina does look peaceful, at least as peaceful as anyone can with sensors stuck to her chest, an IV running into her arm, a ventilator tube and attached hose protruding from her mouth, and another tube dripping her urine into a bag. Jill flashes on *Alien*, the first movie, when the shock of the creature bursting out of the doomed crewman's chest caused her to scream and send her soda and popcorn flying. To her, there's a horror in being possessed by an other, even when that other is life-saving medical equipment.

She shakes off the feeling, settles back in her chair, pulls the novel she's been reading out of her handbag, and opens it to the bookmarked page.

#

What seems days later but has only been a couple of hours, she stands up, stretches. She needs a bathroom break. The nearest Ladies Room is outside the ICU, down a couple of corridors. She considers taking her handbag, then thinks "Why?" The door to the ICU is locked. No one enters without being buzzed in. It's hard to think of a safer place.

As she closes the ICU door behind her, she notices a man approaching. He's tall, white, nice-looking, with regular features and dark curly hair, young, not much more than a boy. He looks stressed, but (just like rumpled) stressed is the normal condition of visitors to the ICU.

She nods to him, an acknowledgement that it's hard to be where they are under the circumstances they're all under, and heads to the bathroom.

#

Grady's punching buttons on his phone as he accelerates. Jill must be back at the hospital by now. Her phone rings—and keeps ringing. Does he have the wrong number? But then he hears her outgoing voicemail message. He says, "Jill, it's Jack. Call me!" He waits a moment, tries again—with the same result. Then he almost hits a construction barrier, hidden by an unexpected curve in the road. The traffic engineers weren't expecting anyone to be doing ninety in this thirty-mph zone. He slows down to sixty, which feels like a crawl. He should find the number for the hospital, call them, talk to their security people.

But he's almost there. Better to focus on his driving. It won't do anyone any good if he wrecks his truck. Keep going.

#

Jill is uneasy. The halls between the ICU and the restroom were empty. The bathroom itself is empty. The building seems deserted.

Don't be silly, she tells herself. You only feel this way because it's late at night. Of course the place isn't bustling. And you're not alone. There are people all around. Just not here.

She pushes the sense of anxiety away. But she's still annoyed at herself: she isn't usually so easily spooked. Pull it together, Jill!

As she dries her hands and drops the paper towel in the waste can, she catches a glimpse of her reflection in the mirror over the wash basin. If she looked rumpled before, she looks disheveled now. This shouldn't matter to her under the current circumstances, but it does. It always does. She's never considered herself beautiful, or even pretty. Her face is too narrow, her nose too long (goes with the face

Jack used to say, then Charlie—you're in proportion, sweetheart). But she's always liked her eyes, blue but not pale, almost a navy, and her hair, too fine but blond all on its own well into her thirties when she had to start helping it out. At the moment, it's straggly (no other word for it), dry and dirty at the same time. Thanks, desert air and desert dust! She'll comb it and brush her teeth. Then she realizes she left her handbag in Gina's room. So she settles for doing what she can to her hair with her fingers.

As she hurries back through the empty corridors to the ICU, still struggling to tune out some residual apprehension, she passes the bank of vending machines. And stops. Suddenly, she's herself again—and hungry. She's amused at how the allure of chocolate, even the stuff found in a vending machine, can shove aside other priorities, like fleeing an unreasonable fear.

She digs in her pockets and finds she has a few singles (which is unlike her—normally bills are straightened out, then neatly aligned in ascending denominations in her billfold). Damn, she's been distracted lately! But right now, she's grateful for the crumpled cash. She looks at the selection: Snickers, Kit Kat, Nestle's Crunch, peanut butter cups...or an energy bar. Oats, fruit. A healthier choice. Better. Have some willpower, Jill. She slips a couple of bills into the machine, pushes a button, and retrieves the bar.

Then she glances at the next vending machine over. Hot chocolate would make the snack complete. It's god-awful late, she's tired, she deserves it. She'll give herself a treat, after all. She tucks the energy bar into her pocket, slides in another bill, pushes another button, and lifts out the steaming cup. Too hot! She pulls a paper napkin from a stack on a nearby counter and wraps it around the hot chocolate. As insulation, it's inadequate. But it will have to do. She'll just be careful.

At the unit's entrance, she pushes the intercom button. When a voice answers, she gives her name and the patient's name. The buzzer sounds, and she slowly opens the door with one hand while holding the cup with the other. She can't believe how hot it still is. She'll be glad when she can set the thing down.

As she passes the central desk, the nurse at the computer calls her over. "Mrs. Whitehurst." Jill stops, puts down the cup, grateful for chance to give her hand a break. "I just wanted you to know," the nurse says, "that her cousin is in there."

Cousin? Not a first cousin, that's for sure. Gina doesn't have any.

Maybe a more distant relative, a second, or a third. Or one of those family friend things where kids grow up together and everybody labels them as if they're blood. Back when she and Jack were married, she knew his immediate family, but she'd never known much about the out-of-state relatives. Has Jack been in touch with anybody like that about Gina's condition? Not that Jill's aware of, but she hasn't been in his company every moment, and there was that hours-long gap when she was asleep in his bed.

"He arrived a few minutes ago," the nurse continues. "Actually, he came by earlier in the evening, but we were changing her, and, well, you know, privacy. And then we were running some tests. We hated to turn him away, especially twice. Just coincidence, but I'm sure it didn't feel good to him. When he was worried and everything. I should have mentioned it to you when you cane in, so you could call him if you needed to. But now he's back." She gives Jill a nursely smile that says, be reassured, all's right with the world.

Still puzzling over who this cousin is, and a bit curious, Jill picks up the cup of hot chocolate, which seems to be denying the laws of thermodynamics, not cooling down at all, and takes the few steps to Gina's room, which is behind the nurses' station and to the right. The door is closed, which surprises her. It's always open unless medical personnel are changing Gina's gown or her sheets, or washing her, or dealing with her catheter, or conducting some other procedure for which they require privacy.

She pushes the door open quietly, taking extra care because of the cup of hot liquid in her hand. As the door swings shut behind her, she sees him—the young man who was walking up to the ICU as she was leaving. His back is to her. He's looking at Gina's ventilator.

She's just about to introduce herself. "Hello," she'll say. "I hear you're…"

Before she can get out a word, she sees him push a button on the machine. What's he doing? Did he just turn off the alarm? Why would…?

He pushes another button. The machine's rhythmic sound stops. Gina's chest no longer rises and falls.

Jill screams.

The door slams open, and Jack charges into the room.

Jill lunges for the respirator. Hot chocolate splashes onto her hand, scalding her. It doesn't slow her down. But the "cousin" is blocking the machine. And Jack is grabbing for him.

In desperation, she throws the cup of hot chocolate—aiming at "the cousin."

And it lands on Jack. Jack howls, but he keeps moving.

The desk nurse appears in the doorway. "Stop!" she commands. "Stop!" But no one's listening.

The nurse tries to get to the respirator. But the two men's bodies are in the way. They're struggling, crashing into equipment, knocking over the bedside table, sending Jill's chair flying.

Jill can't tell who's winning. Jack is in good shape, but the other man is younger, and at least as desperate. "Call 911!" Jack yells. The nurse rushes off.

Jack has his hands on the "cousin," he's fighting to subdue him, to get him down to the floor. Jill looks around for something she can hit him with. Nothing.

The man suddenly breaks free of Jack's grasp, pushes him to the floor, and runs from the room. Jack scrambles to his feet, yells, "Turn it back on," and runs after him.

Jill screams for the nurse, and races to the respirator. She pushes the same button the "cousin" pushed, hoping it's a toggle: off—and on. The regular sound, the clicking that means air going in and out of Gina's lungs, begins again. Gina's chest rises and falls.

#

Grady chases Ben Wendrell out of the ICU, down the hall. He wishes he hadn't been right about where he'd find Ben, or that he'd realized it sooner. But no time to think about that now. The kid yanks open the door to the stairs and disappears through it. Grady's close behind him, but the boy's already out of sight by the time he enters the stairwell.

He expects to hear steps running down. The kid would want to get to the ground floor and out of the building. Instead, he hears sounds above him. Ben's going up.

Grady can't catch the younger man on the stairs, but he manages to gain on him. They entered the stairwell on the third floor, and there are only five stories in the building (tall for Tucson). The stairway has a landing at each floor and two between floors, with the stairs making a ninety-degree turn at each landing. By the time Grady gets close enough to see Ben, they've already passed the doorway to floor four. Good. That means even if Ben increases the distance between them, Grady knows where he's going: floor five.

But Ben passes that door. Grady's just below the second landing between floor four and floor five when he stumbles, twisting his right ankle, smacking his shin on the edge of the concrete step. He goes down hard on the landing.

By the time he catches his breath and struggles to his feet, Ben's disappeared.

Grady limps his way up past the fifth floor, past the door Ben didn't take. All that's left is the roof. Ben could be waiting for him between here and there, hiding around the next turn, pressed against the wall so Grady won't spot him until the last moment—when it will be too late. He could lunge at Grady, send him tumbling backward down the stairs.

Grady climbs cautiously. No need for speed any more, not that he can move all that quickly with his injured ankle.

Landing one.

No Ben.

Landing two.

Still no Ben.

He expects the door to the roof to be locked, but it's not, in defiance of a sign that says, "Must Be Secured at All Times." Maybe someone propped it open for air on a hot September day and forgot about it. Maybe a maintenance man likes to take his cigarette breaks overlooking the roofs of the city.

Grady pulls it open.

At first, he sees only black sky, stars, the moon. Even most nearby buildings are dark at this time of night. Then his eyes adjust, and he can see large pipes, giant air conditioning units. Places for Ben to hide.

Then he hears a voice. "I'm over here."

To his right, across the roof, close by the parapet, he spots the tall, slim figure. And Ben is calling to him.

32

Grady approaches cautiously. He's never liked heights, and the parapet is so low that it's not a real barrier between the solidity of the roof and the five stories of air between him and the ground below. "Why don't you come toward me?" he says. "Let's meet in the middle."

"No," the voice says. "This is where I belong."

Grady's close enough to see the kid lean out, look down, over the edge.

"You don't want to do that," he says. "It'll be okay. Your dad's on his way."

The boy shakes his head. "Won't help."

Grady needs the cops. They must be on their way by now, should be here any minute. He was trained in the basics of negotiating with a jumper. But he's never done it.

He moves closer to Ben. Maybe he can grab the kid, hold him until the police arrive. Although he didn't do so well in the hospital room.

"Back off," Ben says. "Don't come any closer."

Grady holds his hands up, palms facing Ben, to signal that he's stopped.

"You don't want to die," he says to the boy.

"That doesn't matter."

"Sure it does."

"You must think I'm stupid. Nothing matters anymore."

The kid looks down again, puts a foot up on the parapet. Grady blurts, "Don't!"

Ben makes a sound like laughter, but one of the bitterest, saddest sounds Grady has ever heard.

"Don't jump? Is that what you mean." The boy removes the foot from the parapet, places it next to the other one on the solid surface of the roof. "There. Is that better?"

Grady nods. "Yes," he says in the calmest voice he can manage. He hears sirens. The cops—or just an ambulance. Has to be the cops. Then he realizes: the hospital is a large, five-story building. No one knows he and the kid are up here in the dark. He pats his pockets. No phone. He must have lost it during the struggle in Gina's room. Internal security, the police—they'll all have to search the building. He has no way to tell them where he is.

"Okay," Ben says. "Here's what's going to happen. I won't jump. But I'm going to talk now, and you're going to listen. Deal?"

"Deal."

"I never meant to hurt her."

"You hit her. You kicked her. You beat her with a plank that had nails in it."

"No, I meant the other one. Missy. All I wanted to do was talk to her. I wanted her to understand what she'd done. I wanted her to take responsibility. I wanted her to apologize. She wouldn't talk to me. I called and called. The first time she answered and I said who I was, and she did listen, for a minute or so, but then she said she had to go and hung up. After that, if she answered, she'd say, 'Ben, I know how hard it is, but I can't help you.' Or 'I'm sorry for your loss.' Like Hope was a character on some TV show who died from a botched operation or a disease. And then she stopped answering at all. For a while, I'd leave messages, but she never called me back.

"I couldn't sleep, I couldn't eat. When school started, I thought that would distract me. But trying to study was a joke. Finally, I couldn't stand it anymore. So I came to Tucson. I watched her for a few days. I needed to pick my time and place. I didn't want her to be able to walk away. She had to understand that she needed to talk to me.

"It was Friday. She'd gone out every evening, but that night she didn't. She stayed home. I waited. Then I saw the light go off in her living room and on in her bedroom, I thought maybe she had gone to bed early, and I decided it was my best chance.

"The day before, I'd pretended to be delivering a package and knocked on her neighbor's door. I knocked on Missy's door first, for, like, you know, verisimilitude." (Grady hears the SAT word and is reminded that Ben is just a college boy after all.)

"I said I couldn't leave the package because it was perishable, and did the neighbor have a key so I could put it inside. The neighbor said, no, and she'd take it for Missy if I wanted. I should have thought of that, but I didn't, so I said that the sender wouldn't allow it. She shrugged and pointed at the railing. 'She keeps a spare key right there,' she said, 'where anyone with a brain could find it. You could just use it and put the package inside.' I said I couldn't. Regulations. And I thanked her.

"So I knew where the key was. I used it to open the door. No one was around. No one saw me.

"The living room was dark. The blinds were pulled, but I could see enough from a streetlight shining through the cracks around the edges. I opened the door to her bedroom. A bedside lamp was on, but the room was empty. The bathroom door was closed. I could just barely hear music.

"I opened the bathroom door. There was just a little nightlight, but I could see the shape of her. She was in the tub, taking a bubble bath. Her eyes were closed. The music wasn't loud, but she didn't seem to hear me come in.

"I stood there for a moment. Then I turned the light on. And I said something, just her name, I think. 'Missy.' Her eyes were closed, and she opened them really slowly. She was pretty doped up. She had a bottle of wine sitting on the floor next to the tub and a glass on the edge of the tub. The glass was empty. And the bottle just had a little bit left in the bottom. There were a couple of bottles of pills on the counter. The lid was off one of them. The music was coming from an iPod dock. 'Hi,' she said. And she smiled at me. "Who are you, pretty boy?'

"I realized she'd never seen me before. I told her who I was. I told her how it was her fault that Hope was dead. I told her how she'd ruined my life and my parents' lives, and she needed to take responsibility for it. 'Okay,' I finally said, 'your turn.' And she smiled again and said, 'Wanta climb in?'

"And I was so angry. My sister was dead. And this…this whore with her big tub and her bubbles and her music was drinking and drugging and inviting me—this guy she didn't even know—to get into her fucking jetted tub.

"I reached over and I put my hands on her shoulders. And she smiled! Like she didn't have a brain. Like she was floating on some other planet somewhere.

"And I pushed down. Not hard. It didn't take much. She struggled a little, but hardly at all. Like she thought she was a mermaid, or a fish, or something. I kept telling myself to let go, let her up, but I didn't. And once I had her under the water, she just stared up at me and wriggled a little and then she stopped.

"I didn't know what to do. She was dead. I got out of there. All I'd touched were the bathroom light switch, the doorknobs, and the housekey. I turned up the music, I don't know why. There was one of those fancy little guest towels on a ring, and I took it and wiped the iPod controls and the light switch. Then I backed my way out of the place, wiping the knobs as I went. I looked out the little window at the top of the door to make sure no one was out there. I opened the front door, wiped that knob and the key, put the key back where it came from, and left.

"I didn't feel bad about it. Not then. Except that she never apologized. I never heard her say she was sorry."

She was sorry, Grady knew. Her friends at Sapphire were pretty clear on the fact that Missy had changed after the accident. That her drug use became heavier and more frequent. That she drank more. That she didn't talk about it, but she wasn't her old self. Grady would say that what Missy felt was remorse, and that it ran deep. But Ben's not going to believe him.

And it doesn't matter now anyway. Missy is gone. And she was murdered. Maybe she did have some responsibility for the circumstances that ended Hope's life. But Hope was the one who did the drugs, drank the booze, and then got behind the wheel. If she was smart enough to go to college, she should have been smart enough to…

"Why'd you stick around Tucson?" he asks.

"What if she wasn't really dead? What if she told people what I'd done? What if they believed she was the innocent one and I was guilty? Or if she was dead… She deserved it, but other people wouldn't see it that way. I couldn't believe what I'd done. I was going nuts. So I holed up. Stayed in the motel room. Tried to think."

Ben goes silent. Grady waits a moment, then prompts—knowing it's the wrong time to ask it, but driven by his need to know: "And Gina? How did she get involved? She called you, didn't she."

The kid nods, and Grady continues.

"It must have scared the hell out of you when you saw Missy's caller ID on your phone days after you knew she was dead."

"I thought I'd been wrong. That I hadn't totally drowned her. That it was Missy calling, that she'd just been unconscious. I was so relieved. It meant I hadn't killed anyone. It was like a second chance at life. And I thought she'd gotten it now, she must have, what she'd done and how upset it made people.

"So I answered. But it was Gina. She said she knew what I'd done, that I'd killed Missy. That she'd never believed Missy was stupid enough to drown that way, and she'd figured out what happened. She told me enough that I had to believe her. She said she was going to go to the police." (This is both sad and ironic to Grady because Gina wasn't someone the cops were going to listen to. Not about Missy. If only she'd come to him, instead of confronting Ben…) "I said I hadn't done it, that I had info that would prove it, that I'd meet her somewhere and show her.

"We arranged to meet in front of the flagpole at a park. DeAnza park, it was called. She told me how to find it."

Grady knows that park from his days in policing. There were frequent complaints about homeless people sleeping there, drug use, needles in the sand.

"I found it." Ben is saying. "It wasn't far. And she showed up, but I didn't. I was where I could watch her. She waited a while. When she left, I followed her. She walked a long way. I don't know Tucson, but we were already in a bad neighborhood, and I could see that the one we were going into was worse.

"Maybe she went there to buy drugs. Missy was a druggy. Gina knew Missy. And she looked like someone who used. It was late by then. She was kind of waiting, hanging around. Maybe she thought I'd call, I don't know. She didn't call me.

"Then she went into the convenience store on the corner. I saw her come out and ducked into the alley behind the store. She walked right by it, and I was in there, back in the dark where no one could see me. I called her name—it was safe, there was no one nearby who could hear me—and she turned in. Came over. And…

"I didn't want to hurt her either. I didn't want to hurt anybody. But I had to. Once Missy was dead, and Gina… She started it. Don't you see?"

I see that you were a 'good boy' who threw it all away. That you thought because you were a good boy and had always been a good boy and hadn't walked on the grass and had gotten good grades and always made your parents proud that nothing you did could ever really be wrong, that nothing you did could ever destroy your privileged position in life, as a good boy, a loved son, a future college grad, lawyer or doctor or businessman, homeowner, husband, father. You thought there would always be an excuse for you, good boy that you are.

He doesn't bother telling Ben this. Or pointing out what Ben didn't see: that for all her flaws, Gina is loved. And—less important but still tragic—if she dies, Ben will have caused his sister's mistake to metastasize in his parents' lives. Maybe it will turn out that Ben is suffering from an emerging mental illness. That can happen in late adolescence. Maybe testing will reveal that he somehow isn't fully at fault. But he and his parents are all in hell. And one way or another, they'll be in hell the rest of their lives.

"I do feel bad," Ben says. "Not about Missy. About your niece. Even though I had to do it."

"And about your own life. What you're doing to your parents. You feel bad about that."

Ben nods. "Yes." Grady sees tears running down his face. The boy is breaking down.

"C'mon, Ben," he says. "Come with me. Your dad will be here in a few hours. We'll get you some help."

Ben is shaking, sobbing. "I wasn't myself when I did those things. Those horrible things."

Grady moves closer. He's not even sure that Ben sees him.

"Were you drunk? On drugs?"

"Huh? No. No." Still sobbing, no longer even looking at Grady.

"But you weren't thinking straight. You didn't really know what you were doing. You said it yourself." Moving a few steps closer. Keeping his voice soothing, trying for hypnotic.

"Just because you were walking and talking doesn't mean that you were responsible for your actions. You were out of your mind with grief. You hadn't been sleeping or eating. You weren't yourself." He feeds Ben's words back to him, reinforcing the validity of his pain, the possibility that an emotional disability might exonerate him legally, even morally. And it's working. Maybe. He moves even closer.

"The law takes that kind of thing into consideration, Ben. And it should. It'll be okay. We can make it okay…"

He crosses the last few feet, reaches out, has a hand on Ben, moves to grab him… But the boy pulls away. There's a tower hard by the parapet in the far corner, for cell phone transmissions, some other purpose—Grady doesn't know. Ben runs toward it. He's shambling, stumbling, and Grady's after him, propelled by adrenaline, not even feeling his ankle, catching up.

Ben reaches the tower, grabs a cross bar. He's climbing. Up, up, toward the top. Which looks too fragile, as if it can't possibly support him. But people work on these things, don't they? The structure must be strong. It should hold…?

Ben's up there, way up, and he's sobbing. "Just tell my dad when he gets here," he screams, his voice sounding broken. "Just tell him I'm sorry, and I love them."

"You'll tell him yourself."

Ben doesn't answer. The sobbing continues.

Grady looks at the tower. Close up, he can see that it's old. Rusty. Some sort of antenna, maybe a structure that supported a beacon, not used anymore, probably not maintained…

He can't climb up there. He's too old, he's too… No, he's not. He's in the best shape he's been in in years—thanks to his sobriety and all his pre-Iraq training. But he's scared shitless. He always puts it mildly, even to himself, just says he doesn't much like heights. In fact, he's terrified of them. And going up that tower would be dangerous. It could break. Ben could kick him off. Why should he take the risk? Why should he and the kid both die?

Face it, Grady, you don't want to go up there. You don't want to risk your neck for someone who killed a twenty-five-year-old girl and has put your niece in the hospital fighting for her life. Stay on the ground. You can talk to him from here.

But Grady knows he has to do it.

He puts a foot on the lowest crossbar, reaches up, begins to climb. He knows he's injured his right ankle and wonders if he can put this kind of weight on it, but at this point, adrenalin is still masking the pain.

The damn thing sways. He was right. They're both going to die.

"Get off!" Ben screams. "Get off!"

"No," Grady says. "I'm coming to get you."

"You have to get off!" Ben screams again. The tower creaks. "It won't hold us both."

The tower sways even more. It groans as if it's ready to come apart. Every cell in Grady's body, every neuron firing in his brain, is telling him Ben is right. Get down now!

"I've done enough," Ben screams, "I don't want to be responsible for your death."

"Then come down. You're right. This thing won't hold us both. And I'm not getting off until you do. So you have to come down."

"You first."

Gratefully, Grady moves backwards down the structure, feeling it shift with every movement. It's shaking, he's shaking. He's sure they're both about to collapse.

But he's getting closer to the bottom. Four feet, two, one last step...

As soon as his feet hit the roof's tarred surface, he calls out to Ben. "Okay. Your turn."

It's working. He sees Ben move a hand, then a foot. He's beginning the slow backward descent down the tower, toward safety. Another hand...

The door to the stairwell bursts open. Three cops rush onto the roof.

Ben screams, "No! No!"

As Grady watches in horror, the boy dives off the tower. Gone. Falling through five stories of empty air.

33

By seven Friday morning, Rachel's been on the treadmill in the dinky hotel gym for forty-five minutes, and the run isn't making a dent in her stress. She stewed all night, which is unlike her—and she's not happy about it. She prides herself on her calm in a crisis, but this one is getting to her.

She's always careful not to give a subordinate the upper hand—and she didn't do that here. But she's cursing herself for not staying at headquarters and sending some junior field person to Arizona on what has turned out to be a wild goose chase. Fucking poor judgment, Rach.

All the flash has been at Gil's end. And now it turns out, he's been trying to run this thing on his own. The undeniable proof of this: not letting her know immediately that Cujo went stateside and that they were tracking him. Clearly, he was hoping never to have to acknowledge that the guy was at large at all. And, if he was forced to admit they'd ever lost him, he no doubt would have taken credit for getting him back in their sights. He even tried to deflect the blame for the original sin of letting the guy get on a flight out of Baghdad.

Routine, my ass. As if there were some faceless, unreachable bureaucrat sitting in a back room mindlessly stamping papers.

He only read Rachel in when he could no longer avoid it. He might not have flat-out lied to her, but he sure as shit lied by omission.

She's never thought of Gil as devious before. Or maybe she'd thought of him that way (deception is a skill after all, and the ability to hold information close when necessary is a useful tactic) but was naïve enough to believe that he would never dare try to use this skill against her.

She remembers a night, right before her first big promotion, the one that made her his superior. They'd just tied a neat bow on what could have been a messy situation and spent the evening toasting their success with Margaritas. She sensed he was going to make a pass at her, and she was wondering what she'd do about it since she'd always thought he was cute and funny but maybe gay or at least bi. She was asking herself how she felt about sleeping with a colleague (not quite an official no-no since neither of them managed the other) and with a guy who wasn't 100 percent straight.

In the end, they closed down the bar and stumbled upstairs to her room and were so damn drunk that they both fell asleep fully clothed. In retrospect, she was surprised that neither of them fell asleep hugging the toilet and that they managed to collapse onto the (still made) bed.

Then she was promoted, and the option of a romantic liaison, or even just plain old sex, was gone. There probably were women in her field who would have risked their careers for the possibility of love, or at least a very hot version of like, but she wasn't one of them. It had taken too much to finally get where she was.

Before long, Gil became engaged to and then married a perfectly nice, extremely attractive woman who did something with spreadsheets. And when Rachel learned more about his past, she realized he'd never been gay or bi at all. He just picked up more signals and expressed more empathy than any straight guy she'd ever met. She assumed that was one of the things that made him so good at his job. And she knew that if she hadn't worked the hours she did (sixty to his fifty, ninety to his eighty) and given up any thought of having a personal life, she'd still be back in the pack with him.

And now. If this wild card—Pickett on the loose—makes things more of a mess than they already are, there will have to be consequences. A letter in Gil's file? A slap on the wrist, but it would sting. Suspension? A possibility. Demotion? Probably overkill. But who knows?

All of this is premature. Table it for now. See what happens. Focus.

The read-out on the treadmill tells her she's done her six miles. She starts her cool-down.

As she swipes a towel across her sweaty face (even with air conditioning, the gyms in Arizona are too damn hot), she considers what she's got. She's convinced there is a recording, and that its content is explosive. Unfortunately, she's also convinced that Jack Grady doesn't know a damn thing about it.

And she has no fucking idea why Cujo has jumped the fence.

34

Since he left the police force, Grady's never liked dealing with the cops. It's as if his relationship to the boys (and girls) in blue changed the moment he handed in his badge. Even though he still had buddies on the force. And even though a few of those buddies stuck by him, as best they could.

He's not sure when procedures he'd always taken for granted turned into overreaching bureaucracy. When roughing up a perp just a little—only to make sure the asshole got a little bit of what was coming to him —became brutality. When the commonsense setting of priorities, going hard after the cases that got the most play in the media or had the greatest chance of being solved, started looking discriminatory and (often) just fucking lazy. He only knows his disillusionment came quickly and was close to total. And in all his dealings with law enforcement since then, he's never seen much that would change his mind.

Given that there are two deaths and an attempted murder involved here, he'll be going down to the station for major debriefing, no way around it. He doesn't even try to give the cops an argument on that one.

And his ankle needs attention. He's in pain.

But he insists on checking on Jill and Gina before doing anything. He finds Jill frantic, pacing outside the entrance to the ICU. When she sees him limp off the elevator toward her, she breaks down in tears. There's an officer guarding Gina, she says, a nice young woman. A little late, Grady thinks. Talk about horses and barn doors. Clearly no one working either Missy's death or Gina's beating had made much headway putting the pieces together. He wonders if they even tried.

They're buzzed into the ICU. Gina's in the same room, hooked up to the same tubes and machines, looking just the same. A detective arrives to speak with Jill about the invasion of Gina's hospital room. Jill insists she has to stay here, no going down to the department for her.

They compromise. Jill will step out of the room to speak with the officer, and Grady won't leave Gina's side until she returns. The officer pulls Jill into the waiting area outside the ICU. Thirty minutes later, she's back, and it's time for Grady to go. He wants to be kept up to date on Gina's condition. Jill promises to call him as soon as she knows anything.

Two officers escort Grady down to the Emergency Department. His ankle is x-rayed and wrapped. It's a bad sprain, but not a break. He's given written instructions (icing, ibuprofen) and issued a pair of crutches. Then he's warned to keep weight off the ankle for a minimum of forty-eight hours and advised to check in with his doctor. He hobbles to the exit, climbs into the back of a squad car, and it's off to the station.

From the chatter he's heard, he's gathered that the cops will be meeting Ben's father as he gets off his plane. And they've decided to let Mr. Wendrell inform the boy's mother of his death. Which in Grady's view is chickenshit. But he doesn't blame them for passing off that responsibility. It's maybe even kind.

Once Grady's seated at a table in an interrogation room, the detective on call pulls in Bachman, the jerk that Grady butted heads with a few hours after Gina was attacked. Grady's back goes up as soon as he sees the asshole, and Bachman's handshake comes with a sneer.

The questions begin. None of them surprising.

No, he didn't know Missy. No, his niece was not in contact with him between the time he left her sleeping in his apartment about ten a.m. Tuesday and the time she was found unconscious in the alley in the early hours of Wednesday morning.

So how'd he make the connection between Wendrell and Missy and Gina?

He tells them about visiting the crime scene and finding the phone, then using it to track down some of Missy's contacts, who led him to Ben.

The on-call detective, a youngish Hispanic guy named Garcia, scolds him for not turning over evidence from a crime scene. It's a pro forma speech without a lot of fire behind it. But it pisses him off anyway.

He reminds the detectives that their people worked that scene, that he didn't get there until almost twenty-four hours later, that they'd had an entire crew at their disposal (as opposed to his unaided eyes and a petite hooker willing to crawl under a dumpster for a price). He doesn't use the words "incompetent" or "lazy," but his implications are clear. Then he says, straight out, that if he'd given them the phone, they would have stuck it in an evidence box and done fuck all about it.

Bachman's tone has been hostile from the beginning. Now he loses it. He's on his feet, bellowing.

"You think you're hot shit. Well, let me tell you something. You're a motherfucking asshole. You accuse us of sitting on our butts, not working this case. What the fuck did we have to work? You think there were clues all over the place like some fucking TV show?

"We canvassed, talked to everyone who'd admit being in the area, and some who wouldn't. Lowlifes, ninety percent. They're not going to tell us shit. We're the enemy.

"But you know all about that. You were a cop. Not a very good one. I checked you out. You were a drunk. And a fuck up. You got kicked out on your ass. But you were still one of us.

"So you found evidence we didn't. Whoopee for you. Like you never missed anything. Always worked overtime on a case where nobody'd authorize it. Went all out every time, whether the victim was an eight-year-old child or a drugged-out hooker. Like you're some goddamn Sherlock Holmes!"

Bachman's face is tomato red. Grady thinks the man is either going to come across the table at him or have a heart attack. Maybe both.

"And when you found this evidence, what did you do? Did you turn it over to us, the guys that you're accusing of not doing enough? Hell, no. You went off and played detective all on your goddamn own. If you'd brought it to us, we'd have found Ben Wendrell sooner. He'd still be alive. His parents wouldn't be burying their second dead child."

Garcia's trying to talk sense to Bachman, telling him, "Take it easy, Mike, calm down."

Finally, the man sputters to a stop.

He's still looming over the table, still red, still a dangerous instant from violence.

"Take a break, Mike," Gracia says.

Bachman shakes his head. "No."

"Take a break," Garcia says again. This time it's not a suggestion.

Bachman huffs, shakes his head, turns abruptly, bumping the chair he'd been sitting in and sending it crashing to the floor. He leaves, slamming the door behind him.

Garcia doesn't apologize. He doesn't address Bachman's behavior at all. Just continues.

They walk through what happened at the hospital, from Grady entering Gina's room and struggling with Ben, to Ben's flight through the hospital corridors and up the stairs, to the events on the roof, the climb up the tower, Grady talking Ben down, the arrival of the police, and Ben's fatal dive.

Bachman's back, and he and Garcia talk big for a few minutes, threatening to charge Grady with obstruction of justice. But everyone involved knows they're only blowing hot air.

Grady waits while his statement is typed up, reviews the document, and signs it. Bachman leaves, and Gracia turns Grady over to a uniform, a patrol officer who looks about eighteen, to drive him home. While he's waiting at the front entrance for the car to come around, his cell rings. It's Jill. There's no real news, she tells him. The doctors don't think Gina was without oxygen long enough to do her brain any harm (which really means "any further harm"), but they won't know until she wakes up. Which is still *if* she wakes up.

Grady says the right things—at first. He thanks Jill. He tells her he'll come back to the hospital later. He's grateful, he says. He truly appreciates all she's done. But then he tells her she should go home. He wants her to go home. He says that yes, the situation is crap, it stinks just about as much as anything can, but there isn't anything she, or anyone, can do about it. Not a damn thing. He's emphatic. He means it.

There are things he doesn't say.

He doesn't address their recent history. Doesn't mention the sex. Doesn't use endearments or allude to any rekindled closeness. He can't imagine getting into all that right now, and he tells himself that Jill has to be feeling the same. It's the circumstances.

But it's also the turmoil within him.

The drive takes longer than it feels like it should, and the uniform and he don't make conversation. It's full morning by now, people are on the roads. The black-and-white crawls through the downtown area with its narrow, one-way streets. Grady has the kid drop him off around the corner from his apartment. There's an errand he wants to run.

#

An hour later, he's sitting on his couch. There a glass of single malt in his hand, two fingers over ice, and a partially empty bottle in front of him on the coffee table. When the uniform dropped him off, he'd already made his decision, and he wasn't surprised about that. Being sober all these months (more than a year now) hadn't surprised him either, although he realized it would have been a shock to almost anyone who knew him. Abstaining, drinking—two sides of the same coin. A flip. It lands heads, or it lands tails.

He had earned a respite, a break.

A drink.

He told himself, this wouldn't mean anything. Today would be an exception.

When he surveyed the liquor store's shelves, he realized that for the first time in his life, he could afford the good stuff (although he should have expected that since he knew what he had in the bank).

He bought one fifth, not two, not a gallon, warning himself that he shouldn't pat himself on the back for that. More would be only a short walk away.

So he's sipping at two fingers over ice. But this is the third pour. Or the fourth. Or… The bottle's about half empty.

A cigarette's burning down luxuriously between his fingers. An ashtray, one that he made for his mother out of clay when he was in fourth grade, one she kept all those years and had on her dresser when she died, sits on the coffee table next to the bottle. It's already thick with butts. Fuck his smoking rule. Fuck his lease. Fuck his own good intentions, his unrealistic expectations for himself.

The whiskey is strong, but smooth. The flavor's smoky, comforting.

He felt good at first. Calm. Relaxed.

Then he moved into reflection, and now he's sliding into regret.

A lot of what Bachman said was exaggerated, even untrue. Up until the very end of his time on the force (or maybe for a year or two before that depending on how you looked at it), he'd been a good cop. A solid detective. Effective. With an excellent solve rate.

Proud of his performance. But then he devolved, spiraled down, and was correctly tagged a fuck up. Bachman had him pegged.

Shit.

And he didn't treat every case the same, pursue each one with the same energy and dedication. Nobody did. And nobody could. They had to "set priorities." And if they didn't, the brass would set the priorities for them.

And Bachman might be right about Ben Wendrell. If Grady hadn't investigated on his own, Ben Wendrell would probably still be alive. This is true.

But Gina would be dead. Bachman didn't admit to that. And, since she came into the room when Wendrell was turning off Gina's ventilator, Jill might have been killed as well.

Ben would likely have escaped. And after that? He might have gotten away with all of it. Or, since there would have been at least one witness—the nurse who let him into the ICU—the cops might have caught up with him eventually. Either way, there would have been at least one more death at his hands.

And who's to say that when and if he was ultimately confronted, he wouldn't have committed suicide by cop? Even taken his parents with him. The kid had come unraveled, gone over the edge…

Stop it, Grady. You're rationalizing. And you don't need to. You kept Ben from killing Gina, and then you tried to save him. You didn't cause him to drown Missy. Or attack Gina—twice. Or make him jump.

But if Grady had been smarter. Realized sooner that Gina was in danger just lying there in the ICU. Figured things out faster. Handled them better. Been able to coax Ben down off the tower sooner. All he'd needed was just a moment, mere seconds, to have Ben's feet touch the roof before the cops burst through the door.

He can't help thinking about Ben's father, and his mother. There will never be enough healing in the world to contain their heartbreak.

He feels himself skidding from regret into sadness. Watch out, Grady, he tells himself, no one likes a sloppy drunk. But he's not going to get drunk. He's only sipping. He'll stay this side of maudlin.

But there's Gina. The last member of his family. His kid sister's only child. Lying there helpless. Yes, she's a drug user. Yes, she's prostituted herself and done God knows what else.

But she's tried so hard. She didn't ask to be orphaned at twelve. She didn't ask for whatever nasty roll of the genetic dice turned her into an addict.

His wallet is lying on the coffee table next to the bottle of Scotch. He picks it up and pulls out the folio of snapshots, begins flipping through it. The guys in Iraq gave him a lot of shit about this, how he carries photos of the people he loves, two snaps back to back in each of the little plastic sleeves. "You should just keep them on your phone, dude!" they'd say. "This is like back in the old days. My grandpa had one of those."

There's the photo of his mom, taken on her last birthday. She's feigning amazement at the number of candles on her cake, at how many it takes just to form the digits of her age. There's Ally, early in their relationship, on a bright Tucson morning when she insisted on dragging him along on a hike. There's Mattie pushing a pop-pop toy Grady had sent. There's the photo of Gina, smiling and happy at fifteen. There's another one of Mattie in Ally's kitchen, wearing a colander as a hat. There's...

What the fuck is Braydon Malone doing in here? The shot was taken from the waist up, with Malone in full sandbox regalia. It's tucked into a plastic sleeve, back-to-back with another picture of Ally.

He pulls it out.

The snapshot of Malone was printed on plain paper, then cut to fit into the plastic sleeve.

How long was it taken before Malone's suicide? There's the start of a moustache, like a pale gold caterpillar, on the kid's upper lip. He was having a hard time growing it, and it had just become more than a line of yellow fuzz when Grady flew out of Baghdad.

So—did the photo show an earlier attempt at facial hair? Or was it taken right before Grady left Iraq?

He's never used the camera feature (new on his latest cell phone), but he knows about selfies. Did Malone take this one specifically to slip it into Grady's wallet just before Grady went on break from the sandbox? He can't remember exactly when he last looked through the folio of photos, but it doesn't matter. The circumstances tell the story.

He turns the picture over. There's writing on the back. It looks like a web address, but in a format he's never seen. Below it: the word "onionland," and the notations:

bm3366*I

W#ic8+O2!

XY%&sj6w53

He tucks the photo back in the plastic sleeve it came from and puts the folio back in his wallet. He stubs out his cigarette, stands up, picks up the glass of Scotch. There's almost nothing remaining—just a tiny puddle at the bottom, under the ice. He tips the glass up and savors the drops that fall on his tongue. Then he carries the bottle of Scotch to the kitchen counter and pours the rest of it down the sink.

35

Forty minutes later, he's climbing out of a cab at Luis's front door.

Before he called for the taxi, he did the rough mental math on his blood alcohol level. Number of ounces, time, body weight. His best judgment was that he was just under the limit.

But he couldn't be sure.

And his ankle was throbbing.

He went back and forth on it for a couple of minutes. It would be stupid to drive; he'd be just fine, pop a couple of ibuprofen, watch the speed limit. It would be stupid to drive; he'd be just fine...

Then he remembered.

His truck was at the hospital. He'd given the cops his keys so they could move it to the parking structure from the loading zone where he'd left it. At the station, they gave him back the keys, but the truck was still on Tier B, in spot 217.

In all his decades in Tucson, he can't remember ever taking a cab before, but he did it this time. Made the phone call, waited leaning on his crutches on the sidewalk outside his building, rode in the sprung back seat of a ten-year-old Chevy that had more miles on it than GM had ever envisioned, endured polite chit chat all the way.

He was so bored that he found himself noticing things that would have barely registered if he had been behind the wheel. The clutter of signs on Speedway, once "honored" as the ugliest street in America. The neighborhood of one-story 1950s brick houses that looked like they were picked up by a midwestern cyclone and plopped down in the Arizona desert. Closer to Luis's, the small adobes, once dirt-cheap, now becoming fashionable and pricey.

A couple of times, Grady spotted what seemed to be the same vehicle in one of the cab's mirrors. It was an older Chevy SUV, black under a coating of desert dust, with tinted windows. He first noticed it when the cab driver slammed on his brakes to avoid going through a red light and the SUV almost rear-ended them. It had an old Fort Benning sticker on the windshield. Home of the Army Rangers. During his first tour in Iraq, Grady was at first amazed, then amused, at how many of the contractors he met boasted about how they'd been Rangers. Once in a while, it was even true. After that close-up view, he couldn't see what was going on behind them with any kind of consistency, but he thought he glimpsed the SUV when the cabbie first turned off the main drag into a residential area, and then again when they made the turn onto Luis's block. It made Grady uncomfortable. But his discomfort made no sense. He chalked it up to the hyper-awareness of his surroundings that he'd developed on escort duty in Iraq. And his emotional state.

As his driver pulled up in Luis's driveway, he saw he'd been right: the black SUV was there. But it rolled by, on down the street. Park your paranoia, he told himself. Like no one's allowed to take the same route you are? He climbed out of the cab, testing his ankle to see how much weight he could put on it (answer: not much) before retrieving his crutches.

He'd gotten here (finally), but it had seemed to take forever. He'd always known he'd rather drive than be driven. During their long-ago marriage, he and Jill used to have minor disagreements about it. She'd accuse him of having control issues ("typical man"); he'd tell her he just didn't passenge well. At one point, he even claimed that riding shotgun make him carsick. After today, he hopes to never take a goddamn cab again.

He hadn't called ahead figuring that because this time of day is the middle of the night for Luis, he'd have his phone off. And even if he didn't, Grady would be harder to turn away in person.

So he paid the cabbie and sent him off, hobbled up to Luis's door, didn't bother with the doorbell, which he knew couldn't be heard (by design) in the room where Luis slept. Instead, he punched the code Luis had given him on his last visit "just in case you ever need it" into the keypad below the intercom—and woke the guy up.

Now he has to talk his way in.

"What the fuck, man!" the familiar voice says after establishing that the asshole at the door is his friend, Jack Grady. "It's not even noon! I sleep during the day. You know that!"

Grady does know that. And he apologizes. Profusely. He says he's come across information that might lead to something big, something that could even impact national security. "No exaggeration, Luis." But he can't be sure. He might be dead wrong. He needs Luis's help.

It's not that he didn't make a stab at it on his own. Before he called the cab, he tried the characters that looked like a weird URL, keying them into in the search engine on his laptop, but he only got garbage and the search engine's best guess at what he might be looking for: "Do you mean XXX?" He didn't. It took him to a porn site anyway.

The electronic lock on the door clicks. As Grady enters, Luis is rolling down the hallway toward him. He's wearing pajamas bottoms and a Suicidal Tendencies t-shirt. His feet are bare, his hair is a tousled mess, his face crumpled, expression crabby. He looks like exactly what he is: a man who's been rudely awakened in the middle of his sleep cycle. But when he sees Grady, he breaks into laughter. "Oh, man! Look at you! Crutches! This hombre is one of us! How's it feel to be 'differently abled'?"

Grady takes the ribbing with good grace. Luis is right. He's temporarily hobbling around. But a few days from now, he'll be back to taking both his legs and his easy mobility for granted, just as he's done all his life. He's acutely conscious of this distinction, and newly thankful for being what used to be called "able-bodied." He mutters something about "just a sprain."

Luis shoots back, "Where's your handicap placard?" and chortles at his own joke. He reaches up from his wheelchair and claps Grady on the back. "Okay, amigo, I'm up now. You might as well stay."

Grady's ready to get to the business that brought him here, but Luis isn't. "Gotta have a Diet Coke, man. First thing every day. I wake up thirsty. And it's got a touch of caffeine. Lubricates the gray cells."

The wheelchair does a one-eighty, and Grady follows Luis to the kitchen. Luis motors over to the built-in counter-height refrigerator, opens it, and takes out two cans of soda. "I was gonna have you do this, you wake me so early. But I can wheel up to the counter and use both my hands at the same time." "You try that with your foot, man, you'll fall over!" Luis's boast ignores the fact that one of his hands is twisted by cerebral palsy He opens each can by holding it against his chest with his left arm, using his wrist, and pulls up the tab with his good right hand.

Fifteen minutes later, Luis has rolled himself up to the keyboard of one of his computers. Grady's perched next to him on a low stool.

Luis turns to Grady. "So, what you got?"

Grady pulls out his wallet, slips out the folio of snapshots, and slides the picture of Malone out of its plastic sleeve. He turns it over and hands it to Luis.

Luis lets out a long whistle. Grady's surprised. It takes a lot to break through Luis's cool. "Where the hell'd you get this?"

"I think one of the guys on my team in Iraq slipped it in there right before I left. I just found it."

Luis turns to Grady. "*Madre de Dios*. You heard about the dark web?"

Grady has. Sort of. Kind of. He thinks.

"Okay. Well, there's the deep web and the dark web. People get them mixed-up all the time. The deep web is sites that aren't indexed. You gotta know the URL to find one. If you don't, you never see it. There's a lot of different stuff, pages like online banking, services behind a paywall."

"So not sinister."

"Nah. Legit. Think about it. Those pages are hidden 'cause of security. Or privacy."

"And the dark web is different?"

"Oh yeah. Those sites aren't indexed either, man. But they're mostly nasty, or illegal—or both."

Shit. Grady doesn't like where this is heading.

"It's not all *malo*," Luis says. "But there's a lot of really ugly stuff. People selling stolen social security numbers, swiped credit cards. Child pornography rings. Black hat hackers, hackers who don't care what color hat they wear, they're all selling their services. Everything's encrypted: sites, communications. Some people think you can buy just about anything on the dark web. And they're mostly right." Luis shakes his head. "Sick."

In his bleaker moments, Grady has often felt that virtually every large institution—no matter how shiny clean and wholesome it looks to the world—has a dark underbelly. He's never thought about applying that insight to the Internet, but it makes sense. Any complex organism, at least any created by human beings, always includes pieces of the worst of us, not just the best.

Luis is still talking. Grady has never heard such a lengthy speech from him. He's usually a man of few words, keeping himself to himself, much concerned with his own privacy wall.

Each of the screensavers on the computers that fill the long tables running around the room is different. The one in front of Luis shows a samurai wielding a sword. He's moving right to left, slicing the screen into ribbons. When he reaches the left edge of the screen, it reassembles itself, and the samurai twirls, swings the sword, begins slicing again.

"And even if you have the URL for one of those sites," Luis is saying, "that's not enough. You see this word 'onionland'? That's how people talk about a part of the deep web that's accessed by a special browser. One of things it does is hide your IP address. You know what that is and how they can track you by it?"

Because of his godawful experience as a federal target a couple of years back, Grady does. It was something he had to be very aware of during his months on the run.

"And you know about authentication?" Grady isn't sure, but he doesn't want to slow Luis down so he nods. "That's different on the dark web, too. A lotta the time, it's complex. You could need a key, man, not just a password." He draws Grady's attention to the writing on the back of Malone's photo.

"This buddy of yours," Luis asks. "What the fuck was he doing fooling around with this shit?"

Grady knows it can only be one thing. That Rachel was right. Malone has burdened him with a duty he's never wanted. He hopes he's wrong.

"I have an idea," he says. "But I can't ask the guy. Right after I flew out, he killed himself."

"You're kidding, man." Luis crosses himself. "*Mierda.*" Shit.

"His name was Malone. And he wasn't much more than a kid. I think whatever this leads us to has something to do with his death. I think it's why he killed himself."

"Fuck." Luis says it quietly, almost reverentially. "That's really messed up."

Grady silently agrees. It is.

He watches Luis's good hand play over the keyboard. "This is the browser I was talking about," Luis says. He enters the characters of the web address. A screen appears. "This is an entry portal," he explains. "I'm hoping these" (here his twisted left hand indicates the remaining characters written on the photo) "are the key, user name, and password. If it needs other verification, we're screwed."

"I think Malone wanted me to get in."

"We'll see, man. Did this guy know how hopeless you are with technical shit?"

Grady likes to think of himself as barely adequate rather than hopeless. After all, he has some hard-earned basic search skills. And these days, he not only owns but actually uses a cell phone. But he doesn't disagree with Luis's assessment. "Yeah. He used to help me. And once he'd got me untangled, he'd kind of smile because what I was trying to do should have been so easy."

Luis, who's been dead serious, grins. "So when he put that in your wallet, he figured you were smart enough to know somebody like me."

The screen changes. Grady sees a file name that includes a mission designation in the format that was assigned to all their details in Iraq, a date, and a series of upper-case letters separated by commas. Grady immediately recognizes those letters as initials. Personnel. "HP" (Hartman Pickett), three of his buddies, and "BM" (Braydon Malone).

"It's a video," Luis says. He clicks another button. The video plays.

They freeze there in front of the monitor, not speaking. The only sounds come from the computer's speakers. The quality is bad, but maybe that's a mercy. It distorts the cries, muffles the screams.

ON THE SCREEN

A narrow dirt road. Two dusty buildings, one a near-ruin. An ancient mini-van stopped on a diagonal across the road, blocking it.

The right back tire: flat.

Two men, youngish, in t-shirts and jeans. They're dark-skinned with black hair. Iraqis. One of them holds a lug wrench.

A spare tire, its running surface slick, treadless, leaning against the side of the vehicle.

From the back: Three men approach the van. All wear fatigues in a desert camouflage pattern. Helmets. Guns. The accessories of war. They're Americans.

Behind them: their armored vehicle, idling. Not visible: the man left inside at the wheel. (A fifth man is our eyes. He's behind the camera, actually wearing that piece of equipment as it will turn out.)

In the van: one woman, also youngish. She wears western garb, but modest: loose trousers, a long-sleeved blouse, a scarf that covers most of her dark hair.

Also in the van: five children. Three boys and two girls. They range in age from six to ten.

The largest of the three men in camos strides up to the two young men. He shouts at them to get their goddamned heap out of the way.

The young man without the lug wrench gestures at the flat tire. In broken English, he explains that they will change the tire as quickly as they can. Then they can get the van off the road.

The large man in camos doesn't care about the tire. He wants the van out of the way. Now!

The young man explains that moving it with the flat tire will damage the wheel. They don't want to…

The man in camos doesn't give a fuck about their goddamn wheel. He orders them to move. I said now! And I meant now!

The man without the lug wrench climbs into the van, sits in the driver's seat. He's attempting to start the vehicle. The engine won't turn over. He spreads his hands in a helpless gesture. What can he do?

The large man is angry. You won't move it, we'll move it for you. He and his team will push it off the road.

The three men and the man behind the camera approach the van. The man holding the lug wrench raises it. He's making some sort of gesture. I need to change the tire. Or thank you for helping us. Or please don't ruin our van. Or…

The man in camos points his weapon at the man with the lug wrench. There's a click. Safety off? "Drop it!" The man hesitates, maybe stubborn, or confused—or frozen with fear.

His friend yells something in Arabic. Later, we will learn that he says, "Put it down!"

The man drops the lug wrench.

"Damn," the large man in camos says to his team. "Now we've got to search the fucking thing."

He's decided that the van is a risk. Or he wants to pretend that the van is a risk.

To the first young man: "Get everybody out."

The women and the children climb out slowly. "Hands in the air," the large man in camos orders. The first young man translates the command into Arabic.

One of the Americans tells the two young men, the woman, and the children to "Move it!" He gestures. "Over there." They line up along the side of the road.

The driver of the armored vehicle joins the rest of his team, and all of the camo-clad men examine the outside of the van. The man behind the camera runs a mirror underneath the vehicle. They open the engine compartment, all the doors. Finally, they climb inside. They toss out bottles of water, a basket spilling oranges, a few automotive tools. They rip into the seats.

They push the van out of the way. The dusty road is littered with the personal belongings that were in the vehicle.

One of the children starts to cry. The woman raises her voice in anger.

She berates the Americans. And she speaks English. They know what she's saying: "You cannot do this! We are citizens! You have no right!"

The large man in camos aims his gun at her. But then he swings it away from her. He shoots one of the two men.

The children scream. The woman screams. And she's screaming words. But now they're in Arabic......

The video plays for thirty-two minutes. It seems both very short and very long.

When it ends, Grady and Luis are both still sitting there silent, staring at the screen.

#

Grady knows what he's seen. The large man in camos is Hartman Pickett. The video isn't exactly high-def. The man's features are indistinct. But the voice and body language are unmistakable.

He realizes he shouldn't be so surprised.

Besides all the other dynamics of that testosterone-filled house back in Iraq, there are the group conversations. When they're not out on assignment, or eating, sleeping, lifting weights, watching porn, the men talk endlessly. About sports. About cars. About confrontations with the locals, with actual insurgents, with authorities of all kinds. Bragging about how ballsy they were, how they fought, how they shouted them down, showed them what was what, who was boss. There's the usual griping about bureaucracy and—over and over—a lot of bluster about the big stuff they could do if the fucking politicians would let them take the gloves off and go after those towelheads.

There are also reminiscences, admissions of a longing for home, stories about kids, girlfriends, fiancés, sharing of hopes, ambitions, plans for the future. But those are pretty much limited to one-on-one conversations.

When it's more than two men talking (and it's usually at least three or four), there's inevitably a shitload of boasting about women. Lots of raunch. About getting tail and big breasts and fucking the bitches. With a lot of focus on location: blow jobs (or nailing her ass) in moving cars (while driving), at the beach, at 35,000 feet in the bathroom of a commercial jet, in the bare-bones fuselage of a transport, in a club, a Hummer, a tent. Shit, why do you think they let girls join the damn Army? No other reason for them. These days, they practically issue pussy along with your weapon.

Everyone, the men who join in and those who generally don't, is used to the macho, profanity-filled content. Grady tends to move away from the conversations, to relocate and take refuge in his headphones. But a couple of times he caught talk that seemed over the line.

Not simply, "It's not rape just because she's had a few. They all want it. Then they whine about it later. A man has to be a man. The aggressor. That's biology."

He heard that stuff every day.

What stands out for him now are a few crazy discussions he overheard of what war used to be about. What it should be about today. And is to everybody except our pussy government. You'd take a city, grab anything valuable, set fire to everything else, kill all the men, sell all the children for slaves, and the women were yours. Do anything you want with them. That's reality. That's the way the fucking world works. The spoils of war. Kill 'em, work 'em, or fuck 'em.

To the victor and all that.

And underlying it all was the accepted fact that the enemy, the locals, whoever they were talking about at the moment, those creatures are not like us. Don't fool yourself. They're not really people.

No one who was part of the core group argued with that premise. And no one else tried. Because it was pointless. There was no use trying to change their minds, no easy cure for bigotry. And Grady figured a lot of them didn't really believe it. They just went along to get along.

It was almost always Pickett who directed the conversations. And each time Grady heard the speech about the spoils of war (with a reminder that any enemy, by definition, was less than human—a capsule refresher course on racial and religious prejudice), it was Pickett working everybody up, egging them on, pushing them into nastier and nastier territory.

Sometimes, Pickett would start in on the time he'd spent in Afghanistan. He liked to talk about that—and even seemed to hint that operating conditions (at least for him) were different there. More "flexible." That things could happen... He'd kind of smile. He wouldn't elaborate.

The man's bad news. Grady's known that since ten minutes after he met the guy. What the fuck? That was his initial reaction. He didn't get it. Any company with sense would never have hired Pickett. But he thought he must be wrong—or missing something. There was screening. There was training.

So—it's all a lot of noise. The guy's just blowing smoke.

That's what he's always told his rational brain.

But still his instinct never stopped asking the same question: What the fuck?

He's never been able to convince his gut that Pickett's anything but what Grady's mother would have called a wrong one.

Even so, he never dreamed....

36

Rachel is mad enough to spit. Before she ever landed at Tucson International Airport ("international"—as in the occasional commuter jet to Mexico), she was aware that support would be thin on the ground here. But she'd never imagined how thin. The computer guys were good enough, she supposed. And the pair that searched Jack Grady's apartment while she dragged out her lunch with him (and would have helped with the search of his storage locker if there'd been much of anything to search), they were competent. But this bozo she's been stuck with for surveillance. All he was asked to do was stick a tracking device on the man's truck, for God's sake. And he couldn't even manage that.

He'd apparently arrived to carry out his mission just as the target pulled out of his apartment house's parking garage. And he'd called and told Rachel that. "Just missed him."

"Did you follow him?" Rachel asked.

The idiot sounded stunned. That wasn't part of his assignment, he objected. "If somebody had said…"

"Forget it!" she spouted in a fury. They'd take care of it later.

All that was yesterday.

When she woke up this morning and checked her phone and her email and had no further news from the asshole with the tracker, she called him. And asked him. Nicely. Her exact words were: "I assume the device is in place?"

There was a long silence. "Uh," he said at last, "uh…"

She was beginning to get the idea. "You didn't place it?"

Again, he sounded dumbfounded. "Uh, no. You told me to forget it."

That wasn't what she meant, and she started to tell him so, to make sure he understood that only a moron would have…or at least would have asked…

But what was the point?

She brought her frustration under control. "Just go over there now and take care of it," she said through gritted teeth. "And then call me back."

She had just gotten out of the shower and was reaching for the hair dryer when he called. The target's vehicle wasn't there, he said. Was he sure? Yes. Had he checked the target's spot, 308? He had.

Had he walked the structure just in case the target had parked in a different spot (a long shot, but if someone else had happened to be occupying Grady's slot when he pulled in, it was a possibility). No, the numbskull hadn't even gotten out of his vehicle, hadn't walked anything. But he would.

"Do it," she said, teeth still gritted. "Then call me back."

Now, she's dressed and putting the final touches on her makeup when the guy calls again.

The report is the same. The target's vehicle is not in the structure.

This time when she says, "Forget it," she means it the way the bozo understood it the first time.

Could she have avoided this by pulling some strings and tracking Grady's cell phone instead? She supposes so. But it isn't like the man is involved in some major plot—if he's involved in anything at all. So why use that juice here? Better to keep it in reserve for a time when she'll really need it.

She was only checking a box, and then only because Gil brought it up. Since when has she done things by the book when the book doesn't make sense? Since when has she let a subordinate (even Gil) manipulate her into using less than her best judgment?

Jack Grady is single, home on break from a difficult and isolating assignment. Should anyone (including her) be surprised that he has a life? He's clearly fucking that skinny blonde. And he'd said something about a niece in the hospital.

At the same time, she wants to shake the tree one last time. She'll confront him, come on strong, use the threat of a polygraph, confirm to her full satisfaction (instead of the ninety-five percent she's at right now) that Jack Grady knows nothing, possesses nothing bearing on her investigation, and—no matter how willing (or not)—can be of zero help in the current crisis. Then she can legitimately get the hell out of this place and back to civilization.

37

Jill's sitting in the small auxiliary cafeteria that the hospital calls a "café." She's just finished a breakfast of scrambled eggs and bacon bits wrapped in a tortilla and is considering going back up to the counter for a glazed donut. She's noticed that there's something about the stress of bedside vigils that makes people throw their healthy diets out the window. She wants to gorge on pastries. A bear claw. Maybe a cinnamon bun.

This is day three of watching over Gina in the hospital. She's tired and lonely and missing her daughter and her home, even her work. Maybe especially her work if she's honest with herself. And while she's into truth telling, she might as well admit that she's missing her husband. Except that she's not sure about that. Maybe it doesn't work this way for everyone, but in her, rejection builds emotional walls, and when it comes to Charlie, she's feeling pretty damn rejected.

Then there's Jack. Somehow, her pain at what she's convinced is the impending dissolution of her marriage and his pain at his niece's plight reconnected them—in bed, if nowhere else. There was physical satisfaction in their two bodies coming together. Was there also comfort? She's not sure.

After they slept together the first time, she assumed they'd talk about it or at least begin to behave differently toward each other. After the second time, she was too confused to address their lack of conversation on the topic.

Truth is, she's been expecting too much. Between the worry about Gina and the horrible events at the hospital just a few hours ago, there's been no emotional space for that kind of communication. It would be surprising—even shocking—if they had managed it. Jack isn't superhuman, and God knows, neither is she.

She buys a bottle of water and a banana to go, forces herself to ignore the rack of donuts. On one hand, she feels like she should hurry back to the ICU. On the other, there doesn't seem to be any urgency about it. Gina's just the same: lying there unconscious, with the machine breathing for her. They still don't know anything about additional brain damage that might have happened during the time the ventilator was turned off. The duty nurse says they'll probably start running some tests later in the day.

She's realizing she can't do this forever, something Jack has pointed out more than once. But she still has a few hours left in her novel (which would have been a quick read if she hadn't been having such trouble focusing). She can certainly stay at Gina's bedside at least that long.

She thinks of calling Jack, telling him, although not in these words, to get his butt over here, this is his niece—his only close relative—lying in a coma.

Then she feels immediately guilty.

Don't go down that road, she scolds herself. Don't turn your longing to see him (yes, admit it, Jill, that's what it is—whether it's loneliness, lust, or something much more complicated) into anger. If you're tired, he must be exhausted. And he's injured.

She needs to let him sleep.

When they were married, he'd sometimes come back from a shift so beat that he didn't even make it into bed. She'd come out to the living room in the morning to find him sprawled on the couch, snoring. She wonders if he ever does that now or if those were the deep, dead sleeps of youth, if—like her these days—he'll nod off in front of the TV or over a book only to wake up a few minutes later and get himself to bed. She pictures him stretched out on his new sofa in his shiny new, almost-empty apartment. But the space is so un-Jack-like that the image won't hold.

She thinks again—for just a moment—about their love-making. Shuts those thoughts down.

She hopes he's remembered to ice his ankle.

38

As Grady opens the door to his apartment, he sees Rachel sitting on his couch, sipping a cup of his coffee out of one of his mugs.

He's pissed. Her power play is unnecessary.

"I suppose it wouldn't do any good to change the locks." He says it coolly, but with a definite edge.

They both know she's broken the law (she couldn't have gotten a no-knock warrant for something like this). And that he won't do shit about it. He'd be out of his mind to call down the locals on some hotshot from the FBI. Damnit.

Rachel has planned to be confrontational, right in his face. It's her last attempt to salvage something from this mess before she blows town. But she has to admit to herself that this has become a rule-out scenario. At best. And now her gut tells her that playing hard-ass isn't the way to go. She's never been sorry when she's gone with her instincts, so she tries getting cute. "Sorry. I have skills. Sometimes, I can't help using them." She watches Grady swing himself across the room, notes the ace bandage and absence of a cast. "Hurt your ankle?"

"Just a sprain. Tripped on a step." He settles on a stool at the island, leans his crutches against the counter.

"So…" she says, getting up from the couch and walking into the kitchen area. She takes a second mug from a cabinet. "Pour you one?"

Grady knows that this social chit-chat is just lubrication for another round of questions. She has to be getting desperate at this point, so her interrogation will go beyond probing, to invasive, maybe even insulting before her pride will let her give up. And unless he clues her in on what he's found, none of it will get her anywhere because she has no idea what to ask.

He has a momentary urge to stonewall her. But that would let Pickett and his crew get away with what amounts to a war crime. He was always disgusted by the guy, did what he could to keep his distance—which wasn't easy since they were living in the same house. But this…

Cujo. That's what his gang calls him. What a sick nickname. And the asshole's proud of it.

So no, he won't be stonewalling Rachel Greene. The expertise of the FBI is key to bringing this thing out in the open in a thoughtful, controlled way. No matter how rude Ms. Greene's intrusion here, she and Grady share a common goal: to see that the world condemns the men who committed this atrocity (even if she doesn't yet know quite what the atrocity is) but doesn't punish the entire country, or even the other men who are doing the same tough job the best, most honorable way they can.

So…

"I was just going to call you," he says.

"Oh?" She says, pausing in mid-pour. There's weight in his words, so she ignores the fact that he's taken control of the conversation. Something's up.

Grady's laptop is at the other end of the island. "Slide that over to me," he says, indicating the computer. She does.

He opens it, starts it up.

As Rachel watches, all of her attention focused on him and what he's going to do or say next, Grady pulls a thumb drive he brought from Luis's out of his shirt pocket. "I found the video," he says.

She can't believe it. They searched and searched. How could they possibly have missed... "Where?"

He holds up the thumb drive. "It wasn't on this thing. It was on the dark web. Malone left me a map."

He pulls the snapshot of the dead kid out of the same shirt pocket, turns it over, shows her the URL and the other information written on the back, lays it on the counter face up, Malone looking at them. "This was in the photo insert in my wallet."

Rachel is stunned. Why didn't she think of this? Malone was a nerd. Where else would he have hidden a video? Not that she could have found it—correction, that her guys could have found it—without the info Malone planted on Grady. At least one of her conclusions was right, though: Malone had pegged Grady as a man who would not only understand what he was seeing but would bring it to the attention of the right people. Jack Grady is the perfect whistleblower: far from self-righteous, flawed, maybe even morally flexible at times, but principled. And Malone intuited this, realized that Grady would see the incident the same way he did. And would never question that it needed to be brought to light.

She watches as Grady inserts the thumb drive into one of the laptop's USB ports and waits for its icon to appear onscreen. He clicks to open the drive, and she sees the file name, with the mission information and date and five pairs of upper-case letters separated by commas. It's the most recent detail noted as "equipment malfunction" in Malone's log. "Those letters are initials," Grady says. "Braydon Malone, Hartman Pickett, and..." She cuts him off. "I get it."

If there was any doubt left in her mind, it's vanished. She knows the content will be bad, maybe devastating, but she wonders how good the footage itself is. How much can a body cam really show?

Grady copies the file onto the laptop. He double-clicks to open it.

The shock of the new is gone, but that doesn't make what he sees any less gut-wrenching. For him, the only possible reaction, or at least the only appropriate one, is silence. He knows that the video will be discussed, dissected. That the people investigating it will numb themselves out of necessity. That news anchors' and narrators' voices will play over the images in media reports and, someday, in documentaries. And that repetition will lead to desensitization. People can only take so much. Eventually, they become inured to the pain of others.

But for him at this moment, the horror is still fresh.

......*The dusty road is littered with the personal belongings that were in the vehicle.*

One of the children starts to cry. The woman raises her voice in anger.

She berates the Americans. And she speaks English. They know what she's saying: "You cannot do this! We are citizens! You have no right!"

The large man in camos aims his gun at her. But then he swings it away from her. He shoots one of the two men.

The children scream. The woman screams. And she's screaming words. But now they're in Arabic.

The other man tries to shush her.

The woman crouches over the wounded man, touching him, cradling him. He's covered in blood, and she gets it on her hands and arms. She clutches her head. Now blood is on her scarf, in her hair.

"He is dead!" This is in English. "He did not do anything! You will not get away with it!" This is an announcement, loud, outraged.

She's grabbed by two of the men in camos. Held. She struggles, trying to free herself. Will she be killed? Will she be raped?

The children are sobbing. The young man left alive is deathly pale. A wet stain spreads from his crotch down the legs of his jeans.

The leader, the large man in camos, looks the young woman up and down. Then he says, "I'm horny as hell. And I'm no homo. But I'd rather fuck one of you assholes than put my pretty white dick in that dirty sand nigger's cunt."

There is laughter. The other men in camos approve of their leader's thinking and admire the way he has with words.

One of the men in camo gestures with his gun at the young man with the wet crotch. "Fuckin' towelhead pissed himself."

"Can't allow that," the leader says. "Your turn. Go ahead and do it."

Without hesitation, the other man shoots the young man in the stomach; then, as he lies writhing on the ground, in the head.

The young woman is begging the men to stop. Let the rest of them go. She'll take the children and walk away. Just walk away.

"Walk away?" the leader says. "We can do better than that. Let's see you run......"

Rachel is standing at Grady's side watching with him in silence. The video is bad, worse than she expected. More offensive, bloodier, more graphic. What happens to some men when you give them weapons (which these men equate with power) and put them in situations where they have to make quick decisions? She won't use the term "split-second" in describing those decisions, not to herself at least, because these circumstances didn't require that. What they did require was a modicum of common sense and a reasonable level of human feeling. And after this crew made their very bad, very wrong initial choice...

It wasn't—or shouldn't have been—a matter of life and death.

How did these assholes get through screening? What happened to their training?

"Again," she says. "I need to see it again."

Grady restarts the video, then turns away, picks up his crutches and swings his way over to the door wall that leads to the small balcony. He can't watch again right now. It's bad enough that he can still hear the sounds. And they're louder than the first time through. Rachel's turned up the volume. For clarity? To punish herself?

He fixes his gaze on the buildings across the way and the street below. He's doing all he can not to listen. And that's how he misses the other sound behind him.

A deep voice says, "Huh. The bitch and the gimp. Sounds like an old movie. A really stupid one."

39

Grady pivots on his crutches. The man standing there a few feet in from the front door is big—tall, wide, and muscular. He's dressed all in black: black jeans, tight black t-shirt, black ankle boots, like a B-movie version of a current-day ninja. Even the gun he's holding in his right hand is black, not shiny, but dull, business-like metal. Grady knows him. Hartman Pickett. Cujo. "Hello, Hartman," he says over the screams coming out of the laptop. He uses the guy's wussy first name purposely, not wanting to encourage the macho.

Rachel turned when Grady did. Clearly, she didn't hear the man come in either.

He sees her glance across the room. It's a quick look, and she almost manages to hide it, but her eyes dart over to the floor by the couch, to her shoulder bag. Grady noticed earlier that she wasn't carrying on her person, no obvious holster, no unattractive bulges in her clothes. (Like Pickett, she's dressed in all black, silk tee, black jeans, pointy black stilettos. But where he's bulky, she's slim and sleek. No place to hide a weapon.) Her gun's in the bag. Big mistake. Assuming she survives this confrontation, she'll never be so casual about her weapon again. Bad way to learn a lesson.

The video ends. Grady can hear Pickett breathing hard. Maybe he's not nearly as cool as he'd like to seem.

Rachel breaks the silence. "Hartman Pickett," she says.

Pickett smiles. "You can call me Cujo. And thanks for leaving the door open. I didn't even have to knock."

It's Grady's turn to regret a stupid mistake. He flashes on the moment when after fumbling with his keys, managing to unlock the door while leaning on his crutches, and hobbling his way in, he saw Rachel sitting on the couch. He pushed the door shut behind him, didn't check that it latched, let alone take time to lock it.

Pickett waves the gun toward the laptop. "You've been watching Goofy's little movie. Stupid kid. Why would he kill himself over that?"

He waves the gun at Grady. "Hey, Geezer, aren't you going to ask me why I'm here? Why I left one fucking desert for another? Why I'm standing in your piece-of-shit crib? What it is I want?"

Grady's not biting. He doesn't see any upside to playing Pickett's game.

Rachel apparently doesn't see it the same way. "Okay. What is it you want?"

"Cujo. What is it you want, Cujo?"

"What is it you want, Cujo?"

"Oh, let's see. The laptop. And that thumb drive. And while you're at it, you might as well give me that nice picture of Malone lying right beside it. Just in case it's related. Or I get to feeling sentimental."

Grady's thinking they should hold out a little, just a little, to make it seem realistic. And then they should give him the damn things. He doesn't get why Pickett would want the snap of Malone, but the asshole's probably just scooping up everything in sight. And who cares? None of it will do him any good. No matter what he takes out of here, he won't have it all.

Then he realizes that Rachel doesn't know that anyone else has a copy of the video. She doesn't know that Luis was the one who found it (or even that Luis exists). Given a few more minutes before Cujo's intrusion, she would have asked, no doubt about it. And he might have even told her.

But now…

"Put the gun away," Rachel says. Her tone is calm, soothing.

Pickett doesn't reply. He just stands there holding the weapon.

"You're not really going to kill anybody for this," Rachel's tone is cajoling, almost friendly. "It's just a badly shot video. Terrible quality, confusing, hard to see what's going on."

"People died. You can see that."

"I'm not so sure that…"

"Bullshit. I could see it from here. I'm identifiable. And even if I wasn't, some of my buddies are."

"It's a war zone. Things are different. It's hard to draw lines between right and wrong."

Pickett's not buying. "Maybe you know that. I sure as hell know it. But tell that to the goddamn liberal media. You think we wanted to kill anybody? Hell, no. But they'll say we did. They twist things. I'm not having my life ruined for some fucking A-rabs. Those people! They got no gratitude, they got no brains. They bring it on themselves."

Rachel is continuing to spout what Grady recognizes as the standard FBI negotiator's script. What you've done isn't so bad. We can help you. Let us help you. Free the hostages. Put the gun down…

"The people you report to, the people who matter, they'll understand. They've been in these situations. They know you make the best decisions you can. And sometimes things don't turn out well. There isn't any good answer."

Just like in all the movies…

Pickett's no genius, but he's not an imbecile. If Grady can see Rachel's words for the load of hooey that they are, so can he.

But at least the man's still talking. "The people I report to. I guess you mean the guys who hired me, their bosses, those suits sitting behind their fancy desks stroking their dicks. Those assholes have never done squat on the ground. And they're going to protect me from the, what are they calling them these days, 'insurgents'? This thing gets out, how the fuck are they going to do that? If I'm not over there in the sandbox, I'm not making money. If I am over there, those towelheads are going to come after me. You saw what they did to those four contractors."

Grady remembers that horror. They all do. Four civilian contractors were ambushed and killed by an Iraqi mob when they made the mistake of trying to save time by taking a route that went through the city of Fallujah. Their bodies were mutilated, burned—and then hung from a bridge over the Euphrates.

But there's no analogy here. That was five-and-a-half years ago, in March 2004. The images ran 24/7 on every news channel in America, and they were searing. But not everybody in a war zone is a threat. A lot are just ordinary people trying to survive. And except for a small number of steroid-damaged hulks who've long ago said goodbye to their humanity, every contractor in Iraq knows that. Nobody in that broken-down van was coming after Pickett and his crew.

Picket takes a few steps toward Rachel. He's not much more than two body-lengths away. "No, ma'am, I am not putting this gun down. But if you move real slow, we'll all be just fine. Close up that laptop. Put it on the floor and set that thumb drive and that fucking selfie of Malone on top of it. Then move real slow again and slide it over to me. Once you do that, I'll have all I want. I'll walk right out. No harm, no foul. You and Geezer here just go on with your lives."

Do it, Grady's thinking. Give him the laptop and the drive and the photo. Maybe he'll leave. And if he doesn't, we'll deal with it. He's armed, but we're still two trained professionals against one. And we're a lot smarter than this lard-head.

As he opens his mouth to urge her to just give the asshole what he came for, to his horror—

Rachel scoops up his mother's cookie jar and flings it at Pickett. Pickett steps to the side, and the thing crashes to the floor, shattering on the hard tile. Fuck! What does she think...

The plant that Jill gave him is sitting on the island next to the spot where the cookie jar was. Is she going to hurl that next?

No.

She grabs the butcher knife from the knife block, throws it at the man. It's wide, misses by a mile, and falls harmlessly to the floor.

What the hell does she think she's doing? Since when are FBI agents trained in knife throwing?

She can't really have expected to hit him. Maybe she thought she'd startle him enough to give them an opening.

If so, it didn't work.

Pickett is red-faced, almost foaming. Rachel grabs one of the remaining knives from the block and holds it out in front of her. Grady can't believe it. She's really bringing a paring knife to a gunfight.

And Pickett's just as well trained as they are. Rachel can't have forgotten that. Is she trying to rile him up?

Why?

"A piece of advice," he says, hoping to slow Pickett down. "I can tell you're pissed as hell. We're not doing what you want. And Rachel here keeps throwing stuff at you. But you don't want to use that thing." He gestures at the gun in Pickett's hand. The look at Pickett's face says, yes, he does. Grady keeps talking. "Not without a silencer. It'd make one hell of a noise. All these hard surfaces.

"You must have noticed my next-door neighbor when you went by. Oh, you didn't see her? Guess you were pre-occupied. Not as alert as you normally are. Old bag has nothing to do all day but watch who goes in and out and complain. I've been here six days, and she's called the cops on me twice. My stereo was too loud. I was unpacking and dropped a box. Walls like paper. And because she has money and a nephew on the force, they show up. So you shoot that thing, and you're done. Even if you get out of the building alive, you won't be on the loose for long. They'll track you down."

Grady's hoping that Pickett may not want to believe what he's just heard but won't take the chance. That's assuming the man is still rational, though. Looking at Cujo's face and his body language, Grady's not so sure.

He waves the gun at Grady. "Get over there," he yells. "Right next to her."

Exaggerating the extent of his disability, Grady slowly swings his way from his spot by the door wall over to the island.

He has to defuse the situation. "Look, Hartman," he says, trying to sound both reasonable and truth-telling, like a man laying it on the line, which, ironically, he mostly is. "Here's reality. Even if Ms. Greene handed the drive and the laptop to you right now, it wouldn't do you any good. It won't save you. You think I found this video on my own, even with Malone's instructions? You know how shitty I am with computers. I barely know how to turn one of the things on. I had help from an associate. The video is stored on the dark web. He knows where. And he made a copy of the download. He knows what to do with that if something happens to me."

Pickett grins. Grady doesn't like the way this is going. The man seems way too confident.

"Oh. You mean that beaner who lives in the shitty little house with all the fancy computer gear. The one in the wheelchair. Nah. He doesn't have a copy anymore. He doesn't have shit. And I got him to delete the file that was up on that site. Watched it go poof! Destroyed!"

Luis! How did Pickett... Grady flashes on the black SUV he'd noticed during his cab ride to Luis's. He'd disregarded his sense that he was being tailed, convinced himself it was paranoia caused by exhaustion and injury. He curses himself for being so stupid.

"It took a little work. He tried to hold out. Kind of a brave guy, for a gimp. But he's only got one good hand. I pointed that out. And he needs that hand. Without it? Life would be hard. I pointed that out, too. And he agreed with me. Eventually."

"You didn't hurt him!"

"Not much. Just enough so he knew I meant it. Left the place kind of a mess, though. Sorr-eee! But he'll be okay. Oh, I got the impression he's some kind of hacker. And maybe an illegal. He won't be crying to the cops."

Luis would have called Grady. If he could have... Grady pictures Luis in pain, perhaps bound, gagged, maybe unconscious. He's angrier than he's been in years. He wants to charge at Pickett, tear him apart. If Pickett shoots him, well... He's not sure he'd feel the bullet.

He consciously brings himself under control. He can't do anything for Luis unless he gets out of here in one piece.

So now what? If he and Rachel turn over the thumb drive and laptop, Pickett really will be getting what he wants. He can walk out of here confident that no one can ever touch him. There will be no evidence. No proof that the recording existed. No forensics to say that he was ever here. The only thing he's touched has been the door knob, and he can wipe that on his way out. Rachel could try to put together a case to take to the prosecutors, but she'd be laughed out of their offices.

Cujo would win.

Would that be so bad? If it saves them, saves Luis?

Grady doesn't like the answer. Pickett wasn't the only one involved in the atrocity, but he's the one who lit the fuse. And he's going to get away with it. It's not like the man feels remorse. There's no contrition here. Pickett is not going to go in peace and never sin again. He may not like all the trouble he's had to take to deal with the aftermath, but under similar circumstances, Grady has no doubt he'll do the same thing again—or something even worse.

Kids, Grady thinks. You killed kids. And we can see how it happened. None of you were in fear of your lives. You acted like it was target practice. Some of you thought it was fucking funny.

And he threatened—and hurt—Luis.

The world needs to know what Pickett and his "buddies" did in Iraq.

Rachel's still holding the paring knife. Grady knows that she could do a lot of damage with it given the chance. But it's hopelessly inadequate in their current situation. Everyone in this room's been schooled in hand-to-hand combat, taught to fight dirty, no holds barred, in kill-or-be-killed situations. What does she think she's going to do against someone who's stronger, has equal skills, and is holding a gun?

The two of them could charge him, if they could communicate enough to coordinate their timing. But that's a good way to die. And then Pickett would still get the thumb drive and the laptop.

The balance of power is with Pickett. One way or another, he's going to get what he wants. Rachel certainly knows that as well as Grady does.

Grady needs a distraction. If he tries what he's thinking of, he and Rachel may not get out of here alive. But if it brings Pickett's crime out in the open, he's willing to take that chance. And risking her life is pretty much what Rachel signed up for.

So—play on Pickett's weaknesses. His temper and his ego.

"She's got you, Hartman. You don't want to use that gun. You know damn well that shooting that off in here would be a great way to get caught. You need to get your hands on us. But if you get any closer, she'll stick you. And she knows just how to use a blade for maximum effect. And if you don't get closer...well, we can stand here all day. I'm only muscle with half a brain, just like you. But she's a Fed. You think somebody won't come looking for her? She's on a case. She has colleagues. People know where she is. They may even be tracking her phone. And when they come through that door, it's all over. Here you'll be, standing like a moron just waiting for them to come and put the cuffs on."

Rachel gives Grady a sideways look like he's crazy. He's sure she's now the one wondering if he's trying to make the man explode.

Pickett stands his ground, but he looks confused. Grady can almost see the alternatives clicking through his head. Time to push the man a little further. Goal: Send him over the edge.

"Didn't plan this very well, did you? If you'd given it some thought—if you're capable of that—you'd have gotten me alone. As it is, it's two against one. You can get one of us. But the other will get you. The only reason we haven't charged you up to now is that you might screw up when we hit you, and that gun in your hand might go off accidentally and hurt someone. Maybe even you."

He drops his voice a good octave, hoping Cujo will hear the imminent threat in it. "But we won't wait forever."

That does it. Pickett lunges, just three big steps forward, and grabs Rachel's wrist—the hand with the knife in it. He squeezes, and the knife goes clattering to the floor.

But Rachel's kneeing him in the groin and he buckles. The man's on the ground. She's putting him into a chokehold. This gives Grady time to act.

He turns to the laptop. Can't let Pickett and the others get away with this. Can't let him destroy the evidence. He clicks an icon, and his email program is up. He opens a new message.

Cujo's still on the floor. But he's broken the chokehold. He can't tune out all the hurt radiating from his balls, but he's been conditioned to ignore pain, and he's functioning again. He's got Rachel by her right ankle. He's yanking at her, trying to get her down.

But damn the woman is strong. She's pulling away.

Grady drags the video file to the email, puts the cursor in the "To" field, clicks "A," and Ally's email address auto-fills. His finger reaches for the "Send" button. And suddenly Rachel's behind him. Her arm swings across, sweeping the laptop off the counter and onto the floor.

She collapses.

Hurt? He doesn't know.

What the fuck happened?

Pickett's still down, and Grady's on him. But the big guy's recovering fast, and Grady can't hold him. They struggle.

They're wrestling, and Pickett's stronger. He's dragging their tangled bodies across the floor, toward the laptop.

Grady needs help. But Rachel's out of it, lying against the base of the island, eyes half-closed.

Pickett's got his hands on the laptop. He pulls the thumb drive out of the USB port. It's in his right hand. Grady has no idea how damaged the laptop is. He has to keep the thumb drive. He grabs Pickett's hand, trying to force it open. No go.

He gets an elbow into Pickett's gut, but the fucker's built like a tank, and if adrenalin is powering him, it's powering the younger man just as much.

He gets his hands free and tries for Pickett's eyes, but Pickett twists his head away.

Then Pickett slams a foot into Grady's injured ankle. Sudden agony.

Pickett's scrambling to his knees. He's still got the thumb drive.

Grady grabs at Pickett's leg, but Pickett kicks him in the stomach.

Pickett's on his feet. He snatches up the laptop and the photo of Malone.

He's heading for the door. Grady sees the gun, abandoned, under one of the kitchen stools. He reaches for it, his hand's on it.

And Pickett's gone.

Until Pickett stomped his bad ankle, Grady hadn't noticed his injury. Now, it's screaming. He struggles to his feet, but he knows damn well he can't go after the man.

He drags himself to his feet, puts the safety on Pickett's gun, sets it down on the kitchen counter.

The cops may not do anything, but he has to try. And he has to get help to Luis.

His phone is still in his pocket. He pulls it out, ready to call 911.

"Don't," Rachel says.

40

Grady turns. Rachel's up, on her feet, standing over by the couch. There's a gun in her hand, pointed at him. While he was fighting with Pickett, she made it across the room, reached her handbag, retrieved her gun. And he missed it.

He can't believe what he's seeing. "What are you doing?"

"Keeping you from making a mistake."

Huh? "I'm just calling 911."

"Put the phone down."

He's winded, banged up from his fight with Pickett. And still incredulous. Pickett's gun is on the island behind him. There's a good chance he can scoop it up and have it pointed at Rachel before she can do anything about it. But what's the sense in that? He chooses to keep talking. "You can't be serious."

"You don't want to make that call. The cops can't do anything. You know that. Oh, they'll send someone. They'll take hours of our time writing it up. And then nothing will happen. There's no proof. None at all."

"You forgot about Luis. I'm calling to get help to him."

"Luis is your 'associate'?"

"And my friend."

If he expects this to make a difference, he's wrong.

"From what I heard, he won't want the cops involved. Where they go, ICE follows. And I also got the idea your friend may be a bit of a hacker. Maybe a white hat. But I doubt he always plays by the rules. It's not in their DNA. Hackers, I mean. If you want help for Luis, that's us."

"Huh?"

"You and me. We'll go over there. If he's badly hurt, we'll call an ambulance. But if he's taken to a hospital, his immigration status might become a question. So let's not do it unless we have to."

Grady has to admit she has a point. He still has his cell in his hand. Rachel still has her gun in hers. He tucks the phone in his pocket. "Put the gun down," he says.

She tucks the weapon in her waistband. He can't believe she thinks he'll buy that. "Not good enough," he says. "Put it back in the bag."

Rachel makes a face but picks up her bag, places the gun in a center pocket.

"Zip the bag."

She does.

"Okay," he says. "We'll do it your way. You and I will go help Luis. Where's your car?"

She's parked outside, on the street.

They're both silent on the way down in the elevator. As they exit the building, Grady says, "You took a real chance with Pickett. He could have shot you."

Rachel makes a noncommittal sound.

"I guess that's part of the job," he adds.

Rachel nods.

She leads him to her car, halfway down the block. It's a BMW 5 series, black, with a Hertz sticker on the rear windshield.

"Pretty nice ride for a rental," he says. "Especially for a government employee. Those travel expense guidelines must have changed big-time."

"I'm paying for the upgrade." She unzips her bag, takes out the keys, and rezips. "You know what business travel is like. All drab and dull. A girl's got to have some fun."

Grady can tell she thinks they're ready to go. But he's put himself between her and the Bimmer. He holds out his hand. "Give me the keys."

He can see he's managed to surprise her, and even under these circumstances, it gives him a moment of satisfaction.

She refuses. "No."

They stand there on the sidewalk next to the vehicle. Grady keeps an eye on her bag, ready to grab it if she makes a move. Ironically, she's listened to what he's said about Tucson and isn't wearing it cross-body. It's slung over one shoulder instead. Taking it from her would be easy.

"You're not a bad investigator, Rachel," he says. "You're well trained. And you're good at what you do. But you're not FBI. You were, the first time I met you back when you were involved in clearing me of that series of murders. And I liked you. You were the only one who didn't treat me like I was a criminal while you were telling me I was free to go. You were a Fed then. But you're not now."

No response.

"You work for Hammer." The organization that hired him. "And, sure, you've been concerned about preventing reprisals against Americans on the ground in Iraq. But that's been secondary. God knows you don't care about bringing anyone to justice. All you've really been out to do is protect the holy grail of profitability. There have been too many negative stories about Hammer's contractors already. A bombshell fuck-up like this could kill the goose that's been laying all the golden eggs.

"You'll try to tell me that you couldn't have done anything about Pickett anyway. Once he tracked me down and discovered that I'd found the video, he was going to get it away from me one way or another, then do whatever it took to shut me up. You couldn't have stopped him, that's what you'll say.

"But we both know you didn't even try. You didn't get where you are by handling a situation like this so badly. You have skills you could have used. Instead, you threw the fight.

"And you weren't about to let me email the video. The laptop falling to the floor. That was no accident. You pushed it off the counter.

"Then you 'collapsed.' Pickett's younger than I am, just as well trained, and uninjured. You abandoned me to him. And you were counting on him to come out on top. Well, congratulations. You won."

"Grady, I…"

"Sssh. There's nothing you can say that I want to hear. So don't talk. Don't try to intimidate me. You're not going to shoot me, not out here in public. And you will never hold me at gunpoint again."

"Okay, I…"

"Give me the keys."

Rachel drops the keys into his hand. "I know you feel betrayed, but you need to let me help. I can get Luis help without involving the police—or immigration. And you can't drive, not with that ankle."

"Watch me."

Grady hits a button on the fob. A beep and the car is unlocked.

He swings off the curb, over to the driver's side, gets in and drives away, leaving her standing there.

#

It's a good twenty minutes to Luis's, even without traffic. And he doesn't dare speed. A ticket would only slow him down further. Not to mention that he doesn't have the right rental paperwork for the vehicle.

His ankle's giving him hell. He tunes it out.

What he can't tune out are his thoughts. He's cursing himself for not catching on in time.

Right up front, he wondered about jurisdiction. Who investigates something like this? A possible crime by civilians working for a corporation contracted to the Army. Who called in the FBI in the first place? And why? Malone's death was just a suicide. Sad, but not all that uncommon. The recording he made of himself—his suicide note—was enigmatic. But was it really so suspicious? And who looked at it first? Someone who was watching out for just these kinds of things?

Now he knows. The answer in every case is Hammer. And no one called in the FBI. This fuck-up was being handled strictly internally.

He broached the topic of jurisdiction with Rachel right up front, when they met over lunch because she wanted to "catch up." She gave him a song and dance about the FBI not being strictly domestic for years, spouted some stuff about interagency and international cooperation. And he swallowed it whole. His guess is it was all true—as far as it went. It just didn't have anything to do with what she was doing and why she was there.

He should have probed, listened for holes in her story. But he had no clue how these things work between federal law enforcement agencies and military contractors in a war zone. And he hadn't cared. If somebody was coloring outside the lines, it was no big deal. Not his business.

Mistake one.

Then there was the illegal search of his apartment. As a citizen, he'd hoped that wasn't standard practice for the bureau. But, then again, he didn't really care. The boys and girls of the FBI have been known to do worse. So he ignored it.

Mistake two.

He didn't even get the implications of Rachel's unauthorized entry.

The giveaway—too late—was that Rachel wanted Pickett to get—and eliminate—all the evidence. Her mission was to find the video if it existed—just as she said. But she wanted to find it to destroy it.

Her goal was to protect the cover-up. Rachel and her team, whoever they are, must have been checking all along to see if anybody involved was getting shaky, watching over them, making sure nobody was going to talk. Once they ensured that the crime would never become public, they would have found a way to reassure each man who was involved that his ass was covered. Nothing to worry about. Nothing at all.

And they'd also have found a way to let each man know that if his conscience started bothering him to the point where he felt the need for confession, there would be unpleasant consequences.

During the confrontation in Grady's apartment, Rachel needed to make sure that Pickett got away, one way or another. If he had left empty-handed, she would have worked on Grady to find out exactly what other evidence there was. Who else knew about this? Were there copies of the video? To find out, she would done whatever was necessary, from persuasion and seduction to "enhanced interrogation."

He told her she won. And she did.

All that will exist of this atrocity will be rumors and memories. There are mothers and fathers who know their children didn't come home that day. They were with a man and a woman: two teachers, or an uncle and an aunt, or family friends. And those adults didn't come home either.

These parents already realize that their children are dead. But they will never know how they died or who was responsible. Intellectually, they'll acknowledge that it could have been insurgent militia. But their lives have already been torn apart, and now they've lost what was left. They will want to blame the Americans.

Rachel may not see incidents that she recognizes as clear reprisals. No one may be able to tie them directly to these deaths. But they will happen. They will be part of the expanding fabric of violence. And more Americans—and Iraqis—will die because of her.

How long will it take for her to face this reality? If she ever does.

He finally pulls into Luis's driveway. From here, everything looks normal. But when he reaches the front door, it's ajar. He pushes it **open**.

41

As the front door swings opens, Grady calls out. "Luis!"

No answer. But he hears a rhythmic thumping.

Calling Luis's name, he moves down the hall toward the workroom at the back as fast as his crutches will let him. As he approaches the rear of the house, the thumping grows louder.

The door to the workroom won't open. He puts his shoulder against it and pushes. No go. There's something blocking it. And the thumps have stopped. Then he realizes: it must be Luis. He's up against the door and has been banging on it from the other side.

The door is solid wood, so he raises his voice to make sure Luis can hear him. "I'll get you," he says. "Coming through a window."

He and his crutches travel back down the hall to the kitchen and out the side door. Making his way from there to the backyard is a struggle. The area between the house and the wall that divides Luis's lot from the next property is narrow and filled with spiky ocotillo, bougainvillea in full, spreading bloom (complete with thorns), and a large Saguaro cactus. Luckily, the ground is packed hard (normal for Tucson), but his crutches and the need to maneuver around the plants slow him down.

Finally, he reaches the graveled area at the rear of the house. Luis's workroom has two windows, both in the wall that faces the backyard. The blinds are closed, so he can't see in. Pickett's work. They were open when Grady was there earlier in the day. There are no security bars, thank God, but the windows are dual pane. His aluminum crutches are too light to break through.

There's a tool shed against the back wall of the lot. It's not padlocked, but the doors are rusted shut. Grady wrestles with them, finally manages to pull them apart enough to fit his body through the opening.

Everything in the shed is covered with a thick layer of desert that's sifted in. He'd bet no one's been in here in years. Luis can't do yard work or repairs himself, and any workmen he hires bring their own tools.

The interior is dim. He's looking for a hammer, a crowbar—something he can swing with enough force to smash one of the windows. As his eyes adjust, he sees a bag of fertilizer, a decrepit workbench with a vise attached, a few jars of screws, an ancient screwdriver. Then he spots it in the far corner: a sledge. The head is rusted, the wooden handle in sad shape. He awkwardly works his way through the junk over to the sledge and hefts it, hoping the business end is still attached well enough to the shaft to do the job.

He quickly discovers that carrying a sledgehammer while on crutches is an almost impossible task. The fifty feet between the shed and the target window become miles. He tries walking without the crutches. He can't do it. His bad ankle won't support his body, let alone the added weight of carrying the heavy tool. So he leans on his crutches, picks up the sledgehammer, moves it as far in front of him as he can and sets it down again. Then he catches up with the sledge, picks it up, and repeats the process. He wants to call out, "It's okay, Luis. I'm coming." But he doubts Luis would be able to hear him, and he doesn't want to bring the neighbors into this.

Finally, he reaches the back wall of the house. He moves to the window farthest away from the door that Luis's body is blocking, hefts the sledge, and slams it against the panes. The glass is strong. It takes two swings before it gives way.

He uses one of his crutches to clear the pieces of jagged glass that have clung to the window frame, lifts his crutches into the opening, sets them down inside, and then manages to heave his body through, into the room.

He sees chaos: smashed computer screens, hardware that was neatly arranged around the room now in a jagged, teetering pile. Luis's wheelchair is on its side on the floor over against the door—with Luis in it. Luis can't walk, isn't mobile without the chair except in the most torturous way. Tipping him over would likely have been enough, but Pickett either didn't get that or wasn't taking any chances. When Grady reaches him, he can see that Luis is tied in with a power cord around his middle. His wrists are tied to the chair's arms. His mouth is plugged with a sock.

Grady can't even imagine how impossible his friend's struggle has been. After Pickett left, Luis—somehow—succeeded in maneuvering himself, chair and all, to the door into the hallway. Maybe it was ajar, maybe he thought he could get through it. But the door opens into the room. And all he managed to do was block it. To be so physically restricted all his life, and now to be trapped like this…

Grady pulls the sock from Luis's mouth. At first, Luis struggles to get words out due to lack of saliva, but after the first strangled sounds, Grady hears: "Damn, man. What took you so long?"

He unties Luis's arms, removes the cord from around his waist, lifts him from the chair and sits him gently against the wall. Then he rights the wheelchair, deposits Luis in it, and wheels him away from the scene of destruction into the kitchen.

He fills a glass with water. "Here," he says. "Drink."

Luis downs half the water, wipes his mouth. "Not here," he says, "I gotta get back to my room."

Grady starts to roll him down the hall. But Luis reassures Grady that he isn't hurt. Just a few bruises. He makes it clear that he can manage the wheelchair's controls on his own now. And he does.

Grady clears the floor ahead of the chair, leaning his crutches against one of the work tables that line the room and pushing the destroyed equipment out of the way. Luis rolls up to a work surface and brushes aside broken glass.

"It was the guy from the video," he says. "The one leading those other *soldados*."

None of them are soldiers, but Grady doesn't correct him. He nods. "Pickett," he says. "Hartman Pickett, to be exact. His crew calls him Cujo."

Luis just shakes his head. "*Madre de dios. Un mal hombre.*"

If Grady had it to do over, he'd never have left Luis alone.

He can see how it happened. Once Pickett figured out which house Grady had gone into, he parked around the corner and snuck onto the property. He would have had a clear view of the workroom from either of the back windows. The one Grady eventually smashed would have given him a good look as Luis navigated to the site on the deep web where the recording was stored (even though he might not have been able to see exactly what they were doing). And then he would have had enough of a view of the computer screen to recognize the video as it played.

When Grady left the room and then didn't return, Pickett had to get to the front of the house as quickly as possible without being seen. But he didn't get there in time to stop Grady.

Why? Maybe he stuck himself on the giant cactus. Maybe somebody getting mail from a mailbox or walking a dog, or some other activity in the neighborhood slowed him down since he needed to stay invisible. Maybe he was just overcautious. Or maybe it simply took him too long to realize that Grady wasn't going to come back into the workroom.

He must have seen Grady getting into the cab, leaving. If the driver hadn't gotten there so quickly and Picket had moved a little faster, he might have confronted Grady, and Luis might never have had to go through all this. Or he and Luis might have both been dead. Grady rates that one as a toss-up.

Pickett couldn't know where Grady was going. All he could do was assume that there was a good chance Grady was headed home, back where he came from.

At that moment, Pickett had to make a decision: focus on Grady or deal with the situation at Luis's instead and get to Grady later. Unfortunately, he made the logical choice. The one Grady would have made himself.

As Luis fills Grady in, it turns out that Luis isn't hurt because he wasn't a fool. It was clear to him early on that Pickett would do whatever it took to get what he wanted. And what he wanted was the video.

So there was no point in trying to be a hero. He could only fail. And suffer. Maybe even die. "I knew he was *mal*, man. That guy was fucking evil."

But Luis knew he couldn't give in too easily. He held out just long enough that Pickett would believe he was resisting. Then he caved. He didn't see any point in letting the man maim him first. Nature had already done enough. "I let the asshole 'force' me to admit we found the video. I let him 'force' me to navigate to the web site and delete the file.

"The one thing I didn't want to do. I didn't want to tell him that you had a copy. I tried to hold that back. But he said I was lying, that you had it on a thumb drive."

So Pickett saw enough through the window of Luis's computer room to know that. Or maybe he was fishing. "He figured that out on his own," he says to Luis.

Luis shakes his head. "Was the download the only copy, he asked me. Then a little pain. He knew I would give in. I knew I would give in. I didn't want to, but... I admitted, yes, you had it on a thumb drive."

"You did the right thing, Luis. It was the only thing you could do."

Luis shakes his head sadly. "And after he tied me and dumped my chair over, he wrecked everything. My screens, my computers, whatever he could break. *Es una pena.*" A shame.

Grady had to agree. It is a shame. Especially since…

"All this was for nothing," he tells Luis. "Everything you went through, all the damage. He found me. He broke into my apartment, surprised me. I didn't see it coming. And I should have. He got the thumb drive, he took my laptop where I'd uploaded the file, he got away. The evidence is gone."

He hates this. He hates his failure to protect Luis, his impotence in the face of Cujo's assault, his delay in catching on to Rachel's scam. But most of all, he hates that Cujo and his gang will get away with something so horrible.

To Grady's shock, Luis laughs. "How dumb do you think I am, man? First thing I did when you set your feet to walking out the door was copy that file to a different site. One he'll never find. No one will unless I wan' them to. *Está terminado*—done—before you hit the other end of the hall."

"You're sure?"

Luis's face says he is. "How long you know me, amigo? You even have to ask?"

Grady can hardly believe it. He wants to scream with relief, to shout with joy.

The cover-up is over. Cujo is done. For once, the good guys have won.

"Luis," he says, "I always knew you were a genius."

42

Mid-afternoon in the ICU. It's been a long day, hours since Jack left the hospital to go down to the station with the police, hours since he phoned her to let her know an officer was driving him home. Gina's still lying there, just as she's been lying there since she came out of surgery on Wednesday morning. And Jill's still sitting. Still not calling Jack. Still letting him sleep.

She put her novel aside more than an hour ago. Couldn't concentrate. She's caught in a minor hell of fatigue and tension: tired, edgy—and increasingly puzzled over what she's doing here.

Gina did turn to her. But only for Jack's phone number.

Gina did give her as next of kin when she was brought into the ER. And Jill's been thinking that's powerful, took it as a sign that had meaning in what feels like an increasingly incoherent world. Now, with the kind of fresh insight that she sometimes experiences on the morning after a sleepless night, she sees no evidence for that.

Gina was badly hurt, drifting in and out of consciousness. The hospital needed a next of kin. They would have been asking her if there was someone they could contact. Jill can hear it: "Who can we call for you?" They'd be gentle but persistent. If there was no answer, they'd ask it again. And again: "Who can we call for you?"

Maybe Gina was still mad at Jack, maybe in her ruined state, she just didn't remember his phone number (new since she'd vanished from Tucson) or his address (even newer). Maybe all she could manage was to point the nurses at the card Jill had given her on Monday morning, the one she tucked in her pocket before leaving Jill's office.

Or maybe she didn't even do that. Maybe one of the nurses dug the card out of her things, asked if this was someone they could call, and she said "Yes" or gestured "Yes," and that was it. Maybe if by some miracle, she did open her eyes right now, she wouldn't even recognize Jill.

So…

She doesn't mean anything to Gina. Why should she? She's just Jack's ex-wife, a person whose life has been so different from Gina's. She might have been someone Gina would respect, maybe even like, but she wasn't a woman Gina knew. Or who knew her.

But maybe if—when—Gina's eyes open, she will be glad that someone is there. Someone who isn't a doctor or a nurse, someone who genuinely cares on a personal level. Even if that caring is mostly because Gina happens to belong to Jack.

What are you doing? she asks herself. You're not helping this body lying there in the bed. That's not Gina. Gina is gone. At least for now.

She may come back. And when she does, there will be people who will help her. But it's not likely you'll be one of them.

Your dental practice rests on your reputation for trustworthiness and dependability—as least as much as on your medical expertise. Your absence is eating away at that. How many angry patients does it take to turn a reputation sour? Do you really want to lose even part of what you've worked so long and hard to build?

And about your patients. You really do care about them. And they do need you—you, Jill Whitehurst, in particular. When you're a patient, you have to trust the person who puts her hands, needles, sharp instruments, noisy grinders, liquids, solids, stitches, in your mouth. And you don't trust a person who lets you down.

And what about your family? Forget Charlie for now. Who knows what he really wants? You with him there in Denver? Or a new life, a fresh start, away from you before he's too old? Just buy a fucking sportscar, she wants to scream. You don't need to dump your wife!

She can't do anything about Charlie. Not right now. The next move has to come from him, and she doesn't see that happening, at least not for a while, probably never.

But Sophie.

Jill left the house for the ER in the early morning hours on Wednesday. Sophie got herself off to school that day, but since then she's been going to Caitlin's for meals and sleeping. Caitlin's parents must be starting to wonder what the hell is going on. She can imagine their conversations. "And we always thought the Whitehursts were such a together family."

Dysfunction is written all over the last few days. This is Friday, and Jill hasn't given anyone in her life, even her daughter, any firm idea of when she'll be back. Sophie must be feeling lost.

A nurse comes into the room, checks Gina's tubes, her machines. She gestures at Jill's discarded novel. "Is that good?" Jill gives her a smile. "It's okay." The nurse adjusts something on Gina's IV. "Well," she says to Jill as she leaves, "helps make the time pass."

That's it. Jill picks up her book and tucks it into her bag. She walks over to Gina's bedside, straightens her covers (which were already straight) and strokes her forehead. Then she turns away.

She'll go to her own house, clean up, text Sophie, let her daughter know that it's time to come home. They'll order pizza from Sophie's favorite place, curl up on the sofa together, watch a movie. She'll thank Caitlin's folks, explain, maybe send one of those edible fruit arrangements. She'll ask her office manager to come in tomorrow, compensating her well for working on a Saturday. Together, they'll straighten out the schedule.

Before she leaves the room, she texts Jack:

Need to go home. Sorry. No change in Gina's condition.

At the last moment, feeling both foolish and daring, she adds the word "love" and a heart emoji.

43

Rachel's in Dallas. Finally. When you're flying out of Tucson, the word "non-stop" doesn't exist, at least not when you're going anywhere civilized people would want to go. Like New York.

She boarded for the first leg of her trip just after four and endured that for more than two hours, crammed into a tiny metal tube of a plane (okay, it was a jet but with seats that would have been a tight fit for toddlers). Then there was the interminable stretch they spent sitting on the tarmac once they landed in Dallas followed by what was still a ninety-minute layover before her second flight.

At least the American terminal is modern, pleasant even. She found her way to the club and has whittled her waiting time to forty-five minutes with the aid of two well-mixed martinis. Sitting at the bar, she can see a couple of TVs, one tuned to CNN, one to a sports channel, and a screen showing gate information. She's hoping the next plane will be more what she's used to and is crossing her fingers for an upgrade. She's as close to content as she's been since this whole thing began.

She was pissed when Grady left her standing on the curb and pulled away in her rental car. Then she thought, well, the hell with it. I'm done here. And called a cab.

Once she was back in her hotel room, she sent a text to report up the food chain. Then she placed a call to Gil. By the time he got back to her, she was dressed in her travel gear, ready to go with limited time to talk.

She got right to the point. "Pack it up. We're done."

She saw the question on Gil's face and smiled inside while keeping her face appropriately serious.

"I found it," she said.

"Shit!" The shock in Gil's voice gave her pleasure. *That's why I outrank you now,* she thought, *and why I always will.*

"You have the video?" he asked.

This issue of possession was going to be tricky, and not just with Gil. She'd be debriefed tomorrow in New York, and the people she'd be meeting with weren't going to be thrilled with how the whole thing played out. But she knew there was really no problem. Not exactly ideal, but not something that, in the end, was going to cause anybody heartburn. Gil would see that with no trouble at all, and she was confident she could make it clear to her superiors.

"Cujo—Pickett—has it. Or did have it. I doubt it exists any longer. He has no interest in having his fuck-up get out. I'd bet my life that by this time those bits and bytes have been dispersed, strewn to the far winds." Triumph was making her poetic. Who knew?

"Huh?"

"He's erased the damn thing, Gil."

"Oh. Cujo was there? How did…"

"How did he get the video? Long story. And let me answer your next question: Where was it? Dark web."

"So…"

"So you can get out of there. I can't believe any of those guys are going to say anything about their 'unauthorized operation.' I'll bet Cujo's already fired off a carefully worded text or two. Meaningless to anyone who doesn't know what he's talking about, but like a reprieve from the governor to those assholes. No, they're not going to spill. Especially once their great leader returns."

"Makes sense. Most people don't let on about murder."

"Let's not call it that. Let's call it…overzealousness. A serious lapse of judgment."

Gil was silent.

"But leave your man in place for a while. And if he sees any sign that any of that crew of idiots is starting to feel the need for confession, he has to get that info to us stat."

"I'm on top of it."

She'd inadvertently insulted him, she could tell. Gil does know his job, after all. Don't be a poor winner, Rachel, she told herself. Don't gloat over your success. And don't throw his lack of it in his face. Letting Cujo slip through his fingers. And then not admitting it for two fucking days. What bonehead mistakes. "I have every confidence in you."

"We'll lean on them if we have to. But I can't believe it'll be necessary."

Duh. Didn't we just agree on that? Oh, give him a pat, Rachel. He needs it. "I think you're right." Time to wind up this call. She decided to throw him a bone. "And, Gil, see you back in D.C., okay? We'll have dinner."

Just as she was about to walk out the door, there was a call from the front desk. Some guy on crutches had left a black BMW in the loading zone outside the lobby. He told the doorman it was hers and took off. She didn't have time to return the car. She'd get someone from the hotel to do it. It was a minor loose end, but she felt a little disappointed at not being able to tie it up even though it would make her life a bit simpler. She had planned on giving Grady only a few more minutes—just until she walked out the door, and she didn't expect he'd meet her deadline. In fact, she'd been looking forward to reporting the BMW stolen.

Forty minutes until boarding. The level in her glass is getting low. She debates having a third martini. Better not. She'll just nurse what's left. Maybe down a glass of Perrier before rolling out to the gate. Have to stay hydrated. She regards the two large olives on their little plastic sword, plucks one off the spear with her teeth and sucks it into her mouth. She picks up the glass to tip in a little of the remaining liquid, taste it with the olive.

And her attention is caught by something on the television. The one on the right. CNN. The sound is muted. But she can see it. The anchorwoman's solemn face. Then: the routine stop. The men in desert camouflage. Their weapons. The children. The gunfire. The blood. Faces are clear, identifiable. Pickett, his boys.

The words of the crawl: BREAKING NEWS...U.S. CONTRACTORS...IRAQ...ACCUSED...ATROCITY...

......one of the men in camo shoots the young man in the stomach; then, as he lies writhing on the ground, in the head.

The young woman is begging the men to stop. Let the rest of them go. She'll take the children and walk away. Just walk away.

"Walk away?" the leader says. "We can do better than that. Let's see you run......"

"Yarkus!" the woman screams. Run. She's grabbing hands, trying to gather the children up, urging them on. They're fleeing across the rough ground. One small girl stumbles. She falls and sits there crying.

The leader aims. He fires. One boy, running well ahead of the others, is down.

Another man in camo fires. Another child drops.

They're efficient. No shots are fired overhead. Only two miss.

They leave the young woman for last. She screams as her charges die. Then it's her turn.

It's possible that not all the men fire. We can't tell from the video. The man wearing the camera doesn't seem to. The visuals seem to indicate that he might have dropped to his knees at one point. And we see a pile of vomit.

The men in camos drag the bodies to the ruined building and dump them inside. The man behind the camera is ordered to help. He picks up and carries a girl, the small one that tripped and fell, already down before she was shot.

The leader and another of the men are doing something in the building, but we can't see what.

The remaining two men, including the one who is our "eyes," gather the water bottles, tools, and other items from the road and stuff them back into the van.

The men who were in the building return. All four get into the armored vehicle. It drives slowly away.

The man wearing the camera is still filming. Maybe he's forgotten to turn the camera off. All we see is disjointed footage of the inside of the vehicle. A couple of the men are joking. The leader encourages this. "Eight less of those fuckers! That's what I call a good day's work!"

Then someone says, "Now!"

BOOM!

The camera rocks, turns, faces the rear of the vehicle.

Through the back window: the van on fire. Then another, bigger explosion. One large burst. Flames. Smoke.

The commentator pauses the video, tells us that this explosion was the building we saw earlier, the near-ruin.

Again, we look at that burst, seen through the rear window. Cujo and his men are blowing up the eight bodies: the two young men, the woman, the five children.

The blast rips them into fragments of flesh and blood and bone. They shower the burning van, rain down upon the land.

BREAKING NEWS...

ATROCITY...ATROCITY...ATROCITY

Rachel doesn't scream. She's too well trained for that. She freezes instead. But she has most of two good-sized martinis in her, and when the building explodes, she reacts. Her arm moves on its own, her glass slams down on the bar top. The stem shatters. And she's swallowed wrong.

She's coughing, but she can breathe. The bartender comes over to see if she's okay. The couple two stools away express concern. She's cut her hand on the glass, and it's bleeding, but not badly.

She exaggerates her coughing, accepts a glass of water, reassures the bartender that she's all right.

Everyone around her is blaming the broken glass and her small cut on the olive that almost got stuck in her throat. They're all thinking how lucky she is.

But she knows the truth.

That a scandal that will destroy Hammer, LLC is just beginning.

That it will become monstrous and devour everything in its path.

And that her career is over.

44

Jill's sitting on his couch. Grady hasn't seen her since she left Gina's bedside to return to her life. They've traded a few texts about Gina's condition, but that's all. He's happy to see her now, even though he has no idea why she's here.

It's been three days since he and Luis discovered the video and Luis unleashed it on the world. It turned out that destroying computer hardware is harder than Pickett thought. Grady and Luis were able to cobble together a system and re-establish a connection with the web. Then Luis sent the video to a number of major news outlets. And managed to do it anonymously.

The story didn't break immediately. Verification of some sort had to happen first, Grady assumed. And some outlets got it on the air, or the Internet, faster than others. CNN was among the first. Their commentator used careful disclaimers: "appears to be," "we believe," "seems to show."

But the pictures made it clear. Five men wearing American uniforms had murdered eight civilians, including one woman and five children, in a location that had already been identified as an area on the outskirts of Baghdad. The men's insignia marked them as contractors, not military personnel.

The atrocity—and it was one—appeared to have been triggered by what should have been a routine interaction between the Americans and the Iraqis.

The quality of the video was bad (the anchorwoman speculated that it was taken by some sort of bodycam), and the audio was worse. But three of the men's faces were visible. And one of those men, clearly the de facto leader, seemed to be the instigator, the main reason—maybe the only reason—that a passing moment of tension became a horror.

There was no question that picture and sound enhancing techniques would allow identification of those men. And the recording bore a time and date stamp. Investigators would be able to pinpoint the exact assignment that became a mass killing and round up every person who participated.

As the video went viral, some of the commentators stopped being so cautious in their descriptions of the men and used words like brutal, vicious, cold-blooded, cruel, and sadistic.

The cable news panels made noises about tracking down the whistleblower, but so far no one had succeeded. There had been two talking heads, one on Fox and one on MSNBC, who made claims to have this knowledge. Both were wildly off-base. If at some point the authorities did find him, Grady trusted they'd have an interest in keeping his name confidential. And he hoped he was right.

Grady had been deeply concerned about the damage done to Luis's workroom by Pickett's rampage. But even as he and Luis were working to find and hook up the least damaged of the computers, Luis made it clear he wasn't devastated, or even worried. "All this," he said, gesturing at the expensive equipment that had become a pile of junk, "It's just hardware. The important stuff is backed up."

Grady assumed he meant software, tools, data—whatever a computer geek like Luis needed to do his work and whatever he had created. "Where?" he asked.

"Up there." Luis waved a hand at the ceiling, and Grady knew he meant the sky, and that the sky meant the Internet.

Grady is paying to replace Luis's gear. Luis tried to refuse, but Grady knew that there was no other way that he would be made whole. By the time they're done, it will take a chunk out of Grady's bank account, but he's happy to do it.

In the past three days, he's taken over for Jill in the ICU, although his version of a bedside vigil is less intense than hers. Or maybe less dedicated. He thinks of it as "vigil-lite." He visits for an hour or so in the morning, another couple of hours in the afternoon, and an hour in the evening.

The nurses who come into Gina's room keep saying, "Talk to her." He asks if she can hear him. Some say, "We don't know." Others say, "Maybe." His guess is no way in hell. Unconscious is unconscious no matter what pretty fantasies people want to have about it. So he just sits there for all the hours he can bear. On one level, this seems weird and useless to him. On another, he recognizes it as an act of love.

He was on his way home from the hospital on this third day when Jill reached him, and he got to his apartment just in time to let her in. That was fifteen minutes ago, and they've already covered how she is (fine), how her daughter is (great), how her practice is (thriving), how he is (okay), and how Gina is (just the same). He's not sure where the conversation goes from here.

While he's wondering, Jill takes it.

"We need to talk," she says. "First of all, you've changed."

His face must express surprise, maybe concern, because she quickly adds, "No, no. It's good."

Okay. Well, there's the money. But all that means is that he can pay his bills on time and live in what he considers a decent place (and what she seems to feel is a sterile box that doesn't suit him). It must be the other thing.

"You've stopped drinking."

Yup, it's the other thing. He'd like to think that alcohol was never that big a deal in his life, but he guesses that to an outside observer maybe it was. He doesn't think that it played a part in the breakup of his marriage to Jill, or if it did, it was Jill's drinking—which wasn't out of control, maybe not even all that heavy except that she was (literally) such a lightweight. But in combination with his consumption, which was about par for a detective of his age and rank, it led to stupid arguments, unnecessary drama, mutual pain. They went to irrational places together and couldn't find their way back.

He'd been a heavy drinker when he was young, sure. And an incident that happened in 1981 when he was dead drunk had almost cost him his life decades later. As he grew older, his consumption didn't really pick up (he likes to think), maybe even slowed down a little—until Jill left him. And it didn't get really bad until she met Charlie and he knew she wasn't coming back. He'd lost her, and for a while, he lost himself. He'll admit that. But he took care of his mother and his dog, held down a job (except for those dark days after he was ousted from the police force). He still loved jazz, drove too fast, hated wearing a tie. There was that time when he was on the run, but those were extraordinary circumstances. Still…

He doesn't know what to say, so he doesn't any anything.

"Charlie's gone," she says. "For good. I've told you that."

Grady knows she believes it. Or is so worried about it that her mind goes directly (and protectively) to worst case scenario. He's not so sure. Charlie has always seemed like a decent guy to him. Solid, with a good set of values. He's not convinced that the man would just throw away the marriage.

Jill seems to be waiting for him to say something, but maybe she's only pausing. He's probably supposed to be doing what he's heard is called "active listening." Nodding. Giving little verbal prompts like "Uh huh." "Hmm." "Tell me more." But he isn't. It's not in his nature. He's never been any good at that except in an interrogation when he was the designated "good cop."

He guesses he hasn't really changed all that much.

Jill gets up off the couch and stands facing the balcony and the street below. For a moment, she's still. And silent.

"I'm going to take your suggestion," Grady says. "About getting a table for out there."

"That'll be nice," she says. But he's pretty sure he was stupid to mention it.

After another moment, she comes back to the sofa and sits down beside him. "I've been thinking about it," she says. "We were good together."

Huh??? She broke up their marriage, walked out on him. Good together? He's stunned.

And his face must show it.

"Not then," she says. "Now."

Oh. Those times they fell into bed. She'll get no argument from him there. The sex was better than good. It was wonderful. Hell, just holding her was wonderful. It was less than a week ago, but it seems like…a long time.

She puts a hand on his knee. "I think we should give it another try."

He must still look puzzled.

"You and me," she says. "I think we should give it another try."

She's sitting there looking young and vulnerable in her skinny jeans and scoop-top tee, her hair down and loose. She's the sexiest, most appealing woman he's ever seen. Every cell of his body wants to reach out, take her, accept what she's offering.

Without conscious thought, he embraces her. Then they're kissing, he's holding her face up to his, running his hands through her hair. If they could be together again… He's thought all these years that it's all he could ever want of life, to have one more chance to be Jill's partner.

But he can't do it.

He ached for Jill for a long time. The pain of losing her never went away, but it had diminished over the past few years. Even this last week, there was so much else going on that he mostly managed to keep their love-making compartmentalized. He didn't allow it to give him hope. He didn't let himself believe it implied anything more than what it was: terrific sex.

He doesn't want to light the flame again unless there's a good chance it will stay lit—on Jill's part. He has no doubt it would on his. But he doesn't want to be hurt. And he doesn't want to hurt her. As if he ever could or would—at least intentionally.

But he did hurt her years ago, no denying that. Can he guarantee that wouldn't happen again? "Giving it a try" wouldn't be fair to her marriage, or even to her on her own if she and Charlie do actually split up. It would be way too soon. Her single status would be too new, too painful. And it wouldn't be fair to him.

He can't be her rebound guy.

Maybe it would be more than that, maybe it would last. But he can't take that chance.

He pulls away. It's one of the hardest things he's ever done.

"I can't believe I'm saying this, but we can't. Not yet. It's too soon. Let's wait. If you still feel this way in six months, I'll run—not walk—run, from wherever I am to wherever you are. But you're all mixed up right now, and you're not used to that. You said it yourself at one point: you're spinning. I get that. I've been there."

She starts to talk, but he puts his finger on her lips, gently shushing her.

"You need to slow it down, take some time, think things through. You need to give yourself a chance to find out whether your marriage is really over or whether you and Charlie are just going through a rough patch." And—he thinks but doesn't say—to figure out whether it's me you really want or whether I'm just something you've kept tucked away as a fall back.

"Six months?" He sees despair in her eyes. She must have been looking to him for a quick emotional fix to her pain. She knows he loves her. She'd have to be blind not to have seen it all these years.

He kisses the top of her head. She smells so good. "It's not so long."

He says it, but he doesn't believe it. Six months will be an eternity. And the odds are that Jill and Charlie will have put things back together well before then.

He's learned to live with longing, with loneliness. He's learned to accept the reality that there are some things he can never have and that one of them is Jill. In some ways, he'd rather cut it off now. Entirely. Just tell her to go away. Stay away. Forever.

But he's not quite that strong. Six months is the best he can do.

Hope is so hard.

"You mean it?" There's disbelief in her voice.

He does.

"I guess... How funny that you're being the careful one."

The careful one. That was always Jill.

"Um," she says. "I don't like it."

He doesn't either.

He watches her pull herself together, become the Jill he knows.

"All right," she says. "See you in six months."

She picks up her handbag, puts her hands on his shoulders, gives him a kiss on the cheek. It's tender, and he can tell that she means it as a promise.

But he's terribly afraid that—eventually—she will realize it means goodbye.

45

Rachel's always been proud of where she lives. Damn few single women can afford a townhouse in an upscale D.C. neighborhood. She did the interior herself, and she likes to think that it's a reflection of who she is: sleek and smart. Minimalist, but exceptional where it counts.

But tonight the place is getting on her nerves. Even here in the den, the room she's always thought of as her concession to coziness, it's all sharp angles and emptiness. She doesn't even have a cat.

She thought she was so clever, plucking Jack Grady out of his Tucson funk. He was smart and had uncanny instincts. She was convinced that with his skills, experience, and history of cutting corners when he had to, he was a find. She could do something with him. The gig as a contractor in Iraq was supposed to be just the first step.

She had no idea the asshole would get so hung-up on procedure. And she *way, way* underestimated his capacity for self-righteousness. Where the hell does he get off thinking he's so much better, so much purer, than anyone else? And where the fuck did he get the idea that his judgment is so much more goddamned valid than hers?

She knows what she's doing. He doesn't.

It's late, after midnight. She's sipping red wine out of a stemmed glass with a big bowl. The wine is a lovely Pauliac, expensive but worth it, and the glass is simple, elegant crystal. This is her third glass since dinner, takeout (which she didn't eat) from her favorite steakhouse. Maybe she'll open a second bottle. Why the hell not.

She's been angry for days, and with every swallow that anger grows. It's blossoming like the fragrance of the wine, sharp and metallic, and blooming red as blood.

There have been plenty of scandals before—for those who pay attention. With rare exceptions like Abu Ghraib, though, most of the world prefers to look the other way. This one is different.

She's lost her job, or will soon. Even if Hammer doesn't go down the tubes, which she believes is all but inevitable, she's done. Already, she's been demoted. And the person who told her was Gil. They've bumped him up to her old position.

He enjoyed delivering the news. She could tell. Fucking traitor. Like he'd ever be half the team leader she was.

So what next? Does she still have connections who will help her? Will she have to get out there in the market to find out just how tainted she is?

It's all his fault. Jack-fuckin'-Grady. She could have taken him down. It would have been so easy. She should have done it when she had the chance, taken him down, down, down—all the way to the bottom.

Her glass is empty. She pours a little more, just an inch, make it two. And picks up her cell phone.

The call goes directly to voicemail—which really pisses her off. If she was hot before, she's fuming now. Here *she*, Rachel Greene, is taking the trouble to call this nobody in his fucking cow town, and he can't even answer his damn phone!

At the beep, she starts talking.

"I know what you think. You've patted yourself on the goddamn back, told yourself that Cujo and his gang won't get it away with it after all. And you think that this is a good thing. You're picturing those mommies and daddies wrapping their dead kids in some fucking desert shrouds and kissing them goodbye.

"Here's reality. You've seen the explosion. All they'll get is pieces—bones, maybe some clothing. A shoe. How'd you like to say goodbye to a shoe?

"'Okay,' you might be saying to yourself, 'maybe that's not so bad, Maybe it's better than nothing.'." She tips up her glass, takes a sip of wine.

"Do you think we were stupid? We knew those jerk-offs were bad apples, and we would have found a way to deal with them. This way—your way—the world is outraged. Yup. You did manage that!

"But what's the fucking result? Reprisals. Deaths. More insurgents. More deaths.

"Does that nasty little truth make its way into your bubble of moral superiority? Have you ever heard the term 'escalating cycle of violence?' Do you think more people will die this way or the other way? What the hell have you really accomplished?

"I had plans for you, asshole. We could have done some amazing stuff together. You might have had a real career instead of being stuck in this over-the-hill cop, defanged solider-of-fortune crap."

She takes another swallow of wine. A big one this time.

"But you fucked it up. Do you remember whining that you wouldn't get your security clearance because your mickey-mouse desert police force had fired you? I told you, oh no, Mr. Grady, you've got it wrong. You misunderstood all that paperwork. They let you resign. Hah! You were right. They fuckin' fired your ass. But I smoothed that over for you. Made it a non-issue. Some thanks I get.

"That's all. I'm done."

And she can hardly believe what comes out of her mouth next.

"Stay in touch."

But she finishes it well.

"Asshole."

Two hours later during the first of what will be a number of sleepless nights, Grady plays the message.

He listens to the whole thing.

If he'd been talking to Rachel, he would have explained that he had to do it. He had no choice.

Whatever the math of the outcome, which will be hard as hell to measure and could be argued about endlessly, he'd do it again.

And if he'd been talking to her, there's something else he might have told her, a piece of irony that occurred to him as he was on his way to rescue Luis the day of the confrontation with Pickett.

Pickett followed him from his apartment building to Luis's. He's got that. But how in hell did the guy find him?

At first, he couldn't figure it out. Sure, everyone he worked with in Baghdad knew he was from Tucson and some of them had probably registered the fact that he was heading there on his break. But when he hit town, even he didn't know where he'd be living. As a good employee, though, as soon as he signed the lease on the apartment, he called Hammer's headquarters and gave them his new address. Less than seventy-two hours later, Pickett left Baghdad on his way to Tucson.

It's clear that somebody at Hammer reached the same conclusions about Malone's death as Rachel but got there sooner. And wasn't comfortable that she could get the job done. Or was simply taking no chances. Result? They sicced Cujo on Grady, without telling Rachel or her team. Maybe he was Hammer's "man" in the Baghdad house all along. Or maybe they just knew his history and his tendencies.

So while Rachel was playing Grady, Hammer was playing her.

Whatever. At this point, that has no relevance to him. But if she's tipped to it, she must be furious. It's an insult, even a betrayal.

Given who she is, she'll never understand what he did. But he has no regrets, not about distributing the video at least.

There are still some moral absolutes in this world. He has to believe that. There are lines that you just don't cross. No matter what.

He's sorry she feels the way she does. He figures she's losing her job. But that's just too fucking bad.

All of it is what it is. And it has to be that way.

After a moment, he highlights the voicemail and touches "Delete."

46

THREE MONTHS AFTER

When Grady was seventeen, he was really good at doing nothing. If there'd been Olympic events for typical teenage behavior, he could have medaled in hanging out. Now, too much free time just makes him restless. And too much free time is all he's had for weeks.

Seeing his employer's disintegration as reported in the media was like watching the slow-motion implosion of a building. One moment Hammer, Inc. was a fortress; the next a pile of rubble. He'd known long before the company fell apart, though, that the offer he'd had for his next tour would be withdrawn. And it was, within a week after the video was released. Because he was a contractor, not an employee, they didn't even need to come up with an excuse. There was no mealy-mouthed language about over-staffing or changes in personnel deployment requirements, just a simple statement of fact.

By then, though, he wasn't sure that he wanted to do another tour in Iraq anyway. Was he really up for another three months of marathon card games, listening to his music through noise-cancelling headphones, living with a pack of horny, over-competitive men who spent way too much time building their muscles and giving each other shit? He was tired of being the old guy. He was tired of their rap music, their porn. Maybe he wouldn't go back.

It turned out he didn't have the choice. He knew through the grapevine that many of Hammer's subcontractors were making their way to other contracting outfits. But no one wanted him. He was qualified, trained, and experienced. He still had his security clearance. But although no one had overtly tagged him as the whistleblower, word must have gotten around.

No one said anything about that to him. Instead, they told him they weren't currently accepting applications, check back in a few months, or that they didn't have anything suited to his particular strengths. The most honest hiring manager of the bunch said that they were looking for team players and immediately sounded as if he were choking on the implication of what he'd said: that because of what Grady had done, he wasn't one.

He'd been blackballed.

There was some consolation in knowing that Pickett and his boys were worse off. They were back in the U.S., and all of them were under investigation. Just what the charges would be wasn't yet clear, and there were questions of jurisdiction that complicated matters, but none of them would be having fun anytime soon. There were a couple of far right-wing commentators who were calling the men "patriots" and trying to raise defense funds. But although it wasn't a done deal, it looked like commonsense was going to prevail and justice would be done.

"You've been here before," he tells himself. "And you were in worse shape then." When he was kicked off the force years ago, he had no savings and no prospects. And he managed to (sort of) dig himself out of that hole. This time he has money in the bank— enough to last him for months even after replacing Luis's equipment. And he has new skills. Although he's not sure how well they'll transfer to a civilian occupation in a city that's not in the middle of a war zone.

Except for one slip, he's managed to stay sober. It happened when he figured out that his career as a highly paid contractor was over, when his apartment was starting to feel like the sterile box that Jill implied it was, when he realized that Jill was keeping her distance—maybe because she was sticking to their agreement, maybe because she had come to her senses about him.

He went out one night and bought a bottle of Scotch and then another and another and spent most of the next two weeks drunk. He still made it to Gina's ICU room once a day, in the late morning when he was sober, or close enough, for the few hours between coming to after passing out the previous night and the moment when he'd stop fooling himself that he wouldn't be drinking that day.

Then the hospital called to say that Gina was awake. It wasn't the kind of miraculous awakening that's the stuff of medical drama. Her return to the world was gradual. First, she opened her eyes. Then, she began following simple commands. Trying to talk. Getting out a word. Two.

By the time she was transferred to a rehabilitation facility, he was sober again. Maybe it was just his disgust at himself, maybe it was his increasing awareness that he didn't want to live his life this way, or maybe it was knowing that he wasn't totally alone. He still had one member of his family left in this world, and that person needed him.

He weaned himself off the stuff, suffered shakes, felt like hell. But he did it. And he started going to meetings, even "working the program." The first time he said, "Hi, I'm Jack Grady, and I'm an alcoholic," he had trouble getting the words out. He'd never used the term before. Heavy drinker, yes. Even "drunk" during a few epiphanal moments. But not "alcoholic." And he's still not sure how he feels about the terminology. He's "in recovery." But unlike recoveries from other illnesses, this one—he's been told—never ends.

He's been visiting Gina every day, and she's coming along, thinking a little more clearly and functioning a little better each day. Her medical team has been cautious about her prognosis, but they're starting to talk about a meaningful recovery. He's not sure what that means, but he guesses they'll find out.

Today, a crisp Monday morning (this is what passes for winter in Tucson), he's focused on paperwork. He's decided, reluctantly, that his old pal, Andy Davis, a detective in the Pima County Sherriff's Department, is right.

On his brief trip back to Tucson the past spring between his second and third Iraqi tours, Grady had some time to kill before he was due to sign the papers for the sale of his mother's house. And he gave Davis a call.

He and Davis had worked together years ago, before Andy moved over to the sheriff's department from the TPD. He was one of the few on the job who stood by Grady when his career blew up.

They met at a mid-town coffee shop. Davis hadn't changed much in the couple of years since Grady had seen him. His hair was a little thinner, his gut slightly bigger, his jowls a bit more pronounced. But he was basically the same old Andy Davis. There was something comforting in the fact that he was just as Grady left him.

Except. "See this?" Davis pulled up his right sleeve, revealing his bicep. "The patch. Givin' it a real try this time."

Davis caught him up on people they'd both known when Grady was with the TPD. They chewed over the usual law enforcement beefs about lack of overtime/too much overtime—the never-ending cycle of hours, and paycheck, feast or famine.

Then Davis wanted to know about Grady's experiences in Iraq. "So what's it like?" And, to his mild surprise, Grady found that he really didn't want to talk about it.

"Hot," he replied. "Dusty. Like Tucson in June."

Davis shook his head. "Fuck. If you gotta risk your neck, you'd think you could do it somewhere a little cooler."

And the work? Grady repeated the answer he'd been given when he was considering the job and asked for a sense of what a tour would be like: "Months of boredom punctuated by moments of terror."

"Someone said that about Iraq, huh?"

"Someone said that about World War I."

"Asshole."

Out in the parking lot, they stopped next to Grady's rental car. Grady tapped a cigarette out of his pack and lit up. "Just blow the smoke my way," Davis said, and they both laughed. Then they stood there until Grady's Marlboro was down to a butt. Davis told him at some point he'd be done with Iraq and back in town (although Grady wasn't so sure) and that he should get a P.I. license. It was the logical next step, he said.

Grady pointed out that he was currently committed, and making more money than he'd ever dreamed of bringing in.

Davis had an argument-ending reply. "This war won't last forever."

He was right. And Grady wanted him to be right. Any thinking, feeling person wanted the war to end. Davis also made another point. "You'll come back to Tucson eventually," he said, "Where else you gonna go?

"And when you do come back," he continued, "someone will ask you for help, or you'll get your nose into somethin' like you always do, and maybe next time it won't turn out so well. Next time, you might get busted for no license, or interfering with an investigation, or since you're such a fuckin' cowboy, some beef a helluva lot worse. Get the license."

So Grady is doing just that.

He sits at the kitchen counter, opens his new laptop, navigates to the site, reviews the requirements, creates a logon, and sets about giving the State of Arizona all the information it will need to get the process started.

When he's done, he'll drive over to the Humane Society and pick up a puppy. Maybe he can talk his landlord into letting him have it here, maybe not.

If not, he'll move. Or maybe he'll move anyway. Tucson's in a valley surrounded by four mountain ranges, three close-by, one that keeps its distance. You can see at least one set of peaks from almost anywhere. You can see mesquite trees, with their black branches and pale green foliage, and saguaros, sand, rocks, roadrunners, lizards, snakes, the prickly pear cacti that bloom in the spring, and the wild plants with broad green leaves and white, lily-like flowers that shoot up from the desert floor during the summer monsoons. You might be driving along under a bright blue sky and watch a sheet of rain sweep its way across the valley floor miles away. Or look up toward the Catalinas on the north and see dark mountains with white clouds tucked into their crags and crannies.

From his trendy, upscale apartment, he can see nothing. He's in a concrete canyon. And, like Jill, he's starting to wonder what he's doing here.

What does he want with fancy restaurants? He's no foodie. What does he need with all these bars? He can get coffee and club soda anywhere, without the noise and the high prices. What does he need with windows so thick and air conditioning so strong that he never knows if he should be hearing the desert winds, feeling the dry heat of June, or smelling the creosote after a rain?

He's thinking about something with a yard, a driveway where he can park his truck, a fence so the dog can run around, a place with some quiet and some peace.

He's thinking about home.

47

LATER

He heard about it by email. The message came from one of the guys he'd worked with in Iraq, one of the few men in the house who'd never been pulled into Pickett's orbit.

The email asked how he was doing, let him know the guy (who'd almost been a friend) was now with another outfit. Then there was the news: Hartman Pickett offed himself.

There was a link to a story from a local TV station up in Idaho. The gist of it was simple. Pickett had been target shooting earlier in the day and was cleaning some of his guns. (Apparently, he had an arsenal.) He picked one up and shot himself. Speculation was that he'd been distraught, filled with remorse over his role in a purported atrocity outside Baghdad that had received wide media play a while back.

Grady knew better.

First, he was convinced that Pickett had never felt remorseful about anything in his life. He was a vicious brute of a man. Not stupid. Clever actually, even charismatic. But blackly evil in every cell of his being.

Second, Hammer, he'd read, was reconstituting itself. The name was different, but the players were the same. And the other men involved in the atrocity that caused Hammer's downfall were taking pleas. Only Pickett was a hold-out, insisting on going to trial. And even with Hammer officially dissolved, it was easy to see that none of the forces behind the new entity wanted him to testify. No matter how much coaching his attorneys put him through, he'd be poisonous on the stand. He would spew venom. He couldn't help it. It was who he was. And he'd make news. Of the kind no one wanted. The kind that could jeopardize the shiny new venture.

That would raise questions about Hammer's selection process, their training, oversight. The publicity could taint the new company to the point that it might slow down—even derail—the acquisition of government contracts.

Grady had a pretty good idea how they did it. Find one of Pickett's buddies—from an earlier contractor tour in one of the war zones, from Pickett's time in the military, from somewhere. Someone who had skills that suited him for the job and the ability to improvise as necessary. Compensate him well.

Let him visit Pickett.

Catch up on old times. Commiserate about all the crap the pussy government was putting the guy through when they should pin a goddamn medal on him.

Come prepared with a plan that would lead to Pickett's death. See the gun cleaning and seize the opportunity.

Excuse himself to visit the bathroom. Or get a drink of water, or a beer, from the kitchen. ("Hey, Cujo, got a couple of brews? Nah, man, just sit there. I'll grab them.") Slip a latex glove, tight-fitting, almost invisible, over his right hand. Keep that hand out of Pickett's eye line when re-entering the room. Stop close to Pickett on his way back to where he'd been sitting. Maybe lean over, admire one of the weapons, one that had already been reloaded. Pick it up to admire it further. No. No glove. Use one of the cleaning rags to handle the gun. Understandable. It still would have been greasy.

Compliment Pickett on his taste in weaponry. Hold it to Pickett's temple and fire. Wrap Pickett's fingers around the stock, adding those prints to the others Pickett had already left in the fresh layer of gun oil. And gunpowder residue? Not a problem. Pickett's target shooting had taken care of that.

Some other contractor formerly with Hammer (and now headed to the new entity) would be glad to share with the press just how devastated Pickett was, how guilty he felt, how distraught.

Someone else who knew him might have said that he didn't think Pickett was all that remorseful, but that he'd sworn more than once that they'd never get him, he'd never go to prison. Guess he knew that prison was coming and wasn't going to let it happen. The guy was hard core.

Everyone would have been happy to close the book on the whole thing.

There was nothing Grady could do about it. He was only speculating. No one would listen to him.

And that was okay. Even though he wasn't crazy about corporate murder. (And he had to admit to himself that in the less civilized part of his brain he was sorry that Pickett's death had been so quick. So easy. He wouldn't have had time to feel terror. Or pain.)

Whatever.

Fact is, Cujo is dead.

It couldn't have happened to a nicer guy.

AFTERWORD

As Tucsonans will know, I've taken a bit of poetic license with our town's chronology.

The revival of downtown Tucson was still a dream in 2009 when this book is set, although there were glimmers of the rebirth to come. Today, central Tucson is a lively place, with newly built apartments (like the one Jack Grady has rented) and condos, bars, restaurants, entertainment venues, and stores. We even have a modern streetcar, which began running in 2014.

Miracle Mile was added to the Register of Historic Places in 2017. Some of its vintage buildings have already been restored and repurposed, new restaurants have opened, and the area is becoming a hip shopping destination.

Judy Tucker
December 2018

39406775R00176

Made in the USA
Middletown, DE
16 March 2019